HER MOTHER'S DAUGHTER

BRIAN R. O'ROURKE

INKUBATOR
BOOKS

This novel is dedicated to my parents. Thank you for your love and support.

Published by Inkubator Books
www.inkubatorbooks.com

ISBN (eBook): 978-1-83756-295-4
ISBN (Paperback): 978-1-83756-296-1
ISBN (Hardback): 978-1-83756-297-8

PROLOGUE

ONE YEAR AGO

I always forget trash day.

I tie the bag up quickly and hurry out the front door. The rumble of the municipal truck sounds close—looks like I made it just in time.

Trash days make me feel lonely.

My ex used to take out the garbage. Unlike a lot of the other women on the block, I never had to remind him. It was one of the many gross chores he took care of for me, like cleaning the bathroom and killing large insects in the basement and occasionally picking up the neighbor dog's poop, when the little you-know-what was let outside to freely roam the street and relieve himself wherever he wanted.

Not that I miss my ex-boyfriend Matthew. I don't. Not really. It's a good thing *that's* over. At least, it's over for me. It's not so over for him. Matthew still contacts me from time to time, through Facebook or text. It's annoying. The only reason I haven't changed my phone number is pure laziness.

But I do wish I had someone to handle all the gross, icky things that come up in life.

Outside, it's another cold day. If I wait any longer to put up my Christmas lights, the holiday will have already come and gone. Every other house on the block is decorated, putting mine to shame.

Trash bag in hand, I scoot down my front steps in my pajamas and robe. My breath fogs in the cold air. My slippers don't have the best traction, and I nearly slip on the ice that has a bad habit of forming at the edge of my sidewalk. One of these days, a neighbor out for a walk is going to slip and get hurt. I really need to pay somebody to reroute the drain so my runoff gets all the way to the street.

But, you know: money.

I put the trash bag into the can sitting on my curb. Out of the corner of my eye, I spot my neighbor, Rebecca, coming down the sidewalk with a bag of trash herself. Rebecca is my closest friend on the street.

I give her a wave.

"Hey, Becca!"

Her reaction to seeing me is much more muted than I'm expecting. Rebecca is very outgoing and personable. Normally, our bumping into each other would lead to a long conversation. And we haven't gotten together in almost a month now. As a working mother of two kids, Rebecca is always busy, but especially so around the holidays and this time of year. So when I say hello, I'm expecting her to come over. Rebecca normally seizes every opportunity to catch up.

"Hey, Amanda," she answers in as neutral a tone as anybody could muster.

Clutching her bathrobe at her neck, Rebecca turns around, and without another word or even another glance in my direction, she strides quickly back into her house.

Weird.

I don't remember Rebecca ever giving me the cold shoulder before. Maybe she's distracted because the boys are giving her a difficult time this morning. Or maybe she's distant because there's something going on with her husband, Ron.

There usually is.

Those are perfectly reasonable explanations for Rebecca's behavior. But I don't feel they're right. Even when Rebecca is running around like a maniac, she *always* makes time to catch up. Talking to another woman around her age is a joyful distraction to her, a welcome breather in the often-chaotic life of a working mother.

Trying to understand her behavior, I think back to our last few exchanges. I can't recall doing or saying anything that might have offended her without realizing it. I'm expert at keeping my low opinion of her husband to myself, and I can't think of anything else I might have said.

I check my phone to see if I didn't respond to one of her Marco Polos. The last message in our chain is from me to her, so that's not it.

She texted me two days ago to see if I was doing alright. Becca knows that I've been having a hard time at work. I thanked her and said I was fine, not wanting to get into it. We went on to trade a few more messages, but there was nothing else of substance.

Struggling to understand her cold greeting, I turn to head back inside. I shouldn't assume her attitude has anything to do with me. She could be preoccupied for any number of reasons. I'm not married, and I don't have kids, so I don't know what that life is like.

I'll message her later to see if something's the matter. Right now, I've got to get ready for work, just another day in the ninth circle of Hell. But before I get very far, I get that creepy-crawly sensation on the back of my neck like someone is watching me.

I'm not wrong.

Two women who live farther down the block in the opposite direction are out; they're holding steaming cups of coffee and very obviously looking my way. I only know one by name, and I can count on one hand the number of times we've greeted each other in the last year. No one would mistake the three of us for friends.

Thinking they can't possibly be interested in me, I glance over my shoulder to honestly see if they're looking at someone behind me. But there's nothing else to draw their interest.

They're staring at *me.*

I smile and wave tentatively. One of the women looks away, while the other barely acknowledges my gesture.

Sometimes I wish I could live in the boonies. It must be nice when your nearest neighbor lives half a mile away.

Normally I wouldn't give them a second thought. I don't live and die worrying about what the neighbors think. But it is difficult to ignore their strange behavior when it's coming hot on the heels of Rebecca's cold attitude.

As I start toward the house once more, the feeling on the back of my neck doesn't go away. I still feel like there's some-body else watching me, somebody I can't see. Beginning to feel deeply unnerved, I climb my snowy steps.

Before I reach the door, I hear a vehicle speeding around the corner. A white news van with several antennae and a big dish turns onto the street, slowing as it reaches my house.

And then I *realize.*

I suddenly understand why the neighbors and Rebecca are acting so strangely.

My whole life is about to change.

Somebody has figured out who I am.

1

The bookstore is busy, as it usually is, on a Sunday afternoon. I stop by the café for my obligatory cup of coffee. I was up really late last night, and I had an attack of the yawns on the way here. If I don't get a caffeine drip going, I might nod off during this meeting.

While I'm waiting in line, I check my texts. Rebecca has been blowing up my phone lately with everything she has going on at home. She found out her husband, Ron, was cheating on her many years ago, and ever since then, her life has been one long, seemingly unending roller coaster. But there's nothing from her this morning.

As I check my phone, I catch the woman in line behind me looking at me a little more pointedly than a perfect stranger would. Ever since the Big Reveal one year ago, I've had so many random people approach me and strike up a conversation, as if my personal life were any of their business. It's happened so many times that I'm perpetually on my guard these days.

The woman smiles when I catch her trying to look discreetly at me. "Hi."

"Hello."

She's younger than me, maybe mid- or late twenties, and has her frizzy brown hair up in a messy ponytail. She's wearing a gray sweater that's loose at the neck and a pair of mom jeans. She looks familiar.

I turn away from her, hoping this is enough of a social cue to signal that I don't want to engage.

"You're Amanda *Allen*, right?" the young woman asks.

I roll my eyes. The only way to avoid a conversation with this woman is to get out of line. But if she's one of those obsessed people, she might just follow me around the store.

I turn back around. "My name is Amanda *Christie*."

I lean on that last word. Christie. My surname hasn't been Allen for a long time. I've been going by Amanda Christie for a quarter century now, ever since I was a girl.

"Sorry." The woman looks apologetic. "That's what I meant to say. Christie. I ... I just got really nervous. I'm a big fan of yours."

I have two kinds of fans. One of them enjoys reading my suspense thrillers. The other has a sick fascination with my personal history.

It's not often you get to meet an author. And it's even rarer that you get to meet the daughter of a murderess.

This young woman is holding a notebook and a paperback novel. It's a suspense thriller by another author who works in my genre. Then I realize why this woman looks so familiar. She started attending our local writers' group a few weeks ago.

"Oh," I say casually, "you don't have to be nervous. I'm just a regular person, nothing special."

A lot of people claim they want to be rich and famous. Not me. Okay, well, maybe the rich part wouldn't be so bad. But famous? No thanks. I don't like being the center of attention, never mind have people actually fawning over me. While I enjoy what I do, and while I think I'm good at it, it's not like my job is *important*. I'm not curing cancer or running into burning buildings or trying to figure out what happened before the Big Bang. All I'm doing is writing escapist fiction, telling stories that excite and entertain and take people's minds, momentarily, away from their real-life problems.

"Regular person?" the woman says. "Hardly."

My cheeks start burning.

"I mean," the woman goes on, very loudly, "you're a *best-selling* author, for crying out loud."

I smile politely. A couple of people ahead of us in line turn around to gawk at me.

"It's just a job," I say.

"It's just a job that everybody would love to have!"

She's really laying it on thick. I'd like to think I wouldn't act like a fangirl if I ran into John Grisham or Ken Follett, but who knows? Maybe I would.

All the same, the attention is making me uncomfortable.

"I'm so sorry," I say, sticking out my hand. "What was your name again?"

She loses the smile. "You forgot my name?"

My stomach drops. I don't remember speaking to this woman one-on-one before this moment. She's only been to a few meetings before today. Sometimes we go around the room, and everybody introduces themselves, but I can't remember if we did that last week or not. And even if we did, how can she expect me to remember her name? There were probably forty, maybe fifty people in attendance last Sunday.

I'm not one of those self-help gurus capable of that parlor trick where they memorize everyone's name in the room using some two-thousand-year-old mnemonic device.

She suddenly laughs. "Just kidding!" She swats my arm playfully. "You must meet so many people. My name is Sarah. Uh, Sarah Keller. Remember that. One day I'm going to be a bestseller, just like you."

It feels like everybody in the café is gaping at me now. I want to die.

Sarah reaches to shake my hand, but stops at the sight of my palm. "Oh no, what happened there?"

I'd completely forgotten about the thick bandage covering most of my palm.

"Sorry," I say. "I was cutting up an apple this morning."

Sarah frowns. "You've got a little blood there ..."

I pull my hand back. She's right. Some blood has seeped out and dried near the heel of my palm.

"Sorry," I repeat.

"It's okay. The sight of blood doesn't bother me at all."

I fumble in my purse for a tissue, anything to wipe away the blood.

"What were you doing, cutting up an apple?" she asks, like it's the strangest thing in the world.

I really don't like the vibe I'm getting from this woman. Sure, she might be a fan of my work, but some fans are also more than fans, if you know what I mean. And I don't like how she called me Allen. If she's a fan, then there's a good chance she knows I would *never* want to be called by that last name. I haven't done a ton of interviews, but I've made that abundantly clear in each one.

"I mean, why not just eat the apple?" Sarah asks. "Or are

you one of those people who doesn't like the skin? There's a lot of nutrients there, you kn—"

"I cut up my apples to put them in a smoothie."

"Oh, okay. Makes sense."

This line cannot move quickly enough now.

"So, Sarah." I'm struggling here. Most women excel at small talk. I'm not one of them. "What kind of books do you write?"

"The same kind you do," she answers cheerfully. "Mysteries, thrillers, lots of suspense. And murder. There has to be murder. Preferably several. And the grislier, the better, know what I mean?"

I force a chuckle. My books have plenty of murders in them, but I keep the killings PG-13. I don't go into much detail, like some authors do, describing the quantity of blood spilled and the ... you get the idea.

"Have anything published?" I ask.

She shakes her head. "Not yet. I've written, like, three books. Sort of. I mean, one's done, and the other is *blah,* if you know what I mean, and I started a third, but I don't know where it's going. Anyway, I don't know if I'm going to self-pub on Amazon or try to get an agent."

She looks at me expectantly, like she's waiting for some sage advice that is going to be the big secret that changes her life. But I'm afraid I don't have anything special in the way of advice for aspiring authors, other than *keep writing.*

"Well, whatever you decide, keep at it."

She frowns, clearly disappointed by this response. We look at each other awkwardly for a moment. She wants more from me, but every writer's path is different. Some authors find success independently publishing their books online, while others land an agent and thrive working through a more traditional press.

I offer her a tight smile, then turn back around. The line creeps forward. I'm next, thank God.

"What's it like?" Sarah whispers. "Being the daughter of ... do you think it's helped you?"

I grind my teeth.

Either this woman is oblivious to the fact that asking such a personal question when we hardly know each other is incredibly rude, or she realizes but doesn't care.

Turning back around, I look her square in the eye.

"I don't really care to talk about my personal life."

Sarah's face falls. "Oh ... I thought you wanted people to know."

"*What*?"

"I mean, you've done all those interviews."

If she'd actually read them, then she'd know that being the daughter of Kimberly Dawn Allen is not something I care to discuss. Once someone knows who my mother is, they treat me like a curiosity.

A dangerous curiosity.

Though I'm ready to tell this woman what I think of her, I force myself to calm down and be polite. Maybe this woman really is a fan of my work; maybe she has spent time and money reading my stories.

"I do not enjoy being in the spotlight, believe me," I say. "I only sat down for those interviews because the story about my mother had already broken. And, like I told all the reporters, I don't like to talk about that part of my life."

Sarah gives me a knowing smile. "Come on, you can tell me."

I give her a sharp look. "Tell you what?"

"Weren't *you* the one who leaked the story to the press?"

I take a step away from her. "Absolutely not."

She doesn't believe me. "But come on, your sales took off after the world knew who you really were."

"Who I *really* was?" I can no longer be polite. "I've always been me, and I'll have you know that I've worked really hard to get where I am."

When someone suggests—and more than a few people have—that I owe all my success to the fact that my mother is notorious, it really gets my back up.

I've been writing novels for fifteen years now. When other college students were planning where to go for spring break, I was excited to use the week off from classes to get to work on a book. After I graduated from college, I worked full-time jobs for the next twelve years, fitting in writing early in the mornings or late in the evenings. When most people my age were enjoying their weekends off, I worked on my books. It took me seven years to land my first publishing deal. And that was for the *sixth* thriller I wrote. Wanna know how big an advance I got for it?

Four thousand dollars.

Also, that money was spread out over three payments. I got the first third when I signed the deal, the second third when my editor and I finished the edits, and the final third when the book was at last on the shelves, nearly a year and a half after the ink on the contract had dried.

And guess what? That four-figure deal made me one of the lucky few. Ninety-nine point nine percent of aspiring authors don't ever land a publishing contract.

My first published book earned out its advance and even won a small award, but, honestly, I would have made more money working retail at the mall. Over the next five years, I published one or two more books per year. The biggest advance I ever got was eleven thousand dollars. It takes me a good six months to write a book, sometimes longer. In this day and age, eleven thousand dollars doesn't go very far. Trying to live off that, for even half a year, is impossible. That's why, until recently, I've worked a full-time job.

When the story broke that Amanda Christie was actually Amanda Allen, daughter of Kimberly Dawn, I became famous for all the wrong reasons. In a lot of very important ways, it was terrible. My colleagues at work became icy. That promotion I'd been promised went to somebody else. People I considered friends distanced themselves. Neighbors who had always been friendly now pretended like I didn't exist. And everywhere I went, people were watching me. The whole world acted like there was something wrong with me, like I was either broken or perhaps even secretly a killer myself. It didn't help that I wrote suspense thrillers where sick people did some very twisted things.

See, they were all saying, *she's gotta be messed up in the head.*

But I will admit this: having all that unwelcome attention did get people talking about my books. That old saying that there's no such thing as bad publicity proved accurate in my case. My sales began to rise, and the last book I released after what I call the Big Reveal was a bestseller. A lot of cynical people, like Sarah here, think I was the one who intentionally broke this story, knowing it would give my career a much-needed shot in the arm. But it's not true. I never wanted anyone to know who my mother was. That was a secret I was happy to take to my grave. Unfortunately, it's incredibly difficult to talk cynics and conspiracy theorists out of their position. Once they've dug in, no matter what you say, they're never going to believe you.

The only reason she sells, they say, *is because of who her mother is.*

Sure, that story put me on the proverbial map, but if my books were bad, they wouldn't be selling. At best, I'd be a one-hit wonder. But that's not at all what happened. Several older titles on my backlist *also* started selling like crazy. And now my agent thinks my next advance is finally going to be the Big One, six or maybe seven figures.

That sure is a lot of money. And if it happens, I'll be grateful for it. My decision to keep writing only looks like the wise move now, with twenty-twenty hindsight. The truth is, there was no reason to expect I'd ever achieve any reasonable measure of success. In fact, I had every reason to suspect the opposite.

Sarah Keller is watching me like a hawk right now, waiting for me to admit to something that isn't true. She's not at all abashed by my anger. I'm waiting for what should be an obvious apology, but she's not saying anything.

"Excuse me," I say.

I don't want to be anywhere near this woman. I walk right past her, not bothering to get that coffee after all. With how angry I am, I don't need any caffeine to keep me going at this point.

2

In the bathroom, I check my makeup in the mirror and take out my pink comb to work on my hair. No matter how much I brush it out, no matter how much detangling spray I use, my hair knots up worse than a dehydrated marathon runner. My pink comb always reminds me of Mom. She had one just like this when she was a child. I finish up in the bathroom and head out.

The writers' group meets on the other side of the building, where the store holds special events like book signings and activities for kids to encourage reading. The group is open to everyone, from the mega-bestselling to the person who hasn't written a word yet.

Writing is a solitary, lonely profession. People not working in the field don't understand what the life is like. They might shrug off the idea of rejection like it's nothing, but very few of them could handle years of it. Working away and never earning a cent. What little family I have left has been mostly unsympathetic. Aunt Cecelia, the woman who took me in after Mom had to run, has no time for it. She once told me that I chose to be a writer, so I just have to deal with it.

Of all my friends, only Rebecca seems to truly "get it." Thank God for her.

The writers' group was the one place I could go knowing someone would *understand.* Even the successful authors who attend regularly remember what it was like before their big break and can sympathize.

I pass through the MYSTERY section, making my way to the shelf where my novels are.

My books are turned around so they're backwards.

"Not again," I mutter.

Instead of the spine facing out, the pages are facing out. And the one book that is supposed to have its cover looking out is also turned in the wrong direction.

It's not the first time I've discovered my books like this here. Some goofball is *purposely* doing this so my books are more difficult to find. I start pulling them out, one by one, and putting them the right way. Who the heck is doing th—

"Hi, Amanda."

The voice startles me. I didn't hear anybody come into the aisle. Whirling around, I find my ex-boyfriend standing a few feet away.

"*Matthew,*" I say. "You scared the living daylights out of me."

My heart is fluttering. I pick up the book I dropped when Matthew frightened me, then place it on the shelf before facing him again.

Matthew doesn't look good. When we were together, he always had a fresh haircut and a clean-shaven look. He took care of himself and always had nice clothes. Being a real estate agent, the man always had to look presentable, be ready to sell at a moment's notice.

I'm not superficial. I don't care about expensive clothes or constantly fussing over one's appearance. I love a comfy pair of old sweatpants as much as the next girl. But I have to admit, Matthew has let himself go. His hair is long and messy. He hasn't shaved in several days, and the look isn't flattering; he's stuck in that awkward phase between cute stubble and distinguished beard.

Matthew normally dressed up whenever he left the house. *You never know when you're getting a call,* he would say, and like the universe was listening, he'd always get a call and have to run to show some house. But today he's wearing an old pair of jeans under a sweater that used to fit him well but is now a size too small.

Matthew gives me a playful smile and pretends to be apologetic. "Oh, I'm sorry. I didn't mean to—"

"This has to stop," I say.

He tilts his head to the side. That annoying grin is still on his face. I wish I could punch it off.

"You used to like when I scared you," he says.

"I hated it," I say. "And you know that."

"Really?" He pretends to think about it. "Oh yeah, that's right. But I never understood it. We used to watch all those slasher flicks—"

"Matthew," I say, looking him dead in the eye, "you can't keep doing this. It's been over a year now."

His grating smile slips. His eyes turn serious.

"What?" he says innocently. "I can't shop at this book-store anymore?"

"You know the writers' group meets here every Sunday. That's why you're here."

"It slipped my mind, to be honest," he says. "But then when I saw you head into the bathroom, I thought I should say hi. We were very close not so long ago. It would have been rude to ignore you, wouldn't it?"

"Next time, please ignore me," I say.

He adopts a hurt expression. "Amanda, please. I think about you all the time. That lawsuit with my ex is done. It was all a lie, like I told you and—"

"I can't do this." I hold up a palm. "Goodbye, Matthew."

I don't want to get into it with him. Matthew's not someone you engage with, because he doesn't understand the word no, and he doesn't respect boundaries. Give him an inch, he'll take a mile. Then ask how you could be so stingy.

"Wow." He makes a face. "I thought better of you. Don't you care about the truth at all?"

I start walking. "If this doesn't stop, I will call a lawyer."

Before I get past him, Matthew latches on my forearm.

"Wait."

I spin around and rotate my arm very quickly, ripping myself out of his grip. I've taken a few women's self-defense courses over the years. It takes all my willpower not to knee Matthew between the legs.

"Whoa!" Matthew jumps backward, like I'm the aggressor. "Take it easy! I just wanted to talk."

"I'm done talking with you," I say. "Do not put your hands on me ever again."

"Please, Amanda," he says, his voice growing thick. "I really miss you. You were the one. You *are* the one. I swear to you that thing with my ex was a lie. If you'll just hear me out, then—"

"Goodbye, Matthew."

This time he does not try to grab me. I walk away,

making sure not to look back once. When I enter the area in the back of the bookstore, I'm all jittery from the shot of adrenaline. I cannot *believe* Matthew grabbed me. Especially considering why I broke up with him in the first place.

I take my usual seat, on the far-right side of the big table facing the room. I'd much rather sit in the, for lack of a better word, audience section of the room on one of the folding chairs. I don't like being front and center, like I'm some kind of authority figure. But the other published authors insisted I join them up front, and eventually I relented.

I'm a few minutes early, but the room is already full. Ever since my story broke, and especially since my next book turned into a bestseller, the writers' group has been well attended. There must be sixty people here today, probably our biggest crowd ever. There are a lot of new faces too, which is great.

Sarah Keller is sitting in the second row of chairs facing the big table, looking down at her phone with an angry expression on her face. Shaking her head, she quickly types a message of some kind. I hope she's not posting about how "rude" I was to her. She seems like she'd be the type.

I catch a handsome man with brown hair sitting in the third row looking at me. As soon as my eyes find him, he turns away shyly, pretends to be on his phone. Smiling to myself, I keep my eyes on him a moment longer until his baby blues inevitably drift back in my direction. This time, he doesn't look away. Instead, he laughs and nods as if to say: *You caught me.*

He's been coming for a few weeks now, giving me the googly eyes when he thought I wasn't paying attention. His name is Brandon. He's a bit younger than me, I'm guessing, but not *too* much. And right now, we are gawking at each other like a couple of teenagers, having a moment out of one of those dumb romantic comedies. I haven't been with anybody since Matthew ... with everything that's happened in my life, there hasn't been any time.

But I could make time for this guy. He's handsome in that boy-next-door way, with brown hair and those blue eyes and a strong jawline. He's also put together, with nice broad shoulders ...

"Afternoon, everybody."

Ken Willis swoops into the room, carrying two novels (both by him) in one hand and a coffee in the other. He was one of the founders of this group, starting it when he was just a newb and didn't have a publishing deal yet. Like me, he eventually went on to become a midlist author, getting his books published but not really making a living wage at it, until a couple of years ago when one of his sci-fi books went, if you'll pardon the pun, supernova. His newfound success has unfortunately gone to his head. He has a tendency to steamroll his way through these meetings, answering every single question posed, never missing an opportunity to give his opinion even if he has nothing interesting to say.

"Sorry I'm late," Ken says, "but I was busy writing the next bestseller this morning and didn't want to stop."

I don't groan. But I do roll my eyes. A couple of other published authors sitting at the table with me do the same thing. The newer members of the group, on the other hand, eat it up, several of them laughing and a few people in the audience even applauding.

Brandon catches me in that unguarded moment. He smiles and also rolls his eyes at Ken.

Ken takes his usual spot at the middle of the big table and puts his own novels faceup in front of him.

"Thank you all for coming," he says. "I looked over the agenda from last week, where many of you wanted to know what it was like working with a publisher. I thought that was a good place to start, and I happen to have a few thoughts on the matter."

Of course he does.

Ken clears his throat. "If that sounds good to everybody, why don't we get started there?"

We've talked about this a lot recently, so I don't really want to expand on it. But, at the same time, I'm not interested in running the show, keeping minutes, or making sure we stick to an agenda. I'm really only here to socialize and help in what little way I can. So I keep quiet and let Ken drone on and on about the various publishers he's worked with. Eventually I tune him out and look around the audience. Sarah Keller is avoiding eye contact with me, which is totally fine. Brandon can't stop smiling at me, but he makes a real effort to listen to Ken and then the next author who discusses the subject. I spot the older lady—Louann—who always sits in the back row, never speaks except when she's forced to introduce herself, and knits the entire meeting. Just past her is the low divider separating this room from the bookstore proper. I'm about to glance back at Brandon, but then I catch a pair of eyes looking at me.

Matthew.

He's got half his head over the divider, and he's watching me. Before this moment, his behavior has been annoying, but this is the creepiest thing he's done since we broke up, and I begin to worry that he's become unhinged. At first, Matthew respected my wishes and cut off all contact after we broke up. But a few months later, I started getting infrequent and innocuous-seeming texts and messages from him.

> Just wanted to say hi.

> Hope you're well.

> That movie you love is available on Prime.

I was polite but kept my distance, often "forgetting" to write him back when I thought the contact was getting to be too much.

He would take the hint and digitally disappear for a month or two. But then the texts would start again:

> Read your new book—it's amazing!

> Remember that zipline place we always wanted to try? It's closed now. ☹

> Found out my aunt has cancer.

> Do you think you'll ever get married? Do you still not want to have kids?

About a month ago, I told him I needed a clean break. Matthew used that old line about just wanting to remain friends. It was only when I told him I didn't believe him that his behavior became worrisome. Instead of respecting my wishes and going away once I'd called his bluff, Matthew doubled down. He admitted to still loving me and told me we were "destined to be together."

Now he's camped out at the back of the bookstore, gawking at me while I'm in a writers' group meeting. I didn't want to have to go through the pains of hiring an attorney and getting a new phone number, but he's left me no choice. He's obsessed—

"Amanda?" Ken says.

My head snaps around to look at him. "I'm sorry?"

He makes a face, at which several people in the audience laugh.

"Earth to Amanda," Ken says.

"Sorry," I say, red-faced. "I was deep in thought."

"I'll say," Ken responds, prompting a few more laughs, which I really don't appreciate. "Was there anything you wanted to add to the discussion?"

I shake my head and smile politely. "Not really. I think we've covered this a lot recently."

Ken's eyes narrow. He does not miss the barbed comment.

Ken turns back to the group. "Why don't we open up the conversation, then? Does anyone have any questions for the panel?"

The panel. Those words are like nails on a chalkboard to me. Ken likes to sit up here at the big table and pretend like this meeting is one extended book tour press conference, where the important people (mostly him) field questions from the peons. It's so gross.

"Or anything," I jump in. "It doesn't have to be a question. Maybe some news, or something you've experienced lately in your writing?"

Ken's smile remains on his lips, but it's gone from his eyes.

There is the obligatory moment where a large group of people are quiet, each of them looking around the room to see who's going to be brave enough to speak first.

"Come on," Ken says. "We don't bite."

A ripple of nervous laughter carries through the room. The cute guy raises his hand to speak.

"I've got—"

"Did anyone hear about that woman who turned up dead this morning?"

This question comes from Louann, the old lady who's always knitting in the back. She's one of the few people in the group who still wears a KN95 mask.

No one answers. Everybody seems to be at a loss.

Louann carefully sets her knitting materials down on her legs. She's been coming to the writers' group for about a year now, but I can count on one hand the number of times she's spoken.

"Sorry." Louann smiles apologetically. "For blurting that out. But everybody here is always looking for story ideas. Not to exploit someone's death, but this murder is interesting. Anybody who's a mystery or thriller writer should look into it."

"Yeah," someone else chimes in. "I saw it online this morning."

"It's disturbing," another woman adds. "Fair warning."

I notice that Brandon appears to be at a loss, like me. But most in the room seem to know the story. I try to stay off the internet in general, but especially in the mornings, when I want to get some work done. This morning, I was busy slogging through the latest book.

"Oh my God," someone else blurts out, their eyes riveted to their phone.

"Decapitated," Louann blurts out, shaking her head. "Whoever did it, the sicko forced a book into her mouth."

I frown. If I heard her correctly, that's a really odd coincidence.

There are a few gasps of disbelief and the usual outraged chatter that follows such an announcement. One person has to make the obligatory comment about how the world is completely falling apart. Pretty soon, though, everybody has their phone out to check the news story.

Including me.

My heart is in my throat as I do a Google search. I'm dimly aware that Ken is talking, trying to regain control of the conversation, but none of his words actually reach the part of my brain responsible for comprehension. I click on the first link that pops up.

Police have not identified the woman by name, but authorities have confirmed what Louann said.

Talk about a terrible coincidence ...

"Amanda?" Ken says. "Are you alright?"

The room is spinning.

"Amanda?"

I'm able to find my voice and stop the room spinning somehow. Palming the table in front of me, I get my bearings.

"Sorry," I manage. "I was just, uh, shocked to read about what happened."

I pull the travel mug out of my bag and sip from the smoothie I made right before leaving the house. It's still freezing cold, which is a good thing because I'm burning up. When I put the smoothie down, I realize a few people are staring at me.

They must have read my first novel, *Serial Reader*.

It featured a deranged killer. He decapitated one of his victims ...

And stuffed a book into her mouth.

3

My mind is elsewhere for the rest of the meeting, but I manage to fake my way through it.

Decapitations are rare. But they do happen, of course. Anything is possible when it comes to psychopathic killers.

But what are the odds the victim would also have a book stuffed into their mouth?

As the meeting comes to a close, I catch Sarah Keller watching me from the second row. When our eyes meet, she gives me a very strange smile that I try to decipher. She mentioned she was a fan of my work, so I'm assuming she's made the same connection between the death in my novel and this bit of news.

But why smile about it? Is this her way of making me aware she's made the connection? Based on our awkward exchange earlier, I do wonder if she thinks I'm secretly *happy* about this tragic turn of events because it might drum up more sales for my first novel. That's obviously not the case, but disabusing this rude woman of the notion would be more trouble than it's worth.

The less I engage with her, the better.

Sarah only breaks eye contact once Ken announces the meeting's end. Like she's fleeing the scene of a crime, she quickly stuffs her things into a backpack and hurries out, nearly bowling someone over on her way. Though I'm glad I don't have to engage with her again, her unusual behavior has only added to my considerable unease this morning. News of the murder unsettled me, and I've been keeping an eye out for Matthew the whole meeting.

While I gather my things, Brandon approaches the big table. The butterflies start fluttering in my stomach. It's been a while since I've met a nice guy.

"Hi there."

I act like I didn't notice him coming toward me. Picking up my bag, I try to seem surprised.

"Oh, hi."

I flash him what I hope is my best smile. Brandon's clear blue eyes are drinking me in. He sticks out a hand.

"I'm Brandon."

"I—" I almost say *I know.* But I catch myself in time. I want to play this cool. I don't want this cute guy thinking I'm desperate. "I'm Amanda."

We shake hands. His palm is rough, callused, like he works with his hands a lot. Or, judging by the look of him, maybe he lifts big heavy weights.

"I know who you are."

He flashes a nervous smile, which makes him all the cuter.

"Hey, this is totally out of character for me," he says. "I

don't usually walk right up to a pretty woman and do this, but could I buy you a cup of coffee?"

Pretty woman?

My face is a million degrees.

I never did get that coffee I so desperately needed earlier, because Sarah was being so rude.

"I'd love that," I say, my voice cracking a little bit.

His whole face lights up. "Oh, great!"

I check to make sure I have everything in my bag; then we head toward the café. The perfect gentleman, Brandon moves out of the way so I can leave the meeting room first. I keep my eyes peeled for Matthew.

"Is something wrong?" Brandon asks, picking up on my nerves.

I don't want to tell him my ex-boyfriend went from heart-broken to creepy today.

"No, everything's fine."

"What were you going to say?" I ask. "Before that lady brought up that terrible news story?"

Brandon's face gets all red. He scratches the back of his neck.

"Oh, it was nothing."

"Really?" I say. "You seemed like you had a pertinent question, but then the whole meeting went off the rails, and we never came back to you."

He takes a deep breath.

"It's probably dumb," he says. "I'm just getting started on my first book."

"That's great," I say. "What's it about?"

"Uh ..."

His face is bright red. I know the feeling.

Some authors can't wait for someone to ask them this

question. They will talk your ear off for hours about their latest project, boring everyone in listening distance to tears.

I'm not like that.

I *don't* like to discuss what I'm working on. And I find it incredibly difficult to explain a story in a few words. They call it the elevator pitch. I've tried getting better at that, but it does not come naturally to me.

And don't get me started on synopses. They're the *worst*.

"It's hard to describe," Brandon says.

I smile. "I understand."

"What about you?" he asks.

"She writes mysteries and thrillers."

Sarah Keller steps out from between two bookshelves in the Sci-Fi section right in front of us.

"Didn't you know?" Sarah asks Brandon, like she's been part of our conversation the entire time. "She's Amanda *Christie*."

Brandon looks to me, wondering if Sarah and I are friends, very confused by her sudden butting-in. I give him a slight shake of the head and a Help Me look.

"Oh," he says, offering me an apologetic smile. "Sorry, I don't read too many mysteries and thrillers."

"Well, you *should* have heard of her," Sarah says, her voice full of sarcasm. "She's a Big. Time. Author."

I don't want to turn this conversation with Sarah Keller uncomfortable right in front of this cute guy I hardly know. But it needs to be done.

"And didn't you know? She's the daughter of—"

"Sarah," I snap, "I don't appreciate the way you've been speaking to me. Would you please leave me alone?"

Sarah looks offended. While I'm waiting for her to fire

back, I steal a quick glance at Brandon to gauge his reaction. He's giving her a standoffish look.

When Sarah notices Brandon's stony expression, she stops short of speaking. In quite the huff, she whirls around and shoots up the Sci-Fi aisle, disappearing around the corner.

I offer Brandon a sheepish grin. "I'm so sorry. I don't like to talk to people like that, but—"

"But she's a psycho?" Brandon cuts in, with a goofy grin.

I laugh, relieved by his reaction. "I'll tell you all about our first interaction. I mean, if you're into torture."

"Torture away," he says, motioning toward the café.

We make small talk in line while we wait to order. Brandon never once looks away from me, not even when a rather stunning redhead who looks like she's a personal trainer walks right by him. The guy is totally into me, and I'm doing my best not to come off as desperate as I actually am. But I can't help it. A couple of my nervous tics show up. I catch myself fussing with my hair. I worry about smiling too widely, since the teeth in my lower jaw are a little crooked.

After we order, we wait for our coffee by the counter.

"Uh-oh," Brandon says, looking past my shoulder.

I freeze. "Is it her again?"

He nods. "Only this time ..."

"What?"

"Don't turn around." He puts his hand on my shoulder. "Don't look."

I'm dying to see. "What is it?"

"She's chewing out that other guy; what's his name, Ken?"

"I have to see."

"Oh my God," Brandon says, bringing a hand up to his mouth. "She's got a knife."

"What?"

I whirl.

Sarah is not there.

When I turn back around, Brandon is trying not to laugh.

"Not funny."

"You're smiling," he says.

"Did you do that just so you could touch my shoulder?" I ask.

That wipes the smile right off his lips. "Oh, no, I'm sorry, I didn't mean—"

"Got you," I say.

He holds out a palm. "I deserved that."

"Yes, you did." Then I grow serious once more. "But don't ever touch me again."

He looks nervous for a moment. "Oh, you're tough."

We collect our coffees and sit at a small table next to the storefront windows where we can see out into the parking lot. A big truck is moving methodically up and down the rows of cars, throwing salt behind it. They're calling for the first snowstorm of the season tonight.

"Alright," I say after we're settled. "Tell me about your book."

His face is immediately red again.

"It's so *embarrassing* to talk about it. I mean, in my head, it sounds like a good idea. But when I try to explain it to somebody else ..."

"It's okay," I say. "We all feel like that."

"You do too?" he asks, incredulous. "But you're a

published author. And apparently, I should have heard of you."

I laugh. Just because you're a bestselling author, it doesn't mean everybody's heard of you.

"Still happens to me," I say.

"So, you write mysteries and thrillers?"

He's slyly changed the subject of the conversation away from himself back to me.

"Yes."

"Is there murder?" he asks.

"Usually," I say, which is a lie. My books *always* involve murder. I'm fascinated by this savage, inhuman act. I'm sure if I started speaking to a psychologist, they'd have a field day with *that*, considering who my mother is.

Then we just start talking. I tell him all about my writing career and about how great it felt, about six months ago, to give notice at my job. Brandon shares his story. He moved to the area for an IT job several years ago. He was there less than three months when the CEO sold it off to a private equity firm, who forced them to merge with a similar organization, which then proceeded to fire anybody they thought was redundant. Because of how little tenure Brandon had there, he was one of the first to go.

"Ever since then," he says, "I've bounced around. It's more difficult to find an IT job than you think."

That's really surprising. I always figured doing something with computers was a surefire way to make a lot of money.

"So what are you doing for work?" I ask.

"I work here, actually."

"At the bookstore?"

He nods. "Why do you think I offered to buy you a coffee? I get a discount."

I have a good laugh at that.

"I've always loved books," he says. "And always wanted to write one."

"You should," I say. "You should write one about—"

"Hold on." He gives me the palm. "Are you going to suggest I write a book about a supercomputer trying to take over the world?"

"No."

Maybe I was.

"You so were." He points at me. "That's what everybody who knows me says. You're into computers, you should write a book about one."

I give him the best cutesy smile I can muster. "Well, what *is* your book about?"

"It's, uh ..." He looks around the café, lowers his voice. "It's a romance novel."

"Romance?"

"Yeah." He makes a face. "Look, here's the thing. I don't even read them, but they sell really well, you know? And, out of nowhere, this idea came to me. So I just sat down and started."

"I would never have guessed."

He shrugs. "So that question I had, earlier."

"Yes?"

Neither of us have touched our coffees.

He fidgets in his chair.

"When do you write?" he asks. "What time of day?"

I don't know what I was expecting him to ask, but it certainly wasn't this. "Normally first thing, then I take a break to exercise or get housework done. Then I start up again after lunch and work for a few hours."

"But not at night?" he says.

"Only when I'm under a deadline."

"Are you under one now?"

"No."

"Great." He smiles, leans in. "Then that means you're free for dinner tomorrow."

I tip my head back and laugh. He got me, alright. Very quickly, maybe too quickly, I say yes.

"Great. You can tell me who your mother is," he says with a wink.

I feign a smile. I wish he already knew. That way I wouldn't have to worry about his reaction. But now I have to figure out a way to share the story of my mother with this man. It's a story that scares most men away.

4

I'm still riding high when I pull into my driveway. Brandon is very handsome, we share an interest in books, and he's got a good sense of humor. I can't help the excitement I feel. Best of all, he seems like a really nice guy.

Then again, my ex-boyfriend seemed like one too. Matthew had a good job, he was always supportive of my aspirations, and he never let anybody be rude to me. We dated for a while, and I was *this close* to asking him to move in with me. Then his ex-girlfriend accused him of assaulting her.

I was completely shocked when I found out. Even worse, Matthew himself didn't tell me. His ex contacted me to share the damning news. At first, I didn't know what to think. Matthew got angry occasionally, but he'd never laid a hand on me. I think I didn't *want* to believe it because everything was going well in our relationship.

But then I started to wonder.

Matthew hadn't gotten mad *occasionally*. The truth is,

Matthew has a temper. Usually, it's directed toward other men. He has a certain machismo that, I won't lie, was a bit of a turn-on when we first met. I'd never dated a man like that, someone who was constantly out to prove himself to others, who was determined to never let anybody walk over him. Most of the guys I dated were more type B personalities: laid-back, easygoing, humorous, kind. Matthew's very different personality was *exciting* at first because it was such a change of pace for me.

It was only later, after we'd broken up, that I realized that his machismo was just him overcompensating for a lack of self-confidence. I understood that a man who has to constantly assert himself is suffering from some deeper problems.

And there was one time—only once—when Matthew lost his temper with me. He thought one of my old high school friends was flirting with me over text, and we got into an argument. Matthew raised his voice while the neighbors were sitting twenty feet away in the dining room. Rebecca and her husband, Ron, heard everything.

When Matthew and I were alone later that night, I told him how much he'd embarrassed me and that he needed to leave. I didn't break up with him on the spot, but the implication was there. He gently protested, but when I insisted, he grabbed my arm. Now, at the time, I was turning to walk away from him, and he claimed that he hadn't meant to hurt or intimidate me. He just wanted to keep the conversation going. But when I heard about his ex-girlfriend filing charges against him, that unprecedented (and never repeated) moment in our relationship came crashing back. It was like I could feel his hand again, crushing my forearm.

I obviously made the right decision. While his antics

following our break-up were understandable for a while, his behavior today has crossed a line. Now I have to consider obtaining a restraining order, an action I'm reluctant to take. It requires research and paperwork, potentially hiring an attorney, inviting the police into my business, and dealing with government bureaucracy.

Also, I've heard through friends that Matthew has hit a low point. Following the charges brought by his ex-girlfriend, Matthew lost his job as a real estate agent and is now working at the mall, probably earning a fraction of what he used to. The last person he wants to see on his doorstep is a sheriff holding a court order. I don't necessarily want to make matters worse for him, but I must protect myself.

I put Matthew out of my mind and think about my upcoming date with Brandon. I've decided to broach the subject of Mom immediately. If my mother's identity is going to sour him on me, then it's better to know right away.

But something tells me he's not going to mind. That might be wishful thinking, but Brandon doesn't seem the type to hold anything against a person because of who their parents are.

I hop out of the car. The sky is one long wall of gray. That electric smell is in the air, the kind that normally precedes a snowfall.

Parked across the street is a sedan I don't recognize. Two serious-looking men are sitting in it. They both get out of the vehicle and cross the street. It's obvious they're here for me.

"Ms. Christie?" the older one asks.

I stop before I reach my front steps.

"Yes?"

The two men produce police IDs. They have reached the edge of my lawn and are looking up at me from the sidewalk.

"Do you mind if we ask you some questions?" the younger of the two says. He's athletic-looking, tall, with a dark complexion. The wire-rimmed glasses he's wearing make him also appear erudite.

"Sure," I say.

I have a sneaking suspicion I know what this is about.

"Would you mind if we came inside?" the older of the two asks. He's balding and paunchy and wears a crooked mustache. "It's cold out today."

I get the feeling they want to see inside my house without going through the motions of getting a search warrant. Technically I could decline and force them to ask their questions in the December cold. On the other hand, I probably don't want the whole neighborhood watching two detectives question me. Though I have my suspicions, this could be about anything.

It could even be about my mother.

"Of course," I say, forcing a smile.

"Great," the older man says in a neutral tone. "I'm Detective Rooney. This is my partner, Detective Taylor."

They come up the front walk and meet me at the steps.

"If you don't mind my asking, what is this about?"

The two detectives share a look before the younger one responds.

Taylor says, "We'd prefer to discuss that inside."

I keep my voice low. "Is it my mother? Have you found her?"

"No." Rooney shakes his head, then a thought seems to occur to him. "Unless there's something you wanted to tell us?"

"No," I say quickly. "I have no idea where she is."

Taylor smiles. Rooney can't be bothered. Both men,

though, keep their eyes on me until I can't feel any more awkward in their overbearing presence.

"Please come in," I say.

BECAUSE I WRITE mysteries and thrillers, people assume that I know a lot about police work. My friends like to joke that I could commit the perfect crime, while others ask for my opinion on local crime stories, assuming I know the best way to go about catching a murderer. Many of them think I'm a human lie detector, or that I'm like Sherlock Holmes and notice every mundane detail about a room or a person.

None of these things are true.

While I try to keep my plots plausible, they're not *realistic*. And, while I do my research, I'm no police or forensics expert. Mostly I just try to tell an entertaining story and keep my readers guessing.

When I write a book, I'm in a position of omniscience. I know what everybody is thinking, doing, and planning. If I'm not happy with the first draft, I can edit to my heart's content, completely changing storylines and character arcs. All the reader sees is the finished product, where it appears as if I knew everything that was going to happen all along.

The truth is, I know about as much about police work as somebody who watches a lot of Investigation Discovery. I don't think three or four steps ahead of everyone else, like some of my characters are able to in my books. And I certainly don't know how to outsmart real detectives who question suspects every day for a living.

All this is to say that I'm incredibly nervous with these

two detectives in my living room. Rooney has taken a seat on the couch while Taylor remains standing.

"Do you live alone, Ms. Christie?" Rooney asks.

"Yes," I say. "And please call me Amanda."

"Amanda," he mutters. "Right."

Rooney has this habit of expressing everything with an air of incredulity. The way he said Amanda just now, it's like he doesn't even believe that's my real name. I half expect him to ask for my birth certificate to confirm it.

"Christie's your pen name," Rooney states.

"It's my *legal* name," I correct him. "I changed my name when I went to live with my aunt."

He nods, but even that gesture seems skeptical.

"Why did you pick Christie?" Taylor asks. He sounds like he's genuinely interested.

"I've always been a big reader," I say. "I loved Agatha Christie's stories."

"Amanda Christie," Rooney says. "Must work out pretty well for you. Alphabetically, you appear on the shelves right next to her."

I smile. "I've only recently found success. The first eleven or so years, I worked a full-time job to support myself."

"Hmph," Rooney says.

Taylor moves through the living room, changing positions so that he's almost standing behind me.

"Right," Taylor says. "I've heard about that, yeah. What do they call them, midlist authors?"

I have to look over my shoulder to peer at him. "Yes, that's what I am. Was." I laugh nervously. "I still think of myself as one, as you can tell."

Taylor has a tiny notepad out. "Right, I understand that." He taps the side of his head with his pen. "Up here, I'm still playing ball. Sometimes I wake up in the middle of the night in a sweat, thinking I didn't make it to the game. I understand. How about you, Rooney?"

The other detective growls. "Give it a few years."

Rooney really does not like me. And I get the sense he really doesn't like his partner, either. But, of course, that could all be part of their play. They've assumed some pretty obvious roles, with Taylor being the friendly guy and Rooney the nasty one. I wonder if this is how they always do it, or if they change parts depending on the interviewee.

"Where did you work?" Taylor asks, easing his way around to my other side. "What did you do?"

They've got me triangulated now.

"I worked for a media company as a copywriter, later as an editor," I explain.

"Right." Taylor nods. "And where was that?"

Why does he want to know about my last job?

"Uh, the name of the company was Nordel Media," I say. "I waitressed for a couple of years out of college, then finally got hired doing something where I could actually use my degree."

"English," Rooney barks.

I nod.

He shakes his head. Obviously disapproving of my decision to spend four years and a lot of money studying a language I grew up speaking. I've heard that one before.

"How long were you at Nordel?" Taylor asks while he scratches notes.

"Almost ten years."

"Right, that makes sense." He pulls a face, like he's consulting some list inside his head containing information he can fact-check my statements against. "Okay, so you were there ten years. You seem like a nice woman; you must have made some friends there."

"Oh, sure." I look nervously from good cop to bad cop and back again. No idea where this is going. "I'm kind of an introvert, but I made some friends. I still talk to a few."

"Any enemies?" Rooney asks.

His question startles me.

"Enemies?" I shake my head. "I'm not the kind of person who makes enemies."

"Really?" Rooney leans forward on the couch. "What kind of person makes enemies, then?"

"Uh ..." I look helplessly from him to Taylor, but the other detective is looking down at his notepad. "I mean, I'm kind of quiet. I'm not very confrontational—"

"I think what Detective Rooney means," Taylor interjects, "were there people there you *didn't* get along with? You were working at Nordel for ten years, and interacting with, what, dozens of colleagues, right, so chances are during that time period, you and somebody else didn't always see eye to eye. Was there somebody like that?"

A name comes to mind: Megan Patterson. But I push the unpleasant memories away. Megan and I had our differences. But calling her an *enemy* is a stretch.

"Not really."

Taylor makes a face. He was expecting a different answer. I rack my brain, trying to think of somebody who might, if I squint really hard, check that box for him. It's like I *want* to give Taylor something, he's so nice. But, at the same time, I'm also terrified of telling them anything, for fear I'm admitting to something. And I'm also terrified of *not* admitting to something, for fear that makes me later look suspicious. I really wish I knew why they were here—

"Why'd you leave Nordel?" Rooney asks.

"Well ..."

I blush every time somebody asks me this question. As happy as I am, I'm still embarrassed to talk about how my publishing career took off. It's a bit like winning the lottery. I know how hard I worked, but I also know how lucky I am. A lot of very good writers, many of them better artists than me, will never see this level of success for reasons outside their control.

Imagine telling somebody you get to live your dream, while knowing they almost certainly aren't.

Of course, Rooney is likely mistaking my embarrassment for guilt, like I'm trying to hide something.

"My last book became a bestseller. So I got the opportunity to—"

"This was after that story leaked about your mother, right?" Rooney asks.

"Six months or so after, yes," I say.

Rooney's eyes narrow. "No such thing as bad press."

I shake my head. "I don't know about that. I liked my life the way it was before everybody knew who ... before."

"Really?" Rooney asks. "You liked having to work a full-time job to support yourself while you spent what little free time you had writing these books that hardly anybody read?"

He's got my back up.

Taylor rushes in. "Ms. Christie—*Amanda*—" Big smile. "Amanda, I'm sure you were happy when you got your big break. I mean, anybody would be. It must have been life-changing, right?"

I manage, "Yes."

"That must have been really something," Taylor says. "To

walk into your boss's office one day, tell them you were quitting. Did you give them two weeks' notice? Or was it longer,
since you'd worked there nearly ten years?"

I catch something behind Taylor's eyes. A tell. Maybe he
put it there on purpose. I don't know. These two guys have
got me all discombobulated.

I suspect they know what happened at Nordel. But why
are they asking me about it?

"Things didn't end so well," I say.

"Define not so well," Rooney says.

"Everything has context," I say. "I'm a quiet, private
person."

"An introvert," Taylor says, like he's really eager to help
me along.

"Yes." I nod rather than repeat it, like introvert is a dirty
word. "I had—*have*—friends there, but mostly I kept to
myself. And then that story broke, and ... all of a sudden, I
was *very* remarkable."

"That must have been hard," Taylor says with what
sounds like genuine sympathy. "I'm a bit of an intro myself. I
don't like being the center of attention."

There are tears coming. I'm so angry at myself for
showing what Rooney will undoubtedly take as weakness. I
try to bottle them up.

"And it wasn't just at work," I go on, bulldozing my
way through the hard parts of the story. "It was at
home, it was with old friends, it was in yoga class, it
was at the coffee shop, it was everywhere. I was sort of
famous, and I hated it. I had reporters hounding me at
all hours. People I thought of as friends didn't want
anything to do with me. It got so bad, I considered
changing my name—again—and moving somewhere

new. Twenty-five years ago, it was much easier to disappear. I was also a child. But things are different today. I felt trapped.

"All this stress was wearing on me. The quality of my work suffered. I couldn't concentrate. I took a couple of weeks off, but that didn't help. I just had to face all the same people all over again, with them wondering every minute if I my mother was a killer, if I knew where she was, if I was helping her stay hidden. All of them looking at me like I was going to lose my mind didn't help. I made a few careless mistakes at work, and my boss put me on a performance review."

"What's that?" Rooney asks.

I wipe away a treasonous tear. "Well, it's what they do when they're considering firing you. Either you shape up or ..."

"Ship out," Rooney finishes, harshly and unnecessarily.

"And the whole time I was racing to finalize the edits on my book. My publisher demanded I add another twist to the story, but there was nothing. I mean, like nothing." I point to my head. "I couldn't come up with anything."

"Writer's block?" Taylor asks.

I hate that term, mostly because it's not a real thing. It's just something laypeople say to sound like they know what it's like to write a book.

"No," I say. "I mean, I felt like I had finished a puzzle. There were no more pieces to fit in, no room for them anywhere. My editor wanted me to change the puzzle without actually changing it, is the best way I can describe it. Do you know how difficult that is?"

Rooney remains unsympathetic. Taylor's brow knits together above his wire-rimmed glasses.

"It's always easier to cut than pad," I try, hoping that will make more sense.

"Easier to cut, huh?" Rooney asks, and I don't like the way he says it. Not at all.

Taylor's eyes bulge. "So what happened?"

"I forced another twist into the story, very close to the ending. My editor wasn't thrilled with my choice, but it was the best I could do. I was starting to feel like they were getting cold feet and maybe not going to publish—"

"Hold on," Taylor says, outraged. "They can *do* that?"

I nod. "It happens. Basically, they get their lawyers to come up with *reasons*, and next thing you know, there's no book. Or, and this happens a lot, the house complains about the terrible quarter they just had, and then what little marketing budget your book had shrinks or disappears altogether, and when they release your novel, there's no push behind it. It comes and goes, and nobody knows."

Taylor seems outraged. "Comes and goes and nobody knows?"

"But they ended up publishing it, obviously," Rooney says, like he can't be bothered with what was some very high drama in my otherwise dull life. "And it went supernova, and now here you are."

I'm determined to plant a flag at this point in my story. This man might not understand, or even try to, but he will *know* my experience at the very least.

"At the time, things were looking really bad. I wasn't doing well at work, I was worried about the book, and I was dealing with, well, a personal crisis. Perfect storm."

"And then?" Taylor prompts.

I wipe away a few more traitorous tears. "My team over at the publisher brought a new editor in to look at the book. He told me to take out that twist I'd forced into the story, and we went to press, and the book, well, it did great."

"At work, he means," Rooney reminds me.

"Right. I was close to being ... let go. I made another mistake while I was on performance review, a stupid typographical error. I was certain I'd corrected it; in fact, I thought, well, somebody at work seemed like they always had it out for me. I wondered if this person, somehow, tinkered with my edits to make me look negligent or incompetent."

"Who would do that kind of thing?" Taylor asks.

He sounds incredulous, which is a bit puzzling. If people are willing to commit *murder*, then they're obviously capable of erasing someone else's edits in a document to sabotage another person's career.

I shake my head. Something about the way he asks has got me wary. I decide to keep the name of the person, Megan Patterson, to myself.

"Oh, I don't know," I say quickly. "You know when everything seems to be going the wrong way, you start thinking all kinds of things."

As soon as I've finished speaking, I realize how poor that sounded. I don't want them thinking I was having these *crazy* thoughts.

"Like what?" Taylor asks. "What did you think, Amanda?"

"I was afraid they were going to fire me. But my manager knew what was going on in my life, and I think he took some pity on me."

There's nothing like airing your deepest, darkest secrets to two perfect strangers. Yeah, come on in, let me tell you all about how I nearly failed at the most important things in life ... it'll be a blast.

"Anyway, the book came out a month later, and it was *selling.*" I feel the same relief, all over again, thinking about those heady days after the launch.

That was what I felt then: relief. Not joy, not success, not exhilaration. All my worry about losing my job evaporated in an instant—it no longer mattered. And everything I'd been working toward for years had finally come to fruition.

"My publisher called the next day and offered a generous advance on my next title. I took a few days to think about it, even though there wasn't much to think about, and I gave notice at work."

"How did your manager take that?" Rooney asks.

Oh, they already know.

"He was upset. He felt like he'd given me a break and ... well, long story short, he told me to leave."

"So they fired you on the spot?" Rooney asks.

I want to point out that I'd already given notice, but that seems like a distinction without a difference. I nod silently.

"Then what happened?" Taylor asks.

"Then I came home," I say, a little too harshly, so I try to soften my voice. "And I got to work on the next book."

"So no enemies at work?" Rooney asks.

I know what they're doing. The detectives are throwing a lot of questions at me, coming from different angles. They don't want me to get comfortable.

"Like I already mentioned," I say, giving him as hard a look as I can muster. "No."

I want Rooney to know he's not going to push me around.

"Nobody you ever argued with?" he presses.

Argued with.

I'm a writer, so I love words. But here's the problem with them: they're slippery. They're all made up; they can mean many things, sometimes contradictory things. Like the word sanction. It can mean to approve, but it can also mean to penalize.

"Argued with" can mean (1) had a difference of opinion on the phrasing of some copy for a new marketing blast.

"Argued with" can also mean (2) cursed at a colleague while at happy hour in front of an audience.

"Why is this so hard?" Rooney says, making a face. "You're a writer; you know what the word means."

I'm determined to stand my ground with this guy. "Look, *argued with* can mean a lot of things, but since you're detectives, I'm assuming you mean it in a very specific way, so I was thinking back over literally *ten years* of my life to see if anything fits the bill."

"What do you think I meant?" Rooney asks. "Argued with. My partner and I, we argue all the time. What's the big deal?"

"Amanda." Taylor leans in. He must see I'm getting defensive. "We wouldn't be here, asking you these things, unless it was really important. We need your help. Okay?"

"I understand," I say, "but, honestly, there was nobody I argued with at work."

"Do you know who Megan Patterson is?" Rooney asks, suddenly standing up, like he's tired of beating around the bush.

He moves away from the sofa and parks himself on the sill of the big bay window. The insipid light seeping in through the beige curtains makes this stocky man look older, even more rumpled.

"Yes," I say. "We worked together."

"Uh-huh," Rooney says. "Ever argue with her?"

I realize now I've made a mistake. I should have brought Megan up earlier, qualifying that I didn't think of her as an enemy but that we had our disagreements.

"Not at work, no."

I shouldn't have said that. I should have said—

"Listen," I say. "Megan and I did not get along. But we were always respectful to one another. We weren't *enemies*."

Rooney and I stare at each other for a long moment. I almost forget about Taylor even being there, until he breaks the silence.

"Your first book," Taylor says, consulting his notepad, "was called *Serial Reader,* right?"

That confirms it: I know why they're here. But I don't see what Megan has to do with any of this.

"That's right."

"That was about a serial killer, wasn't it?"

Now that I'm certain why they're here, I don't see any reason to keep things coy.

"I saw that story online this morning," I say. "I was wondering if that was why you came."

"Which story?" Taylor asks, playing dumb. He's a pretty good actor. I almost believe him.

"The news story about the person who was found decapitated, with a book crammed into their mouth. That happened to one of the characters in my first novel. Is that why you're here?"

I wait for Taylor to answer, but he doesn't. My eyes drift to Rooney.

"The killer is a failed mystery writer," Rooney says, surprising me with his knowledge of my book. "And they try to frame a successful author for the killings. Is that how it goes?"

It's a bit more complicated than he's making it out to be. But something tells me Rooney isn't interested in literary nuance.

"Yes."

"By shoving a book into their mouth and chopping off their head."

"When I read the news story, I was ..." I notice that I'm actually squirming. "I didn't know what to think. I hope, I really hope, that some sicko didn't read my book and use it as inspiration."

"Amanda," Taylor says. Without my even knowing it, he's practically come up beside me. "When was the last time you spoke with Megan Patterson?"

The realization hits me like a ton of bricks.

5

"Oh my God ... is she ..."

I can't bring myself to ask the question.

"I'm sorry," Taylor says, like he means it. "We can't discuss an open investigation."

"Especially not with a person of interest," Rooney mutters.

Person of interest is a euphemism police use for people who could be suspects.

"Am I ... I haven't seen Megan in *months.*"

"When was the last time?" Taylor says, making a big show with his notepad and pen, like he has to get this detail exactly right. "Do you remember?"

My heart is pumping like I just ran wind sprints.

"Oh, this must have been—can I look at my phone?" I ask.

"Why do you need to look at your phone?" Rooney says.

"The people from work had a happy hour. I hadn't seen them in a while, and they invited me out. I had it on my calendar, so I can give you an exact date. I think that was the last time I saw Megan."

"You think?" Rooney says, folding his arms. "You mean you can't remember if you saw her again after that time?"

"That *was* the last time," I say. "I was just speaking off the cuff, you know, like we're having a normal conversation."

I try to make my tone angry, but instead I sound more frustrated, maybe even bewildered.

"Sure, you can look at your phone if that'll help you, Amanda," Taylor says.

I pull up my calendar, scroll back through the months. It was sometime in the summer. There.

"June twenty-third," I say, holding out my phone like that's going to mean anything to them. "We met at Mel's for drinks. That's—"

"We know where it is," Rooney says.

"Why don't you tell us about the happy hour," Taylor prompts. "Did you interact with Megan?"

That's one way of putting it.

"Look," I say, "I know how this is going to sound, but I honestly forgot all about it. But it was the first time I'd seen friends from my last job in a while. I had a few more drinks than usual and got a little drunk." I pause for a moment, gathering my thoughts.

"Megan and I never really got along. I was quiet and hated being the center of attention. Megan, she was—is—*is* —" I'm drowning here. "—the opposite. She was always in the middle of every drama. One time, she was incredibly rude and very unprofessional in a meeting, where she suggested for all the world to hear that maybe I was spending too much time trying to be an author and should have focused more on my job, like I couldn't pursue my own interests during my free time, and it really bothered me."

"When was that?" Taylor asks.

"Back when I was still working at Nordel," I say. "Maybe two years before I quit?"

"Before you were let go," Rooney has to point out.

I ignore him. "Anyway, it felt great to see old friends at the happy hour, and they were all so pleased that the book was doing well. It turned into a bit of a celebration. But when one of my friends toasted my success, Megan just had to be snarky. She said, *Good for you. While you were busy writing your books, the rest of us were busy picking up your slack.* Now that I didn't have to work with her anymore, and with a few drinks in me, I let her have it."

"What did you say?" Taylor asks.

"I told her how I'd always felt about her, and that I wasn't alone in those feelings. I told her she was self-centered and shallow and petty and had always had something against me for no reason. Outside of those two issues when I was having a really difficult time, the quality of my work was always excellent. I mean, why would Nordel have promoted me three times in the ten or so years I worked there if I did such a poor job?"

"What else did you say to her?" Taylor asks.

"That was it."

"Did you threaten her?" Rooney asks.

I laugh incredulously. I don't think I've ever threatened anybody in my entire life. But Rooney is unimpressed by my reaction and waits for a serious answer.

"No, I never threatened her."

Rooney takes his eyes off me to nod at Taylor.

The other detective flips back a few pages in his notepad.

"You never said, *If you ever disrespect me again like that, you'll be sorry?*"

I do not remember saying that. It doesn't sound like something I'd say, and I would know. As an author, I spend a lot of time listening to my own voice.

But someone obviously told the detectives I said this.

"Who told you that? It's a lie."

"Sorry, Ms. Christie," Rooney answers with a smug grin. "Open investigation and all that."

Fine. He can call me Ms. Christie all he wants. It's not going to unsettle me.

"What else happened during this exchange?" Taylor asks.

"Nothing." I shake my head. "We had our disagreement. Megan was put off when none of our colleagues took her side, so she left very embarrassed."

"And that was the last time you saw her?" Taylor asks. "You're sure?"

"Yes."

"What were you doing on Friday night?" Rooney asks.

Friday was only two days ago, but the moment he asks me the question, my mind goes totally blank.

"I think I was home."

"You think?"

I nod, struggling to come up with any details. "Yes, I spent a lot of time last week working on the new book. I didn't go out much, other than to yoga and the grocery store."

"So you were home on Friday?" Taylor asks.

"Yes."

"Can anybody confirm that?" Rooney asks.

"I mean ... no. I live alone. I didn't have anybody over. I

was probably curled up on the couch and watching that *Great British Bake Off* show. I live a pretty boring life."

Rooney nods, like he's known all along I'd have no alibi for Friday night.

"You were home all day," Taylor says, "stayed in Friday night, woke up here Saturday morning?"

"Yes."

"You never left the house?" Taylor asks.

"I *could* have. Maybe I'm forgetting something, an errand? Nothing stands out, though. It was just a boring Friday night."

"You don't remember if you left the house Friday night?" Rooney asks, like I'm either the dumbest, or guiltiest, person in the world.

"Nothing comes to mind," I say. "All I'm saying is, if I left the house to do something completely mundane, it might have slipped my mind."

Taylor and Rooney share a knowing look. Taylor puts his notepad and pen away. I wonder if these accessories were just gimmicks, part of the act.

"Can you please tell me what this is about?" I ask.

"Sorry," Taylor says, pulling a face. "But we really can't."

"Ms. Christie." Rooney pushes away from the windowsill. "I have to ask you not to leave the area. You are a person of interest in our investigation, and we will likely have to speak to you again."

I stand and hide my trembling hands behind my back.

"I don't know what this is about, but I swear to you I was home on Friday night."

I'm hoping Taylor takes my side, or at least responds reassuringly, but he doesn't say a word. The two detectives are heading for my door. I follow them into the foyer. The coffee I brewed for them is still in the kitchen. We never even got to the point of having a cup—the questions started right away.

"Oh, one more thing," Rooney says, coming to a sudden stop at the door. "Do you mind if we take your phone?"

"What?"

"Your cell phone," Rooney says. "We'd like to see if you've had any electronic contact with Megan or with other people at work."

I don't want to hand my cell phone over to the police. Not because I have anything criminal to hide, but because my entire personal life is on that phone. I don't want them going through my texts, poring over my emails, checking my call log. It's none of their business.

At the same time, I don't want to add to their suspicions. If I had an alibi for Friday night, I might refuse.

"I'm sorry, but do I have to give it to you?" I ask.

Rooney gives me the fakest smile I've ever seen. "Of course not. It'd be voluntary."

"Then no, I'm sorry," I say. "I need my phone. I don't have a landline here, you see."

"Of course," he says, suddenly playing the good cop. "The wife and I got rid of our landline a couple of years back also. I understand. Thank you for your time."

"Sure."

Once they're gone, I shut the door and take a moment in the foyer.

The two detectives have unnerved me. I peek out the window and am relieved to see them drive off.

My relief is short-lived. Surely, they will be back with more questions, unless a lead sends them in a different direction. And, next time, they might come with a warrant to search my home and confiscate my phone.

While I'm mulling this unpleasant thought over, I see my neighbor Rebecca trudging through the snow in my front yard. A moment later, I hear the thud of her snow boots on my porch. She rings the bell.

I wonder what this could be about. Rebecca normally texts before stopping over.

When I open the door, I'm shocked by what I see. Rebecca looks like she's in a panic.

"Rebecca," I say, "is something wrong?"

"I have to talk to you." She looks past me. "Can I come in?"

I could do without any more drama right now, but Rebecca is a good friend. I move out of the way. When the door is shut, she gives me a nervous look.

"It's about the police that were just here."

THE COFFEE I made for the detectives gets ingested after all. Rebecca loves a cup of joe. I steer her away from the living room, where I was just grilled by the cops, and instead lead her into the den. I sit in my favorite recliner, where I do most of my writing, and Rebecca settles on one end of the sofa.

"Did you get my text?" she asks. "I tried to warn you."

I frown. "Warn me?"

She nods. "About the police."

I check my phone, but there aren't any new texts.

"It must not have come through," I say.

"Really? I swore ..."

She pulls out her own phone. It wouldn't be the first time

Rebecca thought she'd messaged me, or typed in a text and missed the SEND button. I love her dearly, but she can be a little scatterbrained.

"I swore I sent it," she's saying. "God, do you think somebody hacked my phone?"

Rebecca can also be a little paranoid.

About six months ago, she *swore* up and down that someone had broken into her house. This apparently happened in the middle of the day, in broad daylight too.

But the locks weren't jimmied, and nothing was stolen. None of her jewelry was missing, and trust me, Rebecca has some nice, *expensive* jewelry. None of our nosier neighbors saw anything strange or observed anyone unfamiliar on the street at the time, while she was out running errands. But Rebecca is convinced *someone* was in her house six months ago, because her junk drawer was messy.

As far as evidence for a break-in goes, it's flimsy. She's also married to a man who can't be bothered to *ever* help with the cleaning and tidying around the house, and she's also got two younger kids, who seem determined to leave a wake of destruction behind them as they run from one room to the next. One time Rebecca found the downstairs TV remote in the upstairs bathroom.

Needless to say, I'm a little skeptical that her house was broken into.

"Rebecca," I say, "it's no big deal. They were already here and gone. What's up?"

She has checked every pocket, but there's no phone in her hand. "I must have left it at home, I'm sorry."

"Rebecca," I say, "what's going on?"

"It's about the police," she whispers conspiratorially, like we're standing in the middle of a crowded public space. "They spoke to me this morning."

I get that eerie feeling, like somebody is walking over my future grave. She's dying to ask me why they were here, but as much as I like Rebecca, I'm not ready for *that* conversation.

"What did they want?"

"They were asking me all about you," she answers. "What kind of neighbor you are, if you're sociable, if I'd ever noticed anything odd about you or your house, if you have a significant other. They even asked me if I'd ever seen an older woman around here ..."

It takes me a moment.

She nods. "Right. They were asking me if I'd ever seen someone about your mother's age here. Of course I told them no."

My stomach is churning. "What else did they say?"

"They asked if you'd *ever* had a boyfriend ... I said yeah, of course, and ... well, then I had to tell them about Matthew."

I don't know if that's good or bad for me. The detectives will very quickly learn of the assault charges filed against my ex-boyfriend. Will that make me appear as someone willing to associate with an allegedly dangerous man? Or, since I ended the relationship with him, will that make me seem more like an honest citizen?

Who am I kidding? I know what Rooney is going to think. That guy seems determined to put me in handcuffs.

"But, uh, that wasn't why I had to speak with you," Rebecca says.

She's looking down now, like she's steeling herself to broach a difficult subject.

"What?" I ask.

"I'm really sorry, Amanda, but they asked me about Friday night."

"So?"

She gives me a sheepish look. "They asked if you left the house at all, and I told them you did."

"What?"

"I'm so sorry, I didn't think, I should have ... but they were cops, and I was a little nervous, and I didn't want to lie, you know, because then it would look like I was lying *for you*, which would make everything worse."

"Rebecca," I say, "I didn't leave the house on Friday."

Her look changes from sheepish to confused. "But you did, Amanda. I was stringing up the new Christmas lights Ron picked up, and I saw you pulling out of your driveway."

I do *not* remember leaving my house Friday night.

"When was this?"

"You don't remember?" she asks, surprised.

"No, I don't."

Rebecca frowns. "It was around eight o'clock."

I think it over. Then shake my head.

"I don't think I went out," I say.

Rebecca gives me a look like I'm crazy, but then she quickly changes her expression. "Oh."

I can't tell if she thinks I'm trying to lie, to convince her she's wrong. This conversation has strayed into very strange territory.

"Amanda, I ..."

It's my turn to force a smile. "Don't worry about it. Maybe you were mistaken about the night, or maybe I went out to run an errand, and it just slipped my mind."

"But why did the police ask me?" she says.

Rebecca's a dear friend, and I have nothing to hide, but I find myself hesitating anyway. After a moment's deliberation, I decide it's better to share what I know.

"A woman I used to work with was killed."

Her hand clamps over her mouth. "Oh my God—was it the woman whose head was ..."

I nod. "That's how—"

Her hand moves from her mouth to palm her forehead. "Oh my! I can't believe I didn't remember. Now I realize why it seemed so familiar. Didn't you write a book where—"

This is one of those times where I'm not happy a friend has actually read one of my novels. I don't let Rebecca finish.

"Yes," I say. "That's why they were here."

Rebecca's eyes drift past me, toward the foyer. Like she's wondering if the front door is locked, if she can get out quickly.

But she manages to recover. "My God, Amanda. Do they think you ...?"

As Rooney was so happy to point out, I'm a person of interest. But I decide to keep that to myself.

"This is their routine. Of course they have to rule me out first, since I knew the woman and because of the similarities to my book. They're just being thorough."

"Of course," Rebecca says, rising from the sofa suddenly. She's barely touched her coffee.

"Right," she goes on. "Makes sense. Hey, I just remembered, I have to get some things done at home before dinner. Can I text you later?"

I see right through the act. Behind Rebecca's fake smile, there's fear. She's wondering if her neighbor, the woman who writes murder mysteries for a living, daughter of a fugitive murder suspect, might have been involved in this woman's death.

"Rebecca," I say, "I had nothing to do with this."

"I know." She's already stepping out of the den. "I'd never think that."

I follow her down the hall, which only makes things worse. Rebecca is practically running by the time she reaches the foyer.

"Really," I say. "It's one of those insane coincidences. That's all."

"Right."

She laughs nervously as she turns the knob for the front door, then stops laughing altogether when she realizes the door is locked.

Rebecca fumbles with the knob, the lock, then the deadbolt. She's really spooked, so I stay on the other side of the foyer, not wanting to further terrify her.

"Rebecca," I say, "you've known me for years. You know I wouldn't ever do anything like this."

She manages to get the door open. Before she leaves, she turns to me with a fearful look in her eyes.

"I know that, Amanda."

She doesn't mean it.

6

I spend the rest of the day starting many different tasks but completing none. Today's events have left me restless, full of nervous energy that I'm unable to productively channel in one direction. After dinner, I try to work on rewrites, but it's no use. I give it up when I realize two hours have passed and I've barely gotten through three pages of material.

I message Miley, an old friend from Nordel, asking if she has time to talk. She's normally good at responding quickly, but she doesn't answer. I wonder if she's avoiding me.

All day long I've been good about staying off the internet, but now curiosity gets the better of me. I search the news stories again about the murder, but no new information has come to light. That doesn't stop people from idly speculating in the comments. One user has the gall to accuse me of the crime, signing off their comment with this line:

She's her mother's daughter.

Despite zero evidence that my mother is even in the area, would know the victim, or would have any reason to kill this person, other commenters have brazenly pointed the finger at her:

She butchered her lover.

The woman's obviously got a screw loose.

It was just the two of us when I was growing up. I don't know who my father is. My mother never told me; she never told anyone.

Whenever I worked up the nerve to ask who he was, Mom gave vague answers and would subtly change the subject. If she intended to reveal his identity when I was older, the murder of the man she was seeing derailed her plans.

When I was young, I romanticized my father's anonymity: he had to be very important, maybe even a soldier or a spy, a man doing vital, self-sacrificing work whose important but dangerous missions would imperil his family if his identity was ever revealed.

I always had a good imagination.

By the time puberty hit and I began to vaguely understand more "grown-up" things, I wondered if I was the product of an embarrassing one-night stand, perhaps the daughter of a man who did not know I existed. Or, even worse, maybe I was the unwanted offspring of a man who did not want to be a father at all. Later, and for good reason, I began to suspect Dad was a married man and Mom was the Other Woman.

But all these thoughts didn't occur to me until after

Everything That Happened. By then, Mom was literally on the run, the prime suspect in a ghastly murder, a woman who made headlines for all the wrong reasons.

I went to live with Aunt Cecelia, my mother's older sister, who had never had children and had never, as she would make abundantly clear, really wanted any. I harbored a grudge toward her for a long time, but now that I look back on my time with her through the lens of adulthood, I better understand that she was really in no position to take me in. Aunt Cece had her own problems; she couldn't hold down a job and picked all the wrong guys. She only took me in out of a sense of obligation. In the few years I stayed with her, we lived in four different apartments. Finally, my grandmother, then nearly seventy years old herself, took me in. She was in failing health, but her mind was still sharp. When I was little, Nan was very loving. But after Mom went on the run, things changed between us. Like Aunt Cece, Nan took me in out of a sense of obligation. She passed while I was in college. As for the rest of my mother's family ... they really don't want anything to do with me.

I text Miley, an old friend from work. It's my usual bedtime, but I'm still wired. I root around in the pantry for a snack. Nothing catches my eye. I try the freezer, not expecting to find anything, but I spot a pint of chocolate ice cream crammed into the corner.

Ice cream!

That's why I left the house on Friday night. I had a craving for ice cream. Despite the hour, I shoot Rebecca a text. She knows how much I like chocolate ice cream, and I've told her about my late-night runs before.

I spoon out a couple of dollops and eat. It's heavenly. When I'm done, I head upstairs for bed. I try reading to settle my mind but can't focus on the story. I turn out my light, but it's no use: sleep won't come.

I toss and turn and check my phone for the hundredth time. Miley still hasn't written me back. I'm assuming the police spoke with her, since she worked with me and Megan for years and attended the happy hour where I got a little drunk and told Megan what I really thought of her.

It's been hours since I texted her, which means she's avoiding me. I'm both sad and angry. Miley was my closest friend at work, one of the few people at the office who was genuinely happy for me when my book was a success. Now I'm worried that I've lost a friend.

I also feel terrible that Megan was murdered. Though we didn't care for one another, I didn't wish her any harm. Whatever our differences, she didn't deserve ... and even though I obviously didn't have anything to do with her death, I can't help but feel some responsibility. Some psychopath might be drawing inspiration from my work. That doesn't sit well.

And what are the chances it's pure coincidence they'd murder someone I know?

I've had all day to think about this, so why did I wait until bedtime to conjure up the most terrifying idea imaginable?

When I tiptoe downstairs, the hairs on the back of my neck are up. I keep waiting for someone to jump out at me from around this corner or out of that doorway. Moving from room to room, I turn on every light in the house to make sure I'm alone and safe.

There's nobody waiting to kill me. Thank God for small favors.

I've lived alone ever since I graduated college. I don't normally get spooked when I'm by myself at home. But I can't shake the suspicion that Megan's killer must know me. Now I'm turning all the lights off again so that someone lurking outside can't see into my home. I peer out front. The street is illuminated by a lot of Christmas decorations. I don't see anyone moving about.

I make my way into the kitchen to check the backyard. I can't see anything because the porch light is off. How could I have forgotten to activate it before I went to bed? I am clearly not thinking. I flip the switch, but nothing happens. The bulb must have blown.

The rear of my property backs up to some woods that extend about a quarter mile to the high school. When I moved in, I loved the semi-seclusion. I could sit in my backyard and not see any other houses or vehicles or people going by. I live in the 'burbs, but the way my property is situated, I get to pretend like my town is more rural, less crowded.

But right now, I am not loving the proximity to the trees.

With that creeping terror still firmly in place, I decide to brave the basement, where I keep the replacement bulbs. I don't like to come down here in the daytime because it's unfinished, and there are always spiders or centipedes waiting to surprise me. It's not any more enjoyable in the middle of the night, when you're worried about an obsessed psychopathic killer on the loose.

I manage to grab a bulb without screaming my head off. Back upstairs in the kitchen, I peer out the door leading to the deck in the backyard. Without the light on, I can't really see much of anything. The trees edging my property are just vague dark shapes in a much larger darkness. I grab a flashlight out of my junk drawer, unlock the door, and step outside.

It's cold. I'm shivering right away. The porch light is just next to my back door. I manage to get the bulb out even with my incredibly cold fingers and screw the new one in. It lights up right in my face, temporarily blinding me. I forgot to turn the switch off inside. I stagger backward, nearly losing my footing on the steps leading down into the backyard.

After blinking away the spots in my vision, I look around. Of course I don't see anybody lurking. It's cold out here, and you'd have to be a fool to think you could hide in the woods behind my property in the middle of December, when the trees are bare, and I can see nearly to the school. I'm being silly.

But when I turn around to head back inside, Rebecca's dog starts barking wildly.

I freeze on the steps between my yard and deck, too terrified to turn around. Lenny keeps barking like he's seen a deer or a rabbit.

Or something else.

I force myself to turn back around. Lenny is an old dog, and he doesn't see or hear too well anymore, so maybe he's just barking at me. There's no one creeping around in the woods, but I can't shake the jittery feeling as I go back up the stairs. I'm beginning to shiver, and I am looking forward to getting back into the heat, but then my eye catches something on the edge of the deck.

It's an envelope.

My blood runs cold.

Over the years, Mom has left me messages before, though it has been quite a while since I received one. But of course I don't know if this is from her.

The envelope is right on the edge of the deck. I wonder why someone would leave it there, of all places; then I realize they didn't. They probably left it on the mat in front of my back door, and when I opened the screen door, I must have nearly pushed it off the deck without realizing.

My hand is shaking, not just from the cold, as I bend over to pick it up.

There is nothing written on the exterior of the sealed envelope. I don't want to open it, fearful of what it might contain. But, at the same time, I have to know who left this for me.

I hurry back inside, lock the door behind me. I'm shivering from the cold, but my shaking hands manage to tear open the envelope anyway.

I gasp.

The note is not handwritten. The words, cut out of magazines and other periodicals, are glued to the page.

It reads—

You should be more careful.

7

The next day, I keep waiting for Rooney and Taylor to show up at my front door with a warrant. I consider contacting a lawyer, but that seems both reactionary and premature. Granted, our conversation was strained, but they can't honestly believe I would murder Megan at all, never mind in such a telling way that would bring immediate suspicion upon myself.

Can they?

I manage to make a yoga class at least. By the end I'm wiped out. Every part of my body is tight today. I'm carrying my anxiety everywhere. I usually feel refreshed after class, but when I drive home, all I am is tired and somehow more tense, and my mind keeps coming back to the note.

Mom has left me messages before. They don't come often, but they're usually encouraging or, at the very least, decipherable. It's unlike her to communicate so cryptically. That's what so unnerving about the strange message—I'm not convinced it's from her at all. But if it's not Mom, then who feels compelled to tell me to be more careful, and about what in particular?

I can't puzzle it out.

Back home, I don't get much writing done. My mind wanders to Megan, the cryptic note, the police interrogating me in my own living room, and the upcoming date with Brandon.

I go back and forth on whether I should cancel with Brandon. With everything that's happened, I don't know if I'm up for a first date tonight.

On the other hand, it's been a long time since I met a nice man. After I broke up with Matthew, I began to wonder if I'd ever get married. I've reached that age where I'm neither old nor young. Many of my friends have already been married and divorced. Some of them have children entering high school. The fact that I'm the daughter of a suspected murderer has not improved my chances.

Either way, that short exchange with Brandon got me excited again about the prospect of a relationship.

While I'm trying to decide on what to do about the date, my eyes fall on the note I found last night. I had the presence of mind to store it in a Ziploc bag in case the police need it later for evidence.

I consider calling Detective Taylor about the note. The gesture might come off as self-serving, but it would at least suggest to them that I'm cooperative and have nothing to hide. But I decide against it. It would involve *talking* to the police again, and once they have me on the phone, or God forbid in person, who knows what they'll decide to ask me about next. The fewer conversations I have with them, the better. Plenty of innocent people have gone to prison for crimes they did not commit, based on significantly less, even more circumstantial evidence than the police have against me right now. It's better I stay off their radar, and hopefully, they'll find a new lead and identify the real killer.

All day I'm like this. Thinking about Megan, the note, the detectives, Brandon. I barely get any work done on the new book. One minute I'm thinking about the best way to cancel the date, and the next minute I'm riffling my closet in search of the perfect outfit.

By not deciding, I've kind of decided. It gets too late in the day for me to reasonably cancel without coming across as rude or flighty or uninterested. So I pick out some clothes: a nice black dress that fits me well, a shawl, some flats. (I don't do heels.)

I check myself in the mirror, pleased with what I see. I'm not a kid anymore, but I still look pretty good. Years of yoga and of conscientiously keeping off the creeping weight that plagues adulthood have helped.

Fifteen minutes later, I pull into the parking lot of the restaurant where I'm supposed to meet Brandon. I'm a bit early and don't want to come across as desperate, so I sit in the warmth of the car, feeling the heated driver's seat against my back. A light snow begins to fall while I'm waiting, lending the night an almost magical atmosphere.

Just as I'm about to get out of the car, my phone buzzes. I really hope it's not the police. Or Brandon canceling on me.

I'm surprised to discover an incoming call from Miley, my old colleague. She's decided to contact me after all.

"Hi, Miley!"

"Hi, Amanda," she says.

Her voice is flat.

"It's so good to hear from you," I say. "Thanks for getting back to me."

"Yeah," she says, her voice still off. "I didn't know whether I should, to be honest."

I swallow hard. "Because of what happened to Megan?"

"Yeah."

"Miley, I had nothing to do with that."

"Right ..." She drifts away from me. "I guess I don't think you did."

"That's not a ringing endorsement."

We used to share a sense of humor. But she doesn't laugh at my poor attempt at a joke.

"I don't know what to think. After how you treated her at the happy hour ..."

"How *I* treated her? That woman was nothing but a ..." Megan is dead. I don't want to speak ill of her, but I can't let this go. "She was a nasty bitch to me the entire time I knew her."

"I guess ... but she never threatened you or anything."

"Threatened?"

"Were you that drunk?" Miley asks, a little edge to her voice now. "You don't remember what you said?"

"Not word for word, no," I say. "And besides, if I recall correctly, you took my side that night."

"Sure," Miley says. "I was on your side. Then ... this happened."

"Miley," I say, sounding like I'm begging now, "I had *nothing* to do with this."

"You told her she was going to regret everything, Amanda. Those were your words. Why would you say that to somebody you were probably never going to see again?"

I don't remember putting it exactly like that. But how can I deny it? I was, admittedly, a little tipsy. My recollection of the evening is shoddy at best.

"I meant it in, like, the karmic sense. Not that I believe in karma, but I meant, if she continued to treat people the way she did me, it was going to come back around on her. You can't go through life walking over everybody and not expect repercussions. I wasn't *threatening* her."

"Uh-huh."

It's maddening and disheartening that a woman I've known for years is capable of entertaining any possibility that I killed someone. If *Miley* can consider the idea, then the police certainly can too.

"Miley, we worked together for a long time. Outside of that night, when I'd had more to drink than usual, did you ever hear me raise my voice? Or say a bad thing about anybody?"

There's a long pause, and she doesn't really address my point.

"The police came by the office," she says. "I had to answer all these questions. I told them about the happy hour."

"Of course," I say. "I would never expect you to lie for me. Like I said, I didn't do this. And I have nothing to hide."

"But you did have something to hide," she says. "For years, you kept your true identity hidden."

"Come on." Is she serious? "Can you blame me? What would you have done if everybody in the world thought your mother was a murderer?"

She doesn't answer that either. "I told them what you said that started the whole argument."

What is she talking about? I'll admit my memory of the evening is hazy, but I am not one to start arguments. I usually avoid conflict.

"Wait a minute, Miley, *she* approached me."

But Miley talks right over me.

"That woman at the bar overheard you calling her a fucking bitch."

"What? I *never* said that. What woman?"

"Amanda, come on. Now you're lying to me."

"I am *not*. What woman? Who are you talking about?"

"The lady at the end of the bar. She was there by herself, minding her own business, when you saw Megan and called her that. Megan sort of overheard you, then cornered the woman and demanded to know what was being said, and next thing anybody knows, you two are practically screaming at each other."

I have no idea what she's talking about. I do *not* remember talking to a strange woman at this happy hour at all, never mind about Megan. That is so far out of character for me, it's ridiculous to even consider the possibility. But Miley is convinced.

"None of that happened," I say, trying to sound confident. "Is this what Megan told everybody after, so she wouldn't come across as a complete lunatic?"

"Amanda," Miley says, again not answering my question, "I'm sorry about this, but I only called because I wanted to say ... I can't be in contact with you anymore."

I'm shocked. Miley has known me for a long time. How can she think I might have done this? How can she think a drunken argument six months ago would lead me to brutalize this woman?

"If you look at it from my perspective," she's saying, echoing my own sentiments, "then you have to understand, Amanda. But I can't—"

"I understand," I say quickly. "Goodbye, Miley."

"Amanda," she says, her voice suddenly regretful, "wait a minute—"

I end the call. The tears in my eyes are threatening to ruin my mascara. I manage to keep them in. I'm late, but I don't really care. After that phone call, I'm totally out of the mood for a first date.

But it's too late to cancel now. Besides, I have been looking forward to this all day.

As I cross the parking lot and reach the entrance, with a light snow falling, I have absolutely no idea how much I'm going to share with Brandon. I mean, I already decided to tell him about Mom. But what about the police, the fact that I knew Megan, and—

"Hey, you!"

I turn around at the sound of the familiar baritone. Brandon is hustling up the sidewalk, hands in his jacket pockets. His cheeks are red.

"I'm so sorry," he blurts out. "There was an accident. I got held up. I hope you weren't leaving. I'm so, so sorry I'm late."

He really is a good-looking man.

His face has a boyish charm. His cheeks are red from the cold weather. Snowflakes are melting in his brown hair.

"Uh, no. I just got here, actually."

"Oh, great." He lets out a breath. "You had me worried. Let me get that."

Brandon comes up right beside me. He smells good. The skin along his jawline looks a little irritated, like he just shaved. He has very nice eyes.

"After you, my lady," he says, with a twinkle, as he pulls open the door.

I giggle at his silly attempt at humor. Most of the men I've dated have been very deadly serious. I don't think

Matthew once cracked a joke, not ever, to be honest. Brandon's relaxed manner would put me totally at ease under any other circumstances. But there's this heavy weight on my shoulders: there are things I have to tell him.

"Thank you, kind sir," I say.

He bows his head, and I suppress a guffaw. The host smiles as we enter. Brandon gives the man his last name, and the host immediately seats us at our table in the corner.

It's a really nice restaurant. Matthew and I had been meaning to come here for a long time, but never got around to it. It is a little fancy for my tastes, but I decided to go with it when Brandon recommended it.

I'm about to take my coat off, but Brandon gets behind me.

"Can I help you with that?" he asks, his breath touching my neck.

"Thanks."

I feel his hands on my shoulders as he helps me out of my coat and hands it to the host. I'm about to sit, but Brandon is there to pull out my chair. This guy sure knows how to be gallant. I sit, and he pushes my seat in.

"You look amazing," he says as he heads for his own chair. "That dress looks great on you."

I feel myself blushing. "Oh, thanks."

Brandon removes his overcoat and hands it to the host, who leaves. Brandon is wearing a sport coat and tie, with a blue shirt that really brings out the color of his eyes. I smile at him as he sits.

"So," he says, "how was *your* day?"

I can't help it. I laugh. "It was something alright."

He unrolls his napkin and places it in his lap. "I could use a drink. How about you? Maybe some wine?"

Yes: wine. I nod.

"Great," he says. "You're going to love their selection."

I take in the posh restaurant. One look at the menu confirms this dinner is going to cost a fortune. I was already planning on splitting the check with Brandon, though I get the feeling he's an old-fashioned kind of guy who will insist on paying it himself.

"So tell me about your day," he says. "Get some writing done?"

"A little," I say. I feel like I'm going to burst. I have to tell him about my mother ... but then what else do I tell him? "How about you?"

He shakes his head. "I was too busy at work. Maybe tomorrow. You know, I shouldn't do this, but whenever I have downtime on the job, I always spend it writing. So I'm kind of getting paid for it, you know?"

I laugh. Every writer I've ever talked to has done this: work on a story while on a job.

"When's your next book coming out?" he asks.

"The plan is March," I say. "My editor has it right now."

"March." He grins ear-to-ear. "That must be really exciting."

"It is."

"You don't sound that excited," he says. "If it were me, I'd be bouncing off the walls."

Our server appears, introduces himself, and offers us the house red. Brandon asks me if I'd like to sample it. I enjoy wine but don't know much about it, so I defer to him.

Brandon completely botches the tasting. He sips it before he smells it, and he doesn't even check its legs. But he approves, and our server pours us two glasses. The server tells us about the specials, but I barely hear a word he says.

Brandon has already picked up on my mood. I *should* be excited about the new book coming out, and I should be excited to be on a first date, but I can't get settled.

Brandon tells the server we need a few minutes to look over the menu. Then he turns to me when we're alone.

"Is everything okay, Amanda?" he asks.

I try to force a smile, but can't quite manage it. My stomach is in knots. I should have canceled. This was not a good idea coming here when—

"Are you feeling alright?" Brandon asks, genuinely concerned. "If you don't like the restaurant, we can always go somewhere else."

The man is trying so hard. It's cute. And his manner once again puts me at ease.

"Brandon," I say, "there's something I have to tell you."

"Okay." He sits a little taller and gives me his full attention. "What is it?"

"It's about my mother." He doesn't bat an eye when I say this. Maybe he already knows. There's only one way to find out. "She is ... she's a fugitive."

It takes a moment for what I've said to register.

"From the law, you mean?"

I decide to rip off the Band-Aid. "When I was a child, she was having an affair with a married man who was murdered. The police suspected her, and she ran."

Brandon goes very still.

"I have a confession also."

He looks left and right, then leans in.

"My mother is a serial killer."

I freeze. For a moment, I wonder if I've heard him right. Then he cracks a smile. "Kidding."

"Oh."

I laugh involuntarily, releasing a lot of nervous energy. But it is an odd joke to make, especially coming on the heels of my sharing Mom's identity. Brandon has an unusual sense of humor.

He's still smiling, but he holds out a palm. "No, really, I have to tell you something."

"Okay."

He nods. "I already knew about your mother. People at the group talk."

"So ... that doesn't bother you?"

He shrugs. "Why would it?"

I want to be happy he's not put off by this, but his attitude is almost too flippant considering the turn our conversation has taken.

"She's not a murderer," I say. "She's a good person who fell in love with a married man."

He nods and grows thoughtful.

"I just wanted you to know. Now. Before, in case this gets serious—"

"Do you want it to get serious?" he asks.

"Um." I sense that my face is suddenly bright red. "I—"

"I'm joking," he says.

I force a laugh. I really need to know how he feels. "So ...?"

"So what?" he says.

I give him an incredulous look. "Don't you want to run screaming out of the restaurant?"

"That'd be a bit dramatic."

"Fine," I say, growing a little frustrated by his coyness. "I mean, do you want to leave, or ...?"

"Why would I want to leave?" he asks.

"I just told you that my mother is a suspected murderer and a fugitive."

"Yeah, but you're not her."

"How do you know?"

He looks at me sideways. "Are you trying to tell me something?"

"No." I manage a laugh here. I cannot believe how chill Brandon is. "But a lot of people would have a problem with this."

He shakes his head no, then sips his wine. "I can read people. I know you're a good person, Amanda."

I wonder if his act is part of some candid camera prank. Nobody is *this* nice.

"You have a good heart," he goes on.

"How do you know?"

"Okay," he says. "Confession time."

Uh-oh. Where is *this* going?

"I've sort of been checking you out at the writers' group." The color returns to his cheeks, though this time the cold winter air doesn't have anything to do with it. "You're the kindest person on the panel. You always take the time to answer questions thoughtfully, and you never—unlike some other people there—talk down to *anybody*. Now, you're a published author who's written a runaway bestseller. With all the success you've had, you could act a certain way—again, like some other people there—but you don't. You're very down-to-earth. You make everybody there feel welcome."

He's embarrassing me with all these compliments. I manage to squeak out a muted, "Thank you."

Brandon continues, "I wanted to approach you last week, but I chickened out at the last second. To be honest, I'm a little shy. It's something I'm working on, and right before I came up to you, that older woman, the one who's always knitting in the back, she approached and asked you to sign a book for her son, remember?"

I nod. "Louann."

"Louann, that's it," he says. "You were so nice to her. When she asked if you could write her son a long note, and then told you exactly what to say, it didn't bother you at all. And then you asked Louann all about her son, and I could tell you weren't just asking for the sake of it. You really wanted to know. It's obvious: you're a nice person."

I was surprised when Louann approached me after the meeting. She never says much, preferring instead to focus on whatever she's knitting. I get the sense there's something a little off about her, but I can't put my finger on what. When I asked about her son, her answers were vague, which I found odd. Why wouldn't she tell me about him, when I was signing a book for the guy?

"Wait until you get to know me," I say.

He waves the honest-to-goodness modesty away. "You can't fake that. Nobody can."

"If I'm so nice, how come you were too shy to approach me last week, then?"

"Well ..." He looks away, his face turning an even brighter red. "You're not just nice, Amanda. You're ..."

"What?" I ask, not following.

"Come on," he says. "Are you going to make me say it?"

Oh. Sometimes I'm oblivious when it comes to men. Matthew used to tell me that all the time.

"Say what?" I answer, giving him a big smile.

He leans forward. "Amanda, you're very pretty."

"Thank you," I say, giving him my best flirty look. "And you're a handsome man, Brandon."

He blushes deeply and can't hold my stare. It's so cute.

"Alright, alright, let's change the subject," he says.

"To what?"

"Well, now you've opened up that can of worms, you have to tell me about your mom."

8

TWENTY-SEVEN YEARS AGO

I open just one eye.

"Come on, baby girl," Mom says. "It's time to get up."

Mom and I have this thing. It's like a superpower. She can read my mind, somehow, just by looking me in the eye. I don't know if all moms can do that, or if just mine can. But she peers into my bedroom, and her two eyes meet my one open eye, and she knows what I want this morning.

Chocolate chip pancakes.

A few minutes later, that mouthwatering aroma reaches me from the kitchen, and I spring out of bed, no longer tired.

"Are they ready?" I call out.

"Not yet, Amanda," Mom says.

"My name is Mandy," I answer.

"No, it's not," Mom says.

This isn't the first time we've had this argument. Amanda is such a *boring* name. It's three whole syllables long, and nobody likes to say names that are *that* long. That's why I tell my friends to call me Mandy. It sounds so much cooler.

When I grow up, I'm going to write books in the winter and be a singer in the summer. Would you ever buy a CD from a singer named *Amanda*?

I race into the living room. Mom says I run everywhere, like it's a bad thing, but it's not *literally* true. I don't run to the bus stop, because I don't always want to go to school. And I don't run to church either, on those rare Sundays she takes me.

I lie on my stomach on the living room floor and turn on the Saturday morning cartoons. My friends don't know I still watch them. They will *never* know that. Saturday morning cartoons are for children. I'm not a child anymore. I'm almost ten years old now.

On the TV screen, the Teenage Mutant Ninja Turtles are crawling through city sewers, on their way to take on this week's villain. Probably Shredder. It's always Shredder.

"You should brush that hair of yours," Mom says.

She's always telling me that. Sometimes I fib and say I have and then later feel bad about it, especially since I'm pretty sure Mom can tell I'm lying by simply looking at my hair. It gets knotty all the time.

As usual, Mom's favorite pink comb is on the coffee table. She's had it since she was a little girl, making it one of her few prized possessions. I grab a hank of hair and go to work with the pink comb.

Mom appears one commercial break later, bearing a big plate of steaming hot chocolate chip pancakes, my favorite, in one hand and a bottle of maple syrup in the other. I sit up on the floor and open a TV tray and slide my legs under it.

"Here you go, sweetheart," Mom says.

She puts the plate on the tray in front of me. I lower my face into the steam lifting off the pancakes and take in a big whiff. They smell delicious. Even though they're too hot, I can't wait a moment longer. Grabbing the silverware, I dig in.

"You're going to choke," Mom says halfheartedly.

I never cut my pancakes small enough. But that's because they're too yummy. I end up stuffing my face till my cheeks puff out.

"They're so good," I say.

Mom gives me a look. "What did you say?"

Honestly, that was what I said. But with all the pancake stuffed into my mouth, it probably sounded like *air so oo.*

Once I clear some space in my mouth, I try again. "They're so good. Thanks, Mom."

"Sure, sweetheart."

Mom loves making me pancakes, and then, this is a little weird, she loves watching me eat them. I douse my stack with the sugary maple syrup, and just to make her happy, I make sure to cut my pancakes into smaller, more bite-sized pieces.

"Mom, can I ask a question?" I say.

She sits on the sofa and leafs through one of her many magazines that are always covering the coffee table.

"You just did."

Eye roll. She always answers like that. "I mean—"

She sticks her tongue out at me playfully. "I know, sweetie. What did you want to ask?"

"You promise not to get mad?"

Mom's smile slips. I'll admit it's a weird thing for me to ask, because Mom *never* gets angry. She has never lost her temper with me. My friends' moms do it all the time with them. But it's never happened with us.

She closes her magazine. "What is it?"

I swallow a big chunk of pancake and put my silverware

down on the plate in front of me. The Turtles have found Shredder. He's up to no good, as usual. I turn away from the TV to look at her.

I've been wanting to ask about her big secret for nearly *two weeks* now. That's a long time to keep from saying something when you're only almost ten years old.

"Who's the man you were sitting in the car with?"

Mom freezes for a moment. I can tell from her reaction that I've seen her doing something she's not supposed to be doing. Like I said, I'm not a child anymore.

Mom tries to act like it's nothing. "Where did you see me in a car with a man?"

"Well ..."

She gives me the Mom Look. "Amanda?"

"When you dropped me at Allie's house, we, uh, rode bikes to Rachel's later that day." I give her my best apologetic look. Mom would never let me ride a bike that far without an adult along for the ride. "And then we went to the playground by Rachel's house."

Mom is blushing. Up until this point, I wasn't *sure* it was her I saw in the car. I mean, I was pretty sure. The woman was really pretty, like Mom, but she was wearing a hat to cover her hair and these big sunglasses. Mom never wears a hat.

But now I'm certain: it was her in that car with that strange man.

"Is he my dad?" I ask.

Mom's eyes get a little watery. "He's a ... friend."

"Is he your boyfriend?"

"No."

Her response comes out fast and loud.

"He's just a friend," she says. "We've known each other a long time."

"Who is he?"

Mom looks stricken. That's how I probably looked a couple of weeks ago when Mom found out I'd eaten all the chocolate chip cookies she'd hidden above the refrigerator.

"Amanda—"

The house phone rings. I've never seen Mom look so happy to answer it. Normally she says things like "Who could *that* be?" or "Who's calling me at *this* hour?" But she jumps off the couch and dashes into the kitchen. I get the feeling she really doesn't want to tell me who this strange guy is. Why was she sitting in *his* car near a playground all the way on the other side of town?

I turn a little bit. I can just see Mom. The phone hangs in the kitchen but right near the threshold separating this room from that one. She answers, then listens a moment.

"What's wrong?" Mom says. "You don't sound yourself ..."

I can see that Mom looks nervous. She catches me watching her, then turns away and lowers her voice.

She listens some more. When she speaks again, she's forgotten to keep her voice low.

"Do you really mean it?"

I swear I've *never* eavesdropped on one of Mom's phone conversations before. Except that time I got the funny feeling it was my father calling. Then I *had* to listen. Can you blame me? Or that other time, when it was really close to Christmas, and it was Aunt Cece calling. My aunt never calls Mom. That's why I knew she was calling to ask Mom what I wanted for a Christmas present. I shouldn't have listened then either, but I couldn't help it. I mean, I was much younger then. I'd only just turned nine.

"I want to believe you, but ... I don't know."

Mom suddenly looks over her shoulder and catches me eavesdropping. I expect to get an earful. I shouldn't be listening in on a grown-up's conversation; it's very rude.

But she doesn't yell at me.

Or look mad.

Instead, she looks ... excited.

"Okay. I'm coming," Mom says, smiling nervously. "I'll see you soon."

She hangs up the phone and stands there for a minute, lost in thought.

"Mom?"

At the sound of my voice, she snaps out of her daze. "Amanda, darling," she says, "I have to go out for a little bit. Can you be a big girl and take care of yourself?"

Mom has only left me by myself a couple of times before, and only when she was running to the convenience store around the corner for cigarettes. Mom doesn't realize I know she smokes.

"Where are you going?" I ask.

Instead of answering, Mom takes my plate away. I'm only half finished, though.

"Mom, I'm still—"

"I don't want you choking on pancakes while I'm gone," she says.

She puts a hand on my cheek and gives me the strangest smile I've ever seen. She seems like she's very excited but also trying to hide that emotion from me.

"I don't know how long I'll be, sweetheart," she says. "Lock up after I'm gone; don't answer the door; don't let anybody in. If you need something, you can always call Aunt

Cece or Nan. You know where their phone numbers are, right? Okay? I have to go now."

"Mom ..."

I get the most horrible feeling in the world. The way she looks, and the way she sounds, I feel like I'm never going to see her again.

"Please don't leave," I say.

"Aww, sweetie, I'm sorry," she says. "But I won't be gone long. I promise."

She gives me a big hug. She usually doesn't squeeze me this hard.

"Mommy, please don't go," I say.

"Everything is going to be fine," she says.

I don't want her to leave.

"I love you, Amanda."

I nod, unable to say it back.

Then Mom rises. She grabs the purse she keeps by the door, her keys, then opens the coat closet. She sticks her arm in deep, like she's reaching for something hidden all the way in the back. It's that strange hat I saw her wearing.

And something else.

A wig.

"I'll be back, sweetie," she says again. "I promise."

9

"That was the last time I ever saw Mom," I say.

Brandon leans back in his chair, runs a hand through his hair. "Wow. Do you think that was David calling her?"

I nod. "The police pulled his phone records. The last call he made was to my mother."

He shakes his head. "Unbelievable. What about his wife, what's-her-name, Lori?"

Not too many people remember Lori's name. After her husband was killed, she dropped off the face of the earth.

Most people do remember her husband's name, though: David West. He and Mom were having an affair. And if you believe the prevailing theory, Mom killed him because he wouldn't leave his wife.

"Lori West," I answer.

"What happened next?" he asks.

He's intrigued by my story. And so far, he's been very polite about asking questions. Brandon hasn't pried or derailed me or tried to jump ahead to the meatier parts of the subsequent investigation and all the wild, lurid theories the tabloids ran with.

"After a few hours passed and Mom hadn't returned, I cried." Thinking about the worst day of my life is making me misty-eyed even now. "Eventually, the police came."

"I'm sorry," he says, like he's personally responsible. "That must have been terrible for you."

"It was. And one of the detectives was really mean to me."

"Why?"

I roll my eyes. Detective Hamlish. I'll never forget him. Rooney kind of reminds me of him, now I think about it. He was just the sort of person whose anger was always simmering, the cynic who never met an honest person in their life.

"I was a minor, a child, and there was nobody else in the house. He was upset they had to get social services involved before they could enter the apartment," I say. "That was hardly my fault, but he took the delay out on me."

The server brings our dinner. Brandon ordered a steak, and I went with the chicken marsala. The food looks great and smells delicious, though I fear my sob story has robbed Brandon of his appetite.

"Oh man," he says, all chipper. "I am so going to eat all of this."

He digs right in, as if he's already moved on from our difficult conversation.

"She's innocent," I say.

He nods. "I believe you."

He's making this too easy.

Sensing my surprise at his reaction, Brandon puts down his fork and points at me. "The apple doesn't fall far. You're a good person, so your mother must be as well."

"How can you be so sure?" I ask.

He smirks. "Am I wrong?"

I can't help but chuckle. "No, but ... most people wouldn't agree with you. I lost some very close friends when that story broke about my identity."

"Some people are assholes." He waves dismissively. "You're better off without those people in your life."

His almost eager willingness to take my side is endearing. I feel myself opening up to him. "That was the worst day of my life. The next worst day was when someone told me that my mother was a murderer."

He mulls that over.

"You were so young," he says. "You can't have understood it all right away."

I shake my head. "You'd be surprised. I knew what murder was by then. And I overheard my family talking about all the evidence."

"Right." He nods along. "Your mother's DNA and the note David West left."

He's done his homework.

The police found strands of Mom's hair not only on David's clothes, but also in the apartment, along with other bits of her DNA. They also found a safety-deposit box with a letter from David inside. He claimed Mom's behavior was growing increasingly erratic and troubling. Though planned on ending the affair, he could not bring himself to admit to the tryst, wanting to spare his fragile wife's feelings. He left the note because Mom had "threatened" him, and he feared for his safety.

"The woman he described in that letter was nothing like my mother."

He smiles sadly, but he must be asking himself the

obvious question: why would David lie? This is essentially a deathbed confession, one of the many exceptions to the rule against hearsay in a criminal trial. I know because I used one as a plot device once.

"I'm so sorry," he says. "That must have been incredibly hard on you."

He's so kind, but I feel like I've monopolized the conversation.

"Enough about me," I say. "Tell me about yourself."

Brandon dabs at the corners of his mouth with his napkin. "Me? I'm boring."

Kind, cute, very fit, *and* humble? Have I hit the jackpot with this guy?

"I doubt that."

"No, really," he says.

"I've told you about my insane childhood," I say. "What about yours?"

I notice how his shoulders stiffen when I ask him about it. "Oh, it was pretty normal."

I've just shared some very intimate details from my childhood, so I'm a bit put off by his reaction.

"Brothers? Sisters?"

"I'm like you, an only child."

"How about your parents? What were they like?"

"Dad wasn't around much. He worked a lot, and then he, uh, died suddenly when I was still little."

"I'm sorry. I didn't mean to bring up a bad memory."

"It's okay," he says, smiling. "That's what I just did to you."

"You kind of did."

We both laugh at that.

He puts his silverware down again and stares off into

space for a moment before continuing, "Mom was heart-broken after he died. She was never herself again. She never remarried; I don't think she even dated anybody. She passed a few years ago."

I feel for him. I know exactly what it's like not to have much time with your parents. I had zero with Dad and not a lot with Mom.

"I'm sorry. Was it sudden?"

He nods sadly. "Very."

I can tell it's a delicate subject, so I don't press him. I ask him about his job, about what he's writing, but Brandon is apparently one of those shy people who does *not* like to talk about himself. If he didn't give off such a nice, warm vibe, I'd think he was being evasive.

We pass on dessert. Brandon excuses himself to use the bathroom. I've got a good feeling about this man, and I'm wondering where things are going from here. But I feel like I haven't been *totally* honest with him. Yes, I told him about Mom, but no, I haven't told him about the police coming to my house. I feel like he should know that, but I'm afraid of scaring him off.

When Brandon returns, he reads me perfectly.

"You have something to say."

I sigh. "That obvious?"

He holds up his hand and brings his pointer and thumb very close together. "Little bit."

"The police came to my house yesterday," I say. "It was about that woman who was murdered."

"You mean the one who was ..." He flattens his hand and wipes it across his neck. "That one?"

"They came to my house because I knew her."

He gapes at me. "You *knew* her?"

I explain how we worked together, but leave out the nasty argument we had six months ago at that happy hour.

"You know, *Mandy*," he says, giving me a wink at the word Mandy, "you lead an interesting life."

I can't help but laugh. I also can't help but wonder why he's so chill about all this. I mean, without coming out and saying it, I just told the guy I'm a person of interest in a gruesome murder inquiry. Seriously, I'm starting to wonder if Brandon is actually *too* nice. There is such a thing. I've flown several red flags tonight, but he doesn't seem to care.

"Do they actually think you ..."

He doesn't finish the question.

"No. I don't know. Maybe." I take a deep breath. "But I didn't."

"Obviously," he says. "You'd never do something like that."

We stare into each other's eyes for a long moment. The sparks are definitely there between us. It's not the first time I've seen that look in a man's eyes. But it has been a *while*.

"I've had a great time tonight," he says.

"Me too."

With a sheepish look, he says, "I'm not usually this forward, but would you like to come back to my place for a drink?"

Oh boy.

Before I can politely tell him no, before I can make it clear that I'm not the type of woman who does things like that on a first date, my mouth is already answering for me.

"Sure." My face is a million degrees. I look around for our waiter. "Could we split the check?"

He gives me a little grin. "I already paid."

"You did?"

"Confession time: I didn't *just* go to the bathroom a moment ago. I also paid for dinner. I asked you out, so I feel like I should treat you. And I didn't want to have one of those awkward who's-going-to-pay conversations. I hope you're not mad?"

"No." This guy. "That was really sweet of you. Thank you."

He winks. "You'll get the next one."

"You assume there's going to be a next one?"

He puts his palm over his heart. "Don't crush my hopes and dreams."

10

This is crazy. This is *crazy.*

I hardly know this guy.

We shared one meal together, where I did almost all the talking. I found out very little about him throughout dinner. He talked about his previous work in IT in generalities and didn't discuss his writing that much. On the other hand, he knows a lot about me now.

But shouldn't that be to his credit? He made me feel comfortable enough to share all those things, and when I gave him several reasons to run screaming from the restaurant, he stayed. That *means* something.

Still, as I follow Brandon back to his place, I can't help but feel nervous. What if this guy's some kind of sociopath who's really good at manipulating people? Maybe that's how he was able to get me to open up that much without revealing anything of substance about himself. Not only have I heard of people like that, I've *written* about them.

I might be nervous because of everything else going on at this moment, too. If this were a normal day in the life of

Amanda Christie, would I even be giving this decision a second thought?

Then again, I did receive that cryptic note that sounds like both a warning and a threat ... what if I'm supposed to "be more careful" with Brandon?

It's difficult to make sense of everything.

Over the years, Mom has left me messages. It doesn't happen often, but it is her way of letting me know she's watching out for me. But if this note was from her, and she was truly concerned, why not just make that clear? Mom would have been direct: stay away from Brandon, he's a bad guy, or something to that effect.

So I don't *think* the note was from Mom, and I have no reason to suspect it was referring to Brandon.

But that doesn't tell me who sent it or what the danger is.

I'm about to call Brandon from my car. When it comes to faking an upset stomach, I'm capable of giving an Oscar-worthy performance. I don't usually eat such rich food; I could use that as a plausible excuse. Also, going back to some guy's place after one date, no matter how nice he seems, is so out of character for me. This is not who I am.

But as I get my phone out, Brandon pulls into a development and turns immediately into a driveway. We're already here. He parks in front of a large garage that looks big enough to fit two cars. I pull into the driveway right behind him.

Brandon has a really nice house. But I'm surprised by the size of it.

It's two stories and big enough for a family of four. He must have made good money while he worked in IT, because I doubt he'd be able to afford the down payment on such a place now given his current job. Or maybe he received an inheritance from his family.

Either way, it'd be rude to ask about money on a first date, and I also don't want him thinking I'm materialistic. One of his neighbors is just getting home and stops before going inside to give Brandon a big wave, which I take as a good sign.

I can always fake a stomach ache inside if I want to leave. I'm nervous, and part of me doesn't want to go in, but this man has been nothing but kind and complimentary and easygoing. That last one is a biggie. He doesn't seem like the type who's going to try to *force* anything. He was also incredibly polite to our server and the other employees at the restaurant, which says a lot in my book.

I've made up my mind.

I get out of my car. The snow stopped while we were in the restaurant and didn't stick on the streets, but there's a thin coating on Brandon's lawn. He hurries over and offers me his elbow, like he's afraid there might be ice, and he doesn't want me to slip.

I take his arm. "Such a gentleman."

He blushes at the compliment as he leads me toward his house. Together we walk up the steps, and he fumbles with his keys for a moment before we go inside. An alarm sounds. Brandon punches in the code on the digital display by the front door, then turns to me.

"Can I take your coat?" he asks.

I smile and give him my back. Very gently he touches my shoulders as he helps me out of my coat. This slight touch sends a tremor through my body. He lays my coat over the banister by the front door.

"I'll leave it right here," he says.

"Okay."

He puts his own coat in the closet in the foyer. "Come in, come in."

I follow him into the kitchen. It's bright and clean. There are a couple of dishes and a glass in the sink, but otherwise, the place is spotless.

"Sorry," he says. "I haven't had anybody over in a while. This place is kind of a mess."

"You should see my house."

He smiles. "I'd like to."

Oh boy.

"Would you like wine?" he asks. "Or something stronger?"

"I'd better stick with wine. And only one. I do have to drive home."

He nods at that, though I can see a little disappointment in his eyes. Brandon opens a bottle of red and pours two glasses.

"How about a tour?" he asks.

"That'd be great."

He leads me from room to room. The house is relatively new, maybe fifteen years old. Brandon is embarrassed when he realizes he's left his gym sneakers in the middle of the living room and quickly picks them up. Seeing him a little nervous, and eager to prove he's not a slob, is endearing and cute. For a guy who lives alone, he really keeps his place tidy.

"I know," he says.

"What?" I ask, puzzled.

"There's not a lot of *stuff*. I'm trying out minimalism."

Now that he says it, I notice that the place is bare, which makes it easier to maintain. With only a few minutes' notice, he could tidy up in time for a realtor to show it.

"Would you like to see the upstairs?" he asks.

He's really asking me if I'm comfortable.

"Sure."

We snake our way back through the downstairs, then up the steps that double back on themselves. He shows me the spare bedroom and his office. We pass a bathroom in the hallway. Opposite the bathroom is the only interior door in the house I've seen closed. Brandon has taken the time to show me everything else, but he breezes right past this door on his way to the master bedroom.

"What's in here?" I ask, giving him a smile.

"That's just storage," he says. "It's messy. If you open that door, something might fall out and hit you."

I playfully reach for the knob. "Now I *really* want to look inside—"

But before my hand can open the door, Brandon closes the distance between us and puts his hand on top of mine.

"It's *really* messy," he repeats. "I threw everything in there, last minute. Seriously, can we not open this door?"

"You threw everything in there?" I ask, playing dumb. "Why'd you do that?"

He scratches the back of his head, looking awkward. "Just in case you wanted to come over after dinner."

His face has turned bright red.

"Oh, I see. You were expecting to get lucky?"

He can tell I'm teasing him, but all the same he looks pained.

"Are you enjoying this?" he asks. "Watching me squirm?"

I have to chuckle. I don't know why I thought for a moment that this guy could be a sociopath. He's totally harmless.

"Oh, yes."

His hand is still on top of mine. "Come on, let me show you the bedroom."

My heart is beating faster. "Okay."

Very slowly, almost reluctantly, he takes his hand off mine. While I trail him down the hall, my phone buzzes. It's a weird hour for me to be getting a text. I don't want to be rude to Brandon, but curiosity gets the better of me. I check the message.

It's from Matthew of all people.

> Hey you – I'm really sorry about showing up at the bookstore. But I needed to see you. I still love you, Amanda. After you broke up with me, I was lost for a while. But I've made a lot of positive changes in my life and want to tell you about them. Would you give me that chance?

I don't quite eye roll. But I do type out a quick response.

> Matthew ~ Enough is enough. We are not together anymore. I'm sorry for everything you've been through. But I've moved on. You need to do the same.

Brandon is watching me. "Everything okay?"

I don't want to tell him that I have an ex exhibiting obsessive tendencies and coming dangerously close to stalking behavior. I've given Brandon enough reasons to run screaming from me already. And everything tonight has gone so well, I don't want to dampen the mood.

"Oh yeah, just a friend," I say. "She's asking me how the date is going."

He gives me a little smile. "What did you tell her?"

"Really well."

Brandon nods, then reaches into the master bedroom to turn on the lights, but he does not enter. Again, I get the feeling he's going out of his way to make sure I don't feel uncomfortable.

I poke my head in, very conscious of how close we are. His king-sized bed is neatly made. A tidy pile of clothes sits on the only chair in the room. Two paperback novels are on the nightstand next to the bed.

I turn to face him in the doorway of the master bedroom.

"You have a very nice house," I say.

"Thanks."

We're inches apart. My heart is beating fast.

"What about the master bathroom?" I ask. "Do you want to show me that?"

He nods about a million times in one second. "Sure."

We step into the bedroom. I don't really care about seeing his bathroom. And he knows that. He's going through the motions of leading me to the bathroom, when he stops mid-stride, realizing I'm in the room but not exactly following him.

I'm not usually this forward, but Brandon has put me at ease. Even though I don't know him well, I feel like I can trust him. My earlier anxieties seem silly now that he's been nothing but a perfect gentleman. He makes me feel *safe*.

Brandon turns and looks me up and down. It's cheesy, I know, but I give him a come-hither smile.

And he comes hither.

"**G**ood morning," Brandon says.

It's early. I squint against the light coming from the master bathroom. Brandon is wearing a towel and nothing else. He sure does have a nice pair of shoulders on him. Broad and chiseled. His hair is wet like he just came out of the shower. Steam rolls out of the bathroom.

I groan something that I hope is intelligible.

"Not a morning person?" he asks, teasing me.

"Not exactly."

He comes over to the side of the bed I slept on and leans over to kiss me. He smells exceptionally nice.

"Do you like French toast?" he asks.

It's only my favorite breakfast ever.

"Yes."

Another kiss. "I'll whip some up. Come downstairs in fifteen minutes. Okay?"

"Okay."

Brandon rubs my shoulder, then starts to leave but stops in the doorway.

"I left out a T-shirt and some sweats. They're on my reading chair over there. You'll be swimming in them, but feel free to wear them if you don't want to put your dress back on."

This guy is awesome.

"Thanks."

I really should get up and put some clothes on, but I don't want to wake up properly just yet. Brandon and I had a really nice time last night, and recalling it is making me feel better. I ball up under the covers to squeeze out a few more minutes of precious sleep.

Soon, the smell of French toast drifts upstairs. Matthew never made breakfast for us. Not that I ever expected it. He was more the type who preferred going to a diner. The smell of breakfast food drifting into a bedroom reminds me of my childhood, when Mom's cooking was the best alarm clock ever.

I slip out of bed. All I've got on is my underwear. The pile of clothes on his reading chair is gone. He must have tidied up this morning while I was still asleep. In its place are the T-shirt and sweatpants. I put them on. Brandon's right: they're much too big for me. But they're comfortable as anything. I tie the sweatpants as tight as I can and then roll the waistband. At least this way they won't be falling off me.

I grab my shoes and dress before leaving the bedroom. I pad along the upstairs hallway. I'm really tempted to peek into that closet Brandon didn't want me to see. His definition of messy and mine are, it turns out, very different, so I'm curious to look inside and see what I find. I'll bet everything is in its place, and if there are shelves, there won't be any dust on them.

I try the handle.

It's locked.

That's strange.

The door does not lock from this side. That means Brandon flipped the lock on the other side and pulled it shut.

Why would he do that?

I smile and shake my head when the realization hits me. He doesn't want me to see anything out of place in his house, not even the storage space where he's tossed everything to hide it away. It's kind of cute.

When I reach the kitchen, Brandon is spatula-ing the French toast onto two plates.

"Oh good," he says excitedly, "you're up. It's ready now. Coffee? Orange juice?"

"Coffee would be great."

He bobs his head toward the Keurig on the other side of the kitchen. "The cups are in the bin underneath."

I pick out a dark roast while Brandon finishes with the French toast. A few minutes later, we're sitting at the small table in his kitchen. He passes me the cinnamon, and I apply it, shall we say, liberally.

"Do you like it?"

"So good," I say. "Your French toast is delicious."

"I'm glad."

I can't believe how comfortable I am around this man. But then again, he's so easygoing and eager to please. I want to tell him he doesn't have to try so hard, but honestly, it's very sweet, and I've never met a man who acted like this before. While the attention is flattering, I do want to know more about him.

"You never told me about your book," I say. "What is it about?"

"I thought I told you," he says, "at the bookstore."

"Yes, you said it's a romance novel. That's literally all I know."

"Yeah, it's kind of a romance ..." He makes an ambiguous gesture with his hand. "I don't really know what to call it."

This is a problem for a lot of new writers. Especially those penning their first book. They come up with an idea; they add different elements so it's "unique." Very often, they'll use tropes from different genres. The result is usually a Frankenstein-like text, a book that's not really this, but also not really that. Sometimes these quirky stories sell well.

But only very rarely.

Most of the time, these half-this, half-that books are a mess, and nobody is interested. Readers will swear, up and down, that they want to read something new, and they might believe what they say with their whole heart. But here's the truth: most readers want something that's *familiar*.

Brandon is not elaborating.

"What is it about?" I ask.

He takes a deep breath, puts his fork down.

"I know you're being polite," he says, "and that's kind of you. But the thing is, it's a little intimidating talking about your book with a bestselling author."

I put my hand over his. "It's alright, Brandon. You don't have to feel that way around me. I'm just a regular person, not some hoity-toity author who thinks she's above every-body else. But I understand what you're saying. I felt that way too, early on. Whenever you feel comfortable, we can talk about it."

He squeezes my hand. "Thanks."

We finish breakfast in a comfortable silence. When we're done, I make a point of clearing the dishes. This man has waited on me enough. I want him to know I'm just as interested in him.

"Are you making the Wednesday meeting?" he asks while I put our dishes in the dishwasher.

I forgot all about it, to be honest. On Wednesday nights, the writers' group usually meets to critique some poor, but very brave soul's work-in-progress. I normally attend, but only to serve as moderator. My agent and editor have strongly cautioned me against reading other people's manuscripts. They've both seen it happen, where an aspiring writer later reads an author's book, squints really hard, and alleges plagiarism. It's a shame it has to be this way, because I'd like to help other writers out. But I also don't want to deal with a lawsuit, no matter how frivolous.

"I'll be there."

He smiles up at me. "Maybe we could grab a drink after?"

12

Once I'm home, I take a nice warm shower, then slip into my most comfy pair of sweats and a stretchy top. I must get some work done today after yesterday's poor effort.

I settle in at my recliner and open my laptop. The Word document is waiting for me, the cursor blinking at the top of a new chapter. I can't remember what was supposed to happen next, so I scroll up in the document to review my outline. My notes jog my memory, but I have trouble focusing. Now that my blissful feeling from last night has lifted, the cryptic note and the visit from the detectives and Megan's gruesome death consume my attention. When my mind wanders, it goes to dark, scary places, and next thing I know, I'm checking the back porch for a new note as well as the doors and windows again.

Relieved to find nothing amiss, I allow morbid curiosity to get the better of me, once more checking online for news of Megan Patterson. Some new stories appear at the top of the search results. Unfortunately, they're merely updates, with no fresh substance.

As I'm closing out the internet, there's a tentative knock on the front door.

My first thought is it must be the police. But then I relax: the police wouldn't knock like that. When they come to your house, they want you to know they're there.

I go to the front door and peer out the peephole. It's only Rebecca, my neighbor. But, judging by her distracted expression, she looks like she has something serious on her mind.

I open the door. "Hey, you."

"Hi." She musters a weak smile. "Are you busy?"

I should be writing, but I can tell something is weighing on Rebecca. "Want to come in?"

"If you don't mind?"

Rebecca stands in the kitchen with me as I brew coffee.

"I wanted to ask how your date went," she says.

I get the feeling that's not why she's here, but I play along. Sometimes, with Rebecca, you have to walk in a few circles before you come to the point.

"Great," I say. "He's *really* nice."

She nods absently. "Where did you go?"

I think I've already mentioned this. But I tell her again anyway.

"How was it? What's he like?"

Over coffee, I give Rebecca all the non-juicy details. I end my story with, "And we went back to his place for another drink."

I'm expecting a bigger reaction than the one I get from her. Anytime a grown woman and a grown man go to one another's place for "a drink," it's pretty obvious what's set to happen next.

But Rebecca looks down into her coffee.

"Did you stay over?"

She already knows I did. Rebecca isn't nosy per se. But I'm willing to bet my next advance that she noticed my car wasn't in the driveway this morning when she was getting the kids out to the bus stop.

"Yes," I admit, a little jolt of excitement going through my body. "He seems like a great guy."

"I think Ron's having an affair," Rebecca says suddenly.

My smile is gone. "Oh my gosh, are you serious?"

She *almost* starts crying. But by some herculean force of will, she manages to keep herself from weeping.

She's still looking down into her coffee. "I've suspected for a while."

I've never liked Ron. But Rebecca is a good friend. We always avoid the subject of her husband because we both know it won't lead anywhere good for our friendship. Without my ever having come out and said anything, she knows how I feel about him.

I could see Ron stepping out on her. He has a wandering eye, and he's not subtle about it. Just last summer, during our street's annual block party, he went on and on about how good another neighbor looked after losing a significant amount of weight, then mentioned slyly that none of the pounds had come off her chest like they do for "a lot of other women."

Even worse, Ron made this comment in front of Rebecca.

"Have you talked to him about it?" I ask.

"I tried this morning, after the kids left for school." She frowns. "He laughed at me like I was crazy."

"What do you think you should do?"

"I don't know. I've heard him talking to somebody on his

cell in the basement at weird hours. And he never used to lock his phone, but now he does."

I feel awful. Rebecca and Ron have been married for almost twenty years now. And while he's not the greatest guy, I know that she loves him.

Rebecca's frown deepens. "It's the same crap he was pulling all those years ago, when we were first married. There was this woman from the office. She was constantly calling and texting, but he always claimed it was work-related."

"Is he talking to someone from work again?"

She shrugs. "That's what he says."

I don't have much in the way of advice. Ron is a piece of work. Then a thought occurs to me.

"How did it end before?" I ask.

"The first affair?" She blushes. "His, uh, co-worker died."

"Oh my God."

Rebecca nods. "It was weird. When Ron told me she was dead, it was in an offhand way, like he hardly knew this person when they'd been calling and texting nearly every day. It was only a year or so later that he fessed up. They'd been intimate for months, apparently. Ron claimed it was purely physical and swore it would never happen again."

Even though I write mysteries and thrillers for a living, I'm not usually a cynical person. That being said, when it comes to Ron, it's not difficult for me to think the worst of the guy. He's boorish, sexist, condescending. I've based a couple of characters in my books on him. Imagine the guy who doesn't realize it's not the 1980s anymore, and you can't treat women like that these days, and you've pretty much got Ron.

"She choked to death," Rebecca continues her story of

Ron's first affair. "They found her with a belt around her throat in her closet. They thought it was, you know, auto-erotic ...?"

"In other words, it looked like an accident?"

She's nodding along with my question. "That's what the police thought, but her family didn't believe it. They hired their own coroner, who said the belt wasn't in the right place. It was a big deal, locally anyway. A lot of people thought it was her boyfriend. Her family were all convinced it was murder."

"Wow. That is *unbelievable*. Why didn't you ever mention this?"

"You and I weren't as close at the time. And it's not something you just bring up later. Hey, you know my husband might have been sleeping with a woman who died under mysterious circumstances?"

A heavy silence descends upon us. Rebecca's eyes dart nervously. She takes a sip of coffee, her first taste, just to have something to do.

"You don't think ..." I start to say.

"No." Rebecca jumps in quickly. "Ron had an alibi."

"Right." I smile. "Of course. Ron's not—he wouldn't do something like that."

"He was out of town for work," Rebecca says.

"Right."

Rebecca moves past me, puts her cup of coffee on the counter. "I should go. You're busy."

"No, it's okay. I can take a few more minutes—"

But she's already heading for the door.

I follow her into the foyer. "What are you going to do?"

Rebecca puts her hand on the knob. "If I find out there's a woman, she's going to be in trouble."

My blood runs cold. Rebecca's words remind me of the cryptic note I found, warning me that I had to be more careful.

Then I have a terrible thought. Could *Rebecca* have left that note for me?

No way. Even though I've never quite laid all my cards out on the table, she knows how I feel about Ron. Besides, if she suspected I was sleeping with him, Rebecca would put the question directly to me rather than leave a vague, threatening note on my porch.

Before Rebecca leaves, she looks back at me over her shoulder.

"He was out again *last night*. He claimed he was entertaining a client. But they were out *late*. And he came home smelling of perfume."

I freeze. Rebecca hasn't accused me of anything. But her tone is suspicious.

"Becca, I was out all night, and you said Ron came ho—"

"I'll talk to you later," she says, her words tumbling over themselves.

And then she leaves even faster.

13

After Rebecca's gone, I don't know what to do with myself. I must stand in the foyer for a good ten or fifteen minutes while my mind whirls. Does my close friend think I'm sleeping with her husband? I don't use the word *hate* often to describe how I feel about someone, but it might apply in Ron's case.

Banner week, so far.

I text Rebecca, telling her how sorry I am and asking if there's anything I can do. I don't go on to proclaim my innocence, though I feel afterward like I should have. I get the crazy idea to have Brandon call Rebecca and give me an "alibi" for last night, but that's silly. Rebecca and I are friends. She's just really emotional right now and not herself. When she's thinking clearly, she'll realize I'd never have an affair with her husband.

I sit down to work again but find it impossible. Now I'm thinking about this mystery woman from Ron's office. When I should be writing, I'm online, delving into old local news stories.

It takes me literally two searches, and I've found what I'm looking for.

Selena Ramirez – Dead or Murdered?

Selena was young, only twenty-five at the time of her death. The woman was active on social media, so there are several pictures available online for the whole world to see. She was a beautiful woman, with dark hair and cinnamon skin and luxurious, pouty lips. She could have been a model, that's how pretty she was.

Going off that fact alone, I find it difficult to believe she was in a sexual relationship with Ron of all people. I mean, he's okay-looking, I guess, but it's not like the studio is ever going to offer him the role of James Bond. This woman, Selena, she could have had any man she wanted. I seriously doubt she would have given Ron the time of day if they hadn't been working together. Then again, stranger things have happened when it comes to men and women. Everybody has their type, and maybe Ron lucked out and just happened to be Selena's.

I scan through the news articles, the details coming back to me now. I tend to pay attention to these kinds of stories, not out of morbid curiosity, but because they give me ideas for my books. At first there was a big to-do over the alleged sexual nature of the incident. The police were quick, apparently, to classify it as an accident—and it turns out my new best friend, Detective Rooney, was involved in the case.

The young woman's family took umbrage, speaking out against the police department's initial findings. I don't have children, but I assume no mother or father wants to believe their child would accidentally die in such a manner. It doesn't surprise me that this explanation wouldn't sit well with grieving parents.

But then I find an article that mentions Selena's boyfriend at the time.

And my heart skips a beat.

Matthew Lopez.

14

It's just a coincidence, right?

I want to believe that. I really do.

But ... my God.

Why didn't Matthew ever tell me he once dated a woman who died under suspicious circumstances? It seems like something that would come up, if not on the first date, at least eventually. I mean, I felt the need to tell Brandon about my mother *and* the police interrogating me, straight away. How come Matthew never mentioned this?

Knowing this, I have all the more reason to believe what his other ex-girlfriend alleged. How could I have been so oblivious when it came to this man whom I dated for quite a while? I cannot believe how blind I was.

Okay, I'm jumping the gun. It's totally possible that Selena's death was an accident *and* that Matthew's other ex-girlfriend made up a story about how he assaulted her. Right?

When my phone buzzes with a text, I literally jump out of my chair.

> I'm sorry about texting you again last night,
> but I really wanted you to—

It's from Matthew. I don't read the rest. Instead, I send him a message:

> Why didn't you ever tell me about Selena
> Ramirez?

I wait. I don't know what I'm expecting him to say. Maybe just by asking the question, that will be enough to make him go away. I don't really want to go through the rigmarole of obtaining a restraining order—

Now he's calling me.

My thumb hovers over the ANSWER icon. What did I expect? Whatever he has to say about Selena, it's probably too long, too convoluted to share over text. And I have no one to blame but myself, since I asked the question.

"Hi, Matthew."

"Amanda," he says, his voice grave, "who told you about Selena?"

"It doesn't matter," I say, my anger automatically rising. I have to keep that in check. If Matthew's dangerous—and I have to assume he is at this point—then yelling at him is not a good idea. "The point is, Matthew, you dated this woman, and she died in unusual circumstances. In all the time we were together—"

"We weren't *dating*," he blurts out. "I hardly knew Selena."

"That's not what the news accounts said."

"Come on, Amanda, do you believe everything you hear on the news?" His voice is getting louder. "Look, we were both young, and neither of us wanted a relationship. We were two consenting adults having sex. That's it. I think I saw her twice, maybe three times. We met at a bar, exchanged numbers, then texted a little bit. The police saw our texts on her phone, and next thing you know, everybody is saying I'm her boyfriend. I wasn't. I found out later that I wasn't even the only man she was *sleeping with*. Of course, by then, the story was old news, and nobody cared."

"Who else was she sleeping with?" I ask.

"I don't know for sure. I heard from a friend of a friend that it was somebody at her office—but why do you care?"

"Never mind that," I say quickly. "Why didn't you ever tell me this?"

"Why would I?" he practically shouts. *"Hey, Amanda, this woman I slept with maybe twice died?* Even though I had nothing to do with it, what would you have thought?"

I don't know what I would have thought. But I wouldn't have dated him for another minute, if I'm being honest.

Matthew is still talking. "That shit was hanging over my head for a few years. They made me take some time off work. I missed out on a promotion because of it, even though the police never arrested me or anything. It had nothing to do with me. I just wanted it to go away. You of all people should understand that."

"We were together for almost a *year*," I say. "We were talking about moving in together, for God's sake. You had plenty of opportunities to tell me this."

"I am sorry. But what do you want me to say? The longer we were together, the harder it was for me to tell you—and, again, I had nothing to do with it. You have to believe me."

I don't respond.

"Amanda." Matthew sounds desperate. Almost feral. "Do you believe me?"

"I don't know *what* to believe, Matthew. Your other ex-girlfriend accused you of assault, and this morning I find out about Selena. Put yourself in my shoes."

"Amanda, I would never hurt you, never in a thousand years. And I would never *let* anyone hurt you."

"What does that mean?" I ask.

He doesn't answer. "I love you. I *still* love you. If I could just come over and explain everything—"

"NO. You are *not* coming over."

"Amanda!" he yells over me. "You have to believe me!"

I don't say anything for a moment. Then, in as calm a voice as I can manage, I say, "Matthew, we broke up *six months ago* at this point. You continue to call and text. You show up in public places when you know I'll be there. Your ex filed charges against you—"

"They were all thrown out!" Matthew yells. "The prosecutor saw through her lies and—"

"Matthew," I repeat as calmly as I can, "regardless, you keep trying to insert yourself back into my life when I've made it clear I don't want to have a relationship with you. Now, do I have to go to the police station and file for a restraining order, or are you going to leave me alone once and for all?"

"You only broke up with me because my ex was making up all those lies," he answers in a dark tone. "But now that she's been exposed, you won't even give me a second chance. That's bullshit, Amanda!"

"Don't yell at me," I say, my voice trembling. "And answer my question."

"Go get your restraining order. You've already ruined my life. It can't get any worse."

I'm shocked by his abusive language. For a moment, I sit

there, with the phone still up to my ear, completely stupefied even after Matthew ends the call.

My whole body is shaking. When I stand up, my legs are like Jell-O. I want to sit back down, get my bearings, but I know I have to do something. There is no denying it now. I can't believe I didn't see things clearly before this: Matthew has a really bad temper and is clearly unbalanced. He's not just that ex-boyfriend who hangs around a little too long after a breakup.

He might have killed Selena. He might also have assaulted his ex. Just because the prosecutor didn't bring charges doesn't mean he's innocent.

I grab my coat and purse and jump in the car. The skies are clear, the sunlight reflecting blindingly off all the fresh snow.

I've never been inside a police station. You'd think I have, what with the books I write. What a police station looks like isn't all that important in my stories, so I generally just make it up as I go.

This one is only a few years old, a part of the township's new administrative complex. Inside, the station is bright and clean. A young woman wearing a blue uniform takes my information and hands me a form to fill out. I find an empty seat in the waiting area.

I don't hold back when the form asks me to describe my alleged stalker's behavior. Poring over all my texts and missed calls from Matthew over the last six months, I detail a string of behavior that, when I look back and take it all in, seems embarrassingly obvious now.

"Ms. Christie?"

I look up to find Detective Taylor standing over me.

"Oh," I say, fidgeting in my chair. "Hello, Detective."

"Nice to see you again. I'd like to talk to you about that."
He pushes his glasses up his nose and nods at the form I'm filling out. "Would you come with me?"

"Uh, sure."

I follow Detective Taylor through the station. It's busy in here, with police typing away at their desks or on their phones. Detective Rooney is in an office, speaking to an older woman who looks like a civilian. He spots me passing through the interior of the station, his mistrusting eyes tracking me. I don't know whether to wave or not and decide against it. It's not like we're friends.

Taylor brings me to his desk, pulls a chair up beside it so I can sit.

"You're here to file a restraining order against Matthew Lopez?" he asks.

"That's right."

"I see." He turns, briefly, to look at his computer monitor. I can't see it from this angle. Taylor punches a few keys. "Did something happen between you two recently?"

I end up explaining everything I wrote on the form, which is kind of annoying. Taylor interrupts several times, makes me go over different interactions, circles back to earlier incidents. It's all a bit exhausting. People don't live their lives recording everything in their perfect memories. At several crucial junctures in my account, I have trouble recalling exactly what Matthew said or did. By the end of Taylor's questioning, I feel like I have a flimsy case for a restraining order despite the fact that Matthew just literally cursed me out on the phone. So I bring up Matthew's connection to Selena Ramirez. Taylor's eyebrows rise at this. He types notes on his computer. I go to ask him about the next steps in the process, but the detective changes gears.

"Tell me, Amanda," Taylor says, slipping casually back to my first name, "did Matthew ever meet Megan Patterson?"

"Yes," I say, a little jarred. "As a matter of fact, he did."

"Hmm."

"They met at a happy hour back when I was still working at the company."

"The one time?" he asks. "Or did Matthew meet her multiple times?"

"It was several times."

"How about at that last happy hour? The one where you and Megan got into a disagreement?"

"No," I say. "We were no longer together then."

"But you were still in communication with Matthew, weren't you?"

"He was still in communication with me is a better way of putting it."

"Either way," Taylor persists. "Did you tell him about this exchange with Megan?"

"Yes."

Taylor nods along with my statement, as if this confirms something he already knew.

"Did Matthew and Megan ever have words?" Taylor asks.

What the hell's your problem with Amanda, you bitch?

I want to slap my forehead. Those were Matthew's words to Megan at an earlier happy hour. How could I have forgotten?

It wasn't an official work function, just some colleagues deciding at the last minute to meet up for drinks. Someone suggested that significant others be invited. I texted Matthew and let him know I was running late. He arrived a few minutes before me. Megan was already there. Ridiculous woman that she was, she didn't stop to think this man she'd never met before might be my boyfriend and continued to gossip about me. Matthew, who knew of my strained relationship with this woman, immediately shut Megan down with that comment.

After I arrived, Miley pulled me aside to share the story. At the time, I was happy Matthew had so boldly stuck up for me. He knew Miley but not anyone else there, but that didn't deter him. Miley, on the other hand, was less approving of his intervention, noting that "everyone" felt like Matthew had taken things too far. It wasn't just the fact he'd called Megan a bitch. They had all agreed that his tone was threatening.

At the time, I wrote off Miley's concerns. Having been on the receiving end of Megan's thinly veiled criticisms and cattiness in the past, I knew how infuriating she could be. And Matthew was not the type to let anyone badmouth his girlfriend.

I share that story with the detective.

Taylor's face betrays nothing. I can't tell if he already knew about that "bitch" comment by Matthew, or if this is the crucial piece of information that will send their investigation along a new path.

"I see," he says, a moment later. "How did Megan take that?"

"From what I heard after, not well."

"Did you and Matthew ever talk about Megan? Before, or after this incident at the bar?"

Incident. He makes it sound so dirty.

"Sure," I say. "She and I were not on friendly terms, and we had to work together frequently. Naturally, she came up a few times in conversation, but it wasn't like we were talking about her every night."

Taylor nods thoughtfully. "Did he ever express a desire to get back at Megan for the way she talked to you at the bar during that last happy hour?"

I rack my brain. "No, not really. When we talked about Megan, he always asked what *I* was going to do about her."

"What did *you* do about her?"

"Nothing," I say, shaking my head. "I always kept things professional at the office. The only time I wasn't cordial was much later, when I was no longer working there."

"How did Matthew feel about you doing nothing?"

"He wasn't thrilled. He kept telling me I had to confront her. In fact, there were times he put a lot of pressure on me to say something, but I wasn't comfortable and didn't feel it was necessary."

"And when you told him you weren't going to do anything, how did he respond?"

"Actually, he was kind of judgmental about it. This was one of the reasons I ended the relationship. Not because of Megan specifically, but because Matthew had a way of telling me what to do."

"I see. And ever since you ended the relationship, he's been trying to get back together, right?"

"Yes."

"And like you said, Matthew could be a bit overprotective at times. Right?"

"Yes."

"Did Matthew read your books?"

"Oh yes," I say. "He enjoyed them."

"He read them more than once?"

"Yes."

"*All* of them?"

I know where this is going. "Yes."

"He would have read the book where a character is decapitated?"

I nod.

I came down here thinking Matthew might have assaulted his ex-girlfriend and, maybe, either accidentally or intentionally killed Selena Ramirez. Now Taylor has got me wondering if he also murdered Megan Patterson out of some sick, twisted desire to impress or protect me. Maybe decapitating her and stuffing a book down her throat was his way of signaling that he'd done the murder *for me.*

I cannot believe I am even having these thoughts. While Matthew isn't in the best state of mind right now, I can't imagine him killing Megan Patterson simply because the woman previously insulted me months ago.

"Amanda." Taylor sits back and pushes his glasses up his nose once more. "I'm just going to come out and ask you this. Did Matthew ever express any desire to hurt Megan Patterson?"

"No," I admit.

"Even when you told him you weren't going to do anything about the way she was treating you at work?"

"That's right," I say. "He never said he would do anything like that."

He looks past me. I turn to follow his eyes and spot Rooney lumbering our way. The older detective is a big man with quite a presence. A couple of younger policemen move quickly out of Rooney's way, who doesn't bother to acknowledge their overly polite show of deference.

Rooney stops behind me. "What's up?"

Taylor's eyes drift to a conference room. "Got a minute?"

"Sure." Rooney looks down at me. "Everything alright, Ms. Christie?"

"Not really," I say. "I came here to request a restraining order."

"Is that so?" he says, like I'm making this up. Before I can answer, Rooney bobs his head toward the conference room. Taylor apologizes and asks me to wait, promising they'll be right back.

They're not right back. The two detectives talk for at least fifteen minutes in the conference room. I can see them through the glass, but I don't watch because that would look suspicious. While I'm waiting, I check my phone just for something to do. I've missed a call from Brandon, and I've got a few texts from Rebecca in the queue—

> Sorry I dumped all this on you, Amanda. But I didn't know who else to talk to. My sister won't listen when it comes to Ron. She just tells me to leave him. But she doesn't have kids, she doesn't understand.

And this one—

> Do you think he's having an affair? You're my friend, and I respect your opinion. I really want to know.

This is a difficult question to answer. People tell you they want your honest opinion, but more often than not, they don't. I see it happen all the time when new writers send their works-in-progress around to the group, all but begging for critical feedback. Then, when we workshop the manuscript at the next meeting, the same writers get their backs up, dig in, and defend literally every creative decision they made.

All of this is to say, I don't know if Rebecca *really* wants my honest opinion. As her friend, though, I feel like I should give it to her.

As I'm typing, however, the door to the conference room opens, and Rooney strides toward me. He takes Taylor's seat, folds his hands on his paunch. Taylor remains standing, looking a bit out of place at his own workstation.

"Ms. Christie," Rooney begins, "I'm wondering why you waited till today to tell us about Matthew."

"Well, I didn't come here to talk to you specifically," I remind him. Rooney doesn't get to revise history. "This behavior of his has kept up for too long. When we were on the phone today, he would not promise to leave me be, and then he yelled that I'd ruined his life."

Rooney puffs his lips out. "I'm a bit stumped, though, why you didn't think to mention that Matthew called Megan a bitch before? Or why you didn't think to tell us about Selena Ramirez prior to this morning?"

"I didn't know about *Selena* until this morning."

"How's that?" Rooney asks, cupping an ear like he's hard of hearing.

I tell them about my conversation with Rebecca. Rooney does not try to mask his disbelief. He simply finds the chain of events too incredible. Even I have to admit these random connections seem like too big a coincidence. Taylor, for his part, is not openly skeptical; instead he's focusing on taking notes.

"Okay," Rooney says, "so I'll take you at your word that you didn't know about Selena till this morning. That still doesn't explain why you didn't talk with us about Matthew when we were at your house."

"Honestly, I didn't put the two things together."

"Come on," Rooney says. "You write mysteries and

thrillers. You tell stories about cops and criminals. I read that one where the person gets their head chopped off. It actually wasn't bad."

Actually wasn't bad. Gee, thanks.

Rooney is still talking. "You went through several police interrogations in your book. You know how these things work and—"

"That's fiction," I blurt out. "This is real life. You're both cops, so you don't know what it feels like when you're a civilian and two police officers show up at your door, asking you questions about a woman you did not like, who was murdered *like that*. Honestly, I never put it together that my ex-boyfriend might be ..."

I let that hang.

Rooney makes a face like what I just said is utterly ridiculous. "Ms. Christie, let me ask you an honest question. Are you afraid you're our prime suspect in Megan Patterson's murder, and you came down here today to file this restraining order against Matthew as some kind of subtle way to throw us off our game and make it look like Matthew could be a suspect?"

"No!" I'm standing up, outraged. "No! I came here today for help. I didn't even ask to speak to you or Detective Taylor. This is, this is ridiculous. My ex-boyfriend is stalking me. His ex-girlfriend filed assault charges—"

"Which were dropped." Rooney interrupts my tirade. "Her story was full of holes."

I continue on like I haven't heard him. "—and I come to find out that he was seeing this other woman who died under mysterious circumstances—"

"He was cleared as a suspect," Rooney interrupts again.

"—regardless, the point is, I came here for help, and now

you're accusing me of trying to get my ex-boyfriend in trouble for murdering Megan Patterson."

Rooney holds out a palm. "I didn't accuse you of anything, Ms. Christie. All I did was ask a question."

"Don't hide behind words," I say. "You're being totally disingenuous."

"Disingenuous. Going to have to look that one up." Rooney shakes his head. "I don't know what I think yet. We're still exploring a bunch of angles in this case, Ms. Christie."

"Fine." I stuff my phone into my purse, then look at Taylor. "Is there anything else I have to do with that form?"

"No, Amanda," he says very calmly, like I'm overreacting. "I'll make sure it gets where it needs to go."

"Fine," I say again. "Then I'm leaving now."

As I storm out of the police station, I feel the eyes of the two detectives—and everyone else—on me.

15

After I get home, I really try to work on the book, but I can't stop thinking about Matthew or Rooney's latest barely veiled accusations. Every few minutes, I find myself lost in thought or pacing the house angrily. For two hours I make an effort to work, but it's not happening. Not today.

It's quite possible that Matthew *did* kill Megan Patterson, the more I think about it. And if that's true, how is he going to react to my telling him, once and for all, to leave me alone?

I make an early yoga class at the gym and manage to work out some of my energy, which is a mixture of angry and nervous. By the time class is over, I'm feeling a little better, but I'm still on edge. The restraining order is an absolute must, but I'm thinking it's not enough. If Matthew is truly obsessed with me, if he's got it in his head that I've ruined his life and he can't live without me, then what good is a piece of paper telling him to stay away going to do? I need more than that.

Instead of heading home after the gym, I drive about twenty minutes out of town to the gun store. Ironically enough, Matthew brought me here once before and showed me how to shoot at the range attached to the back of the shop. Firing a weapon was both terrifying and exhilarating. Matthew offered to buy me a handgun for protection, but I didn't want a weapon in the house.

But now that idea doesn't seem so crazy. The truth is, I'm a single woman living alone, who's being stalked by an unhinged ex-boyfriend, and some sicko has copycatted a murder in one of my novels to kill Megan Patterson. If someone is intent on harming me, an alarm system and a restraining order are not enough.

I pull my coat on so I don't treat the owner of the gun store to a view of a thirty-something woman in sweaty yoga gear. I must look horribly out of place when I enter, because the man with the long gray beard standing behind the counter looks up at me like I've got a flat tire or need directions.

"Can I help you?" he asks.

"Yes," I say, feeling the eyes of another customer on me. "I, uh, I need a gun."

The man with the gray beard smiles. He's missing a tooth.

"Then you came to the right place."

ON MY WAY HOME, I check my phone and remember I have to call Brandon back and respond to Rebecca. I text Rebecca to ask if she'd like to come over tonight to "watch a movie," which is our code for "talk about stuff." Over the years, we've sent each other that message many times. I add in another text, rather flippantly:

> BTW, filed a restraining order against Matthew today. Good times.

Then I call Brandon.

"Hey, Mandy," he says.

After the day I've had, it's so good to hear his voice. I can't wait to see him tomorrow night for drinks, after the writers' group meeting at the bookstore. I almost wish he'd ask me to come over tonight, because I'm not really in the mood for sleeping alone at home with Matthew steaming. But I still have to play it cool with Brandon. I don't want to tell him just yet about the restraining order—I mean, what guy wants to deal with an obsessive ex-boyfriend who, by the way, might just be a double murderer? I've only been on one date with Brandon, so expecting him to protect me from Matthew is a big ask at this point.

"Hey, you," I say. "How's it going?"

"I'm so glad you called. It's a slow night here."

"Did you steer any customers to the letter *C* in mysteries and thrillers?"

He laughs. "You know what, I did. Hey, let me tell my manager I'm going on break. Then we can talk for a few minutes, okay?"

I hear Brandon talking to somebody and the sounds of him moving through the store. "Hey, I'm back. So tell me everything. What did *you* do today?"

I am prepared to lie to him. I can tell him all about my boring little day, where I wrote (or *tried* to) for a few hours and went to yoga. I'll make a joke about how I'm the most inflexible person in the class, how the seventy-five-year-old man with several joint replacements puts me to shame. Then I'll bowdlerize my conversation with Rebecca; all I'll say is: my friend came over, and we had coffee; it was a blast. But as I open my mouth to speak these pure fabrications, I find I can't. I. Just. Can't. I need to have an honest conversation with someone, and it just so happens that Brandon is actually interested.

"My day was crazy. I found out my friend's husband might be having an affair. His name is Ron. Ron might have also had another affair years ago with a woman who was sleeping with my ex-boyfriend around the same time. This woman died under mysterious circumstances. Then I went to the police station to file a restraining order against my ex. While I was there, the two detectives investigating Megan Patterson's death accused me of making up stories about my ex so they would suspect *him* of Megan's murder. I didn't get any work done after all that, but I managed to make yoga. I needed to do something physical to take my mind off everything else."

There is a long pause. I fear I've gone too far. Should I have lied and pretended like my day was totally nor—

"Wow," Brandon says. "Are you serious?"

"Yes."

He chuckles. "You sure lead an interesting life, Amanda Christie."

Then I'm laughing too.

"So ..." he says, and I can hear the smile in his voice. "How *was* yoga?"

Now he's got me in stitches. "Are you for real, Brandon?"

"For real what?"

"I basically told you my life is complete and utter chaos.

I'm a murder suspect, and my ex-boyfriend might be stalking me. And you're just … *okay with that?*"

"Like I told you last night, Mandy," he says, and I love the way he says Mandy. It's like suddenly our thing. Nobody else gets to call me that. "I can tell you're a good person. I'm sorry you've got all this going on, but none of it is your fault. I'm just, uh, honored, actually, that you'd share it all with me."

Honored? Is this guy for real? Here we go again—can anybody be this nice in real life?

"But before we go on," he says. "Is there anything *else* you wanted to tell me? I mean, now's the time. No reason to hold anything else back."

He's laughing again. Before I can stop myself, I say: "Someone left a note at my back door."

He stops laughing immediately. "A note?"

"You know in those old movies, when the kidnappers cut out words from magazines because they don't want—"

"Right, yes."

"That's what it was like."

"My God." He's not laughing now. "Mandy, this is serious. Did you tell the police?"

"Not exactly."

"Why not?" He sounds worried. I don't know what it is about the note that's got him so spooked compared to everything else. "What did it say?"

"It said I was in trouble and to be careful."

"Jesus." I can hear him switching the phone from ear to ear. "You've got to tell the police. What if it was Matthew?"

I wasn't thinking that originally, but now I have to admit, it's a real possibility. In fact, it makes real sense from Matthew's macho perspective. What better way to get back in your ex-girlfriend's life? Trick her into thinking she's in danger. Then she'll call the strapping ex-boyfriend for help. My head is spinning. It's time for me to admit something. "Mom might have left me that note. And if she did, I don't want to tell the police."

"Your mom is around?" he asks, sounding almost excited.

Mom has warned me before, but I'm not yet ready to share that with Brandon.

"I have no idea," I answer quickly. "But now that all this came out about Matthew, I'm wondering if it was him."

"But if it *is* your mother, do you think she knows something about Megan's death? Was she warning you about it?"

I sense this is his way of asking me indirectly if I secretly communicate with Mom.

"I don't know why she would know about Megan," I answer carefully, not wanting to let on that Mom and I have ways of getting in contact with one another.

"I just assumed ..." Brandon says before taking a deep breath. "I'm going to do something crazy and say what I'm thinking. Here goes. She's your mother. You two must love each other. I assumed you still talked."

He pauses to take another breath. I don't fill the silence.

Brandon goes on. "If you're not comfortable sharing that with me, then I completely understand. I hope I didn't overstep."

There's something about Brandon that makes me trust him. He's so sincere and thoughtful, I find myself letting my guard down.

16

TWENTY-FIVE YEARS AGO

A unt Cece knocks on my bedroom door way too loudly. I mean, it's not like I'm listening to music, and it's not like I'm watching TV (she won't let me have a TV in my room). She knows what I'm doing. She knows I'm quietly reading. She really doesn't have to bang on my door.

"Amanda, I'm coming in," she announces.

Before I can object, Aunt Cece throws open the door. She has curlers in her hair and a lit cigarette dangling out of the side of her mouth. She's always smoking. It's gross.

"Reading again?" she asks, looking down at the paperback in my hands.

I dog-ear my page and put the book on my nightstand. I sit up in bed a little taller.

"You're always reading," she says, like it's a bad thing. "What did I tell you about that?"

I roll my eyes. It's a powerful gesture, one I learned from her. Mom never did that to me.

"Amanda." She comes into my room, sits on the edge of

my bed. "I'm just trying to help you. No man is gonna be interested in a woman who's always got her nose in a book. Believe me."

If all men are like the guys Aunt Cece brings home, then I don't want one. I mean, some boys at school are kind of cute. And if Johnny Roakes kissed me, I'd kiss him back. But marrying one? Uh-uh. No way.

"I like reading," I say.

Which is the understatement of the year.

After everything that happened with Mom, I stopped talking to people. It wasn't hard. The few close friends I had before, they either didn't want to be friends anymore, or they weren't *allowed* to be friends anymore. Yeah. Their parents told them they weren't permitted to associate with a girl whose mother was (allegedly) a murderer.

By the time I got to my new school, with my new last name, I was used to not having any friends. Being by myself was *normal*. I still wanted friends, but I didn't even remember how I made them in the first place. When I was little, it was easy. All I had to do was show up at the playground, and somebody would be there, and for an hour or so, we'd be best friends.

When you're twelve, almost thirteen? It's not like that anymore.

The rules of friendship are completely different now. The dumbest things seem to make the biggest differences. It matters how you dress, what shows you watch, what music you listen to, who you think is hot. (If you don't think anybody is hot, then you have to pretend.) All of it is so ... mysterious and scary now.

So I retreated into books. Aunt Cece doesn't read. She thinks it's a waste of time. But there's a library down the street. I walk there twice a week and check out books. The good thing about my aunt not reading is she has no idea which books are too "grown-up" for me. I basically read whatever I want, even stuff I know Mom probably wouldn't let me.

"I know, sweetie," Aunt Cece says indulgently, like she's talking to a child who's just said they enjoy talking to imaginary friends. "Listen, this is my first night off in a couple of weeks, and there's this really great guy coming over. It'd be nice if we could eat a meal together. So do you think you could, you know?"

She bobs her head in the general direction of the front door to our apartment.

I arch my eyebrows. It's summertime, so it's still light out, but it won't be for long. "You want me to leave?"

"Just for a little bit, hon," she says. "I'll give you some money; you can maybe go get a slice of pizza and an ice cream. Wouldn't that be fun? Why don't you call a girlfriend up to meet you?"

I don't have any friends I can call. She knows this.

Aunt Cece completely misunderstands my reluctance. Unlike my mother, who would know exactly what I was thinking just by briefly looking into my eyes, Aunt Cece never has a clue. It's so annoying. I was hoping she'd develop this superpower over time, but I've been living with her for three years now, so I know at this point it's not happening. I guess it's only a thing between mothers and actual biological daughters. Aunts and nieces? Not so much.

Cece rubs my shoulders. She thinks I'm too scared to go out by myself, like I'm a child or something. But that's not what I'm afraid of. I'm scared of *being seen* out and alone by my peers. "You're getting to be such a big girl now."

"How long do—"

"He'll be here in thirty minutes. It'd be great if you could give us a couple of hours alone. Here you go."

She stuffs a wadded-up twenty-dollar bill into my hand. Cece does not have a lot of money. This is the most cash she has ever given me. She must really be trying to impress this guy. And, naturally, she doesn't want him meeting the niece of her fugitive sister on their first date. That involves too much explaining. It puts guys off, as she says.

I groan. "I don't feel like walking down to the pizzeria. It's, like, five blocks."

"The exercise will be good for you." My aunt's eyes run up and down my body. "Too much reading, and you'll get fat. Then no man will want you."

I'm not fat. And even if I were, so what? Would that mean I'm a bad person? Seriously, Aunt Cece is, like, clueless sometimes.

Before I can protest further, she leaves the room. I close the door, check myself in the body-length mirror. I'm wearing ratty old shorts and a T-shirt I only wear around the apartment because it's too small. I change out of my clothes and put on something more presentable: jean shorts and a tank top. Before leaving, I grab the paperback I'm reading and stuff it my back pocket. *Jurassic Park*. I just got to a good part. Somebody's about to be eaten.

It's a humid night. By the time I reach the pizzeria, I'm in a sweat, and it's then I remember I forgot to put on deodorant. I just started doing that recently, but I always forget. Outside the pizzeria, I make sure nobody's watching, and I quickly whiff under my arms. Yep. I smell.

Great.

It's at that exact moment I spot two boys from my grade

walking right toward me. Dennis and Ivan. They're, like, the two most popular and good-looking guys in the whole middle school, and I'm pretty sure they just spotted me sniffing my pits.

Red-faced, I pretend I don't see them and duck into the pizzeria.

Bad idea.

The pizzeria is *crowded*. And not only that, but it's filled with a lot of kids from school. I want to *die* right now. They're all here with each other, and I'm here by myself. Literally twenty sets of eyes turn to stare at me. All of my classmates have this look on their face: *Who invited her?*

Nervously, I smile and say hi as I stride toward the counter. Several people can't help but laugh because of how awkwardly I'm acting. Everyone is watching me, which makes the simple act of ordering two slices of pizza and a soda like the most difficult thing I've ever had to do.

The bells hanging over the door ring. I know, without looking over my shoulder, that Dennis and Ivan have come inside. I pay the man working the cash register and then slide over to move out of the way. There's a small table for two people by the front door. I hurry over to it and sit so I'm sort of looking out the window.

Which doesn't help.

Now that it's starting to get dark outside, I can see the reflection of the store interior in the window. A lot of my classmates are very obviously talking about me. The man working the register calls out my order a minute later.

Oh no.

I was hoping someone would bring it to me. But now I have to walk back through the pizzeria with everybody watching. For a moment, I consider forgetting all about the pizza and running out of there. I'm *so* embarrassed. But that would probably look even worse, so I take a deep breath and rise on shaky legs.

Dennis and Ivan are sitting with a group of girls at a booth near the counter. I know all the girls. One of them called me a bookworm last week, like it was some kind of insult, and everybody laughed in the girls' locker room. She's red-faced and giggling right now as I walk a little too quickly to get my food.

Dennis throws his head back and sniffs loudly.

"Hey, Ivan," he says. "Do you smell something?"

Ivan mimics his best friend. He takes a big inhale through his nose.

"Oh, *God,*" Ivan says, covering his nose and making a face like he just discovered someone else's vomit in a toilet. "What *is* that?"

I know they're talking about me. Unfortunately, everybody else in the pizzeria knows they're talking about me too.

"Smells like someone didn't use deodorant," Dennis says.

As I collect my two slices of pizza and soda, everyone in the shop bursts into laughter. Totally embarrassed, I take my food outside. I've lost whatever appetite I worked up walking all this way. I walk a block to sit on a bench looking into the park.

And I cry my eyes out.

By the time I'm done, the makeup Aunt Cece doesn't want me wearing just yet is probably all messed up on my face. Using the two paper-thin napkins the man at the counter gave me, I try to wipe my face as best I can. What a horrible night this has been.

I'm about to start crying again, but then I hear them coming. Dennis and Ivan and three girls. They stop at the street corner, half a block from where I'm sitting. I try to make myself disappear, hunching down low on the bench. But it's pointless. I know they can see me.

One of them takes out a pack of cigarettes. Dennis and Ivan are lighting up when one of the girls points in my direction and lowers her voice. The group starts laughing again.

Why can't they just leave me alone?

I stand and throw my uneaten pizza into a nearby trash can. They're still laughing when I hear Dennis say—"God, it *stinks* out here too!"

I can't even turn around and look at them. I'm so utterly humiliated. Aunt Cece wonders why I read so much, and here's one big reason: no character in a book is ever this much of a jerk to me. I pick up my soda and am about to hurry away when I realize the laughter behind me has stopped.

I peek over my shoulder.

A woman wearing jeans and a black hoodie that hides her face has approached the group. The girls are no longer laughing maniacally. As a matter of fact, they look scared. The three of them have backed away from their position on the corner, like they want to return to the pizzeria, but they're afraid to turn around.

Dennis and Ivan don't look much better off. The woman is speaking to them but very softly. From this distance I can't hear what she's saying. She points at the two boys, her voice rising sharply now to bark an order at them: "Apologize!"

Dennis is tall for his age. He's on the basketball team. Ivan isn't tall, but he's a wrestler. Not a month goes by at school where he's not getting into a fight with somebody. These two kids should not be intimidated by a woman who is shorter than and clearly not as strong as either of them.

But their faces are pale, their eyes wide.

Dennis's mouth flaps like that of a fish on dry land for a moment before he turns in my direction and raises an apologetic hand.

"I'm sorry, Amanda," he calls out.

"Louder!" the woman says.

"I'm *really* sorry!" he practically shouts.

The woman points at Ivan and hisses something I miss.

"I'm sorry too!" Ivan announces, even more loudly than his friend.

The three girls are backing away. Once they reach the corner, they break into a run. The woman is still talking to Dennis and Ivan, who both look like they want to bolt. But fear is rooting them to the spot.

"Yes, ma'am," Dennis says, using a word he's probably never uttered before: ma'am. "I promise."

"Me too," Ivan adds quickly. "I swear. I'm sorry. We're sorry."

"It won't happen again," Dennis adds, in a quavering voice.

The woman flicks her wrist dismissively. A gesture telling them *leave now*. Dennis and Ivan don't dawdle. They back up and then take off, like they're running the forty-yard dash in gym class.

I can't move. I don't know who this woman is. But I have my suspicions. She comes up to Dennis to about the same point I do. Okay, I don't know how I know, but somehow, I'm sure of it: this is my mother.

I haven't seen her since that horrible day.

Very slowly, the woman at the corner turns in my direction. She keeps her hood up and peers in my direction. I can't see her face, not really. She gives me a little wave. I'm too scared and amazed and dumbfounded to react. She reaches into the pocket of her hoodie and takes out an envelope and holds it out for me to see. Then she bends at the knee and carefully places it on the sidewalk. Before I can think of anything to say, she turns the corner and strides away. By the time I reach the corner and look down at the envelope on the sidewalk, she's gone.

17

"What did the note say?" Brandon asks.

"I won't always be around. But I'll always be looking out for you."

"That is just ... *wow*."

I haven't ever told anybody this story before. Not even Matthew, my most serious long-term boyfriend up to this point. And yet here I am, sharing this secret with a guy I've been on one date with. What has come over me?

"I guess Dennis and Ivan never bothered you again," he says.

I laugh. "No. In fact, they went out of their way to avoid me."

"I'll bet."

He doesn't know the half of it. Not so long after this incident, Dennis's girlfriend made fun of the T-shirt I was wearing in gym class. Aunt Cece wasn't always the best at buying me clothes when I'd outgrown the ones I had. Anyway, I'd shot up, and this T-shirt was showing off my belly. I've always had a little bit of a tummy, and this girl found it hysterical. She embarrassed me in the locker room before class by pointing it out to everyone. But by the end of the period, after she and Dennis had had a chance to talk, she came right over and apologized immediately.

It wasn't the only time Mom terrified somebody who wasn't treating me respectfully ...

"Did you ever see her again?" Brandon asks.

I almost admit that I have but decide against it. I've already shared enough with this man I hardly know.

"You know, I'm not sure," I say. "But tell me about your parents. Is your father famous for allegedly doing something terrible?"

"No," Brandon says quickly. "No, not exactly."

"Oh, now *that* sounds interesting. Tell me about him."

"I don't really like to talk about my parents," Brandon says.

"Come on," I say, a little miffed by his unwillingness to share things with me. "After everything I told you?"

"Mandy, I didn't know Dad well, and ... look ... he was killed. I don't really want to talk about it."

Now I feel horrible about pressing him. "I'm sorry, Brandon. I didn't mean to pry."

"And Mom ... she already had problems, but when Dad ... she was never the same."

"I'm so sorry," I say.

"It's okay. I know you didn't mean anything."

For a moment we're silent. He's definitely gone over his fifteen-minute break, so I'm expecting him to say goodbye.

"Alright, alright." Brandon sighs. "I guess I've got to tell you. I mean, it's only fair."

I don't want him to feel like he's obligated to divulge personal details.

"Brandon, if you don't want to—"

"Dad was abusive. A little toward me, but mostly toward Mom. They split up, and—well, actually, Mom and I ran away. One night, when he went out to do his thing, she had me pack a bag, and we left. We stayed at a women's shelter while it got sorted out. It wasn't until the police arrested Dad that we were safe to leave. Mom was too scared to press charges, so the police couldn't build a case and had to let him out."

"My God. What happened next?"

"Well ... his life was ruined. Even though the police didn't bring charges, word got out about what had been happening, obviously. He lost his job, and then his drinking problem only got worse."

"I'm so sorry. How old were you?"

"Young. I was ten years old when we left."

"That's about the same age I was."

"I know," he says. "I'm starting to think ..."

"Starting to think what?"

"Do you believe in fate?" he asks.

Oh boy. Are we seriously having this conversation? Already?

"Not really."

"Yeah, I don't really either." He laughs. "But it's interesting how similar our childhoods were."

"Yes."

"Anyway," he goes on, "now that I've totally freaked you out, I might as well finish the story. We moved halfway across the country and changed our names. I found out a few years later that Dad liked to rough women up in general, not just Mom. While they were still married, he would go out and meet other women. He could be charming, you know? He seemed like the most harmless man when you met him."

I can't help my brain sometimes. It goes to very dark places all on its own. I blame my childhood. Anyway, right now my brain is going to this lovely place: Brandon is charming and seems like the most harmless man I've ever met. Did he get that from his father?

Did he get anything *else* from his dad?

"One woman came forward, then another, then several more. There was even—I didn't hear about this until I was older—talk of Dad having, uh, accidentally murdered one of them. Like, in a fit of rage. But there wasn't enough evidence to make that charge stick."

"My goodness," I say. "That must have been really hard on you."

"It was difficult not having a father when I was growing up, especially when I was becoming a man myself. By then, Mom wasn't doing great herself. She was an addict ... I don't know if she got that way because of Dad's abuse or if she was always that way. A few years after we'd gotten out of that particular mess, she had latched onto this new guy. He was a step up from Dad. A tiny step, that is. He wasn't *physically* abusive, but he was really hard on her—emotionally and mentally, you know—and then, eventually, on me. The minute I graduated high school, I was out of there."

I can hear how much the past still haunts him.

"It's nothing to be ashamed of, Brandon," I say. "None of this was your fault. You were a kid."

"I know," he says. "But people look at you differently when you tell them these things. Do you know what I mean?"

"You know I do."

He laughs a little awkwardly. "Dumb question, I guess."

"My extended family really wanted nothing to do with me," I say. "Mom was always the outcast. The girl who never wanted to go to church, who didn't apply herself in school, you know? To them, she was that loose girl who got herself knocked up and then wouldn't tell anybody who the father was.

"Aunt Cece kind of took me in by default, because nobody else would. None of them ever were brave enough to look me in the eye and say this, but I figured it out: they think Mom killed David West. They distanced themselves from me, like I was diseased or something. I should really have gone to live with my aunt Mary because she had two kids of her own who were around my age. But that didn't happen. She passed a few years ago from cancer. Want to know what she told me on her deathbed?"

"What?"

"It wasn't quite an apology, but she explained why she didn't take me in. She was afraid that whatever devil had gotten into Mom had passed to me. She didn't want me growing into a monster like my mom, living in the same house as her children, my cousins."

"Jesus."

"Yeah," I say, a single tear escaping my eye. "That didn't make me feel great."

"That's terrible."

"It wasn't easy," I say, feeling more tears coming. I want to tell this man I hardly know everything, especially now that he's opened up to me. But I also feel I should lighten the mood a little. "Do you still want to grab a drink tomorrow night, after I told you all this family trauma stuff?"

"Are you kidding?" He laughs, such an easy, ready laugh. "Of course I do. I can't wait."

"Me either."

"Mandy?"

"Yeah, what is it?"

"Is there anything I can do to help right now?"

He is just the sweetest.

"I mean," he says, "not that I'm *trying* to invite myself over—"

"Oh, sure."

"—but, well, would you like me to come over tonight? Your ex sounds, not to be rude, a little *off*. If you'd like somebody to be there, I could come over."

"That's so sweet, Brandon," I say.

I'm about to take him up on his offer when my phone buzzes. Rebecca responded to my text:

Can I come over in 15?

Rebecca was not herself earlier. Her relationship with Ron has always been rocky, but now it seems like it's coming to a head. She's my friend; she really needs me. And I want to make sure she knows, without a shadow of a doubt, that I'd *never* fool around with Ron behind her back.

"I was ready to say yes," I tell Brandon, "but my neighbor is coming over."

"The one whose husband ... dot-dot-dot?"

"Dot-dot-dot." I chuckle. "That's him."

"Okay, got it. Well, if you change your mind, and I don't care how late it is, you can always text. Or call. Seriously."

"You're the sweetest."

I can almost hear him smile down the phone at that. "Alright. I'll see you tomorrow night?"

"I'm looking forward to it."

I have this warm feeling when I end the call with Brandon. Even with everything going on in my life, even with Matthew being Matthew, and this horrific murder, talking to Brandon makes me feel giddy. I haven't been lucky when it comes to men. Prior to Matthew, I'd been in two serious relationships, and when I eventually worked up the nerve to share my identity, it wasn't long before I was single again. One man broke up with me on the spot after we'd been dating for *months*. The other took his time—a whole forty-eight hours—to conjure up vague reasons about why our relationship wasn't working for him.

Then there's Matthew. While he didn't judge me for who my mother is, he has his own share of issues. And ever since that story broke about me, I haven't been on a *single* date.

Maybe my loneliness and lack of options are making me more trusting than usual. But Brandon *seems* like a genuinely good guy. I can talk to him. And I love how he opened up. Vulnerability is attractive when it's real. When Brandon shared, I could tell how difficult it was for him to talk about his father and childhood. It wasn't part of some calculated, sociopathic ploy.

Fifteen minutes pass, but still no Rebecca. This happens a lot. Her definition of time and mine are very different, but to be fair, I'm not married, nor do I have two children to manage while holding down a job.

While I'm waiting, I try to get a little work done. Try being the operative word. Every word I write gets deleted a minute or so later. I get frustrated and find myself closing the document and sifting through my email instead. As always, I'm close to maximum capacity on my storage. I sort by size, so the largest emails are at the top of the queue. They're mostly chain messages from friends or the few odd family members who still actually talk to me. Most have attachments. I decide to be merciless, deleting the ones I haven't even opened. The process gives me the feeling of being productive at least.

And then I get to an email that's not from a family member or friend.

It's from Sarah Keller.

I must have completely missed this email when she sent it. It's nearly three weeks old. Yikes. I was never great with email, and now that readers are reaching out to me in droves, I'm even worse. Maybe this is why Sarah was so nasty to me at the writers' group the other day, because I never responded to her message. Even though she was very rude, I'm starting to feel bad.

I open her email and regret it immediately. There are several chunky paragraphs that go on and on. Without reading them, I scroll to the bottom of the email. This note must be ten thousand words—long enough to be a novella.

To use Brandon's euphemism about Matthew, Sarah is clearly a little off.

I circle back to the beginning of the email, where Sarah writes all about the first time she picked up one of my books and how the character in it reminded her of herself. Then the email takes a sharp left turn, and Sarah is telling me all about her childhood, how her own mother was in trouble with the law and how difficult that made everything. My mind is reeling from all the information she provides. To use a writer's expression: it's one long info dump, digression interrupting digression, most of it about people for whom I have no context. And to sum up, she details the many dozens of reasons why she's a writer and why she thinks I can help her become a bestseller too.

This is creeping me out. Sharing your life's story, all your hopes and dreams, with a perfect stranger over email is not the behavior of a well-adjusted adult.

Ken, the other bestselling author of the group, warned me about getting messages like these, and I half didn't believe him. He likes to self-aggrandize, and I thought he was pretending he was well-known enough to get crazy emails from obsessive fans. But if *I* got one, maybe Ken wasn't making it up.

Sarah has also attached not one, not two, but *three* Word documents to the email. According to a postscript at the bottom of her message, these are the three manuscripts she's been working on. One is complete, the other is mostly complete, but she doesn't know how to finish it, and the last is just the opening chapters, but she's the most excited about it of the three. In a post-postscript, Sarah realizes she didn't tell me what to do with any of these attachments and explains she'd like me to read them *all,* because she just knows I'll like them, and maybe we could even co-author one or more than one if I feel good about them?

I've already filed a restraining order this week. I don't feel like going back to the police station tomorrow to file another. Sarah's rude behavior at the bookstore only seems odder, more jaded and stalkerish now that I've read this email. Even if she was angry that I didn't write her back, she could have simply asked me if I'd seen her note. That would have been the most reasonable place to start that conversation.

I'm very tempted to give her another piece of my mind. But I don't think that will be received well. I have to keep my response professional while also nipping this in the bud, before Sarah gets any more ideas that are completely out of touch with reality. I don't even want to imagine what it would be like to work with her.

Hi Sarah,

I'm very sorry, but I just saw your note. I'm not great with email. Please forgive my belated response. Working on one book, never mind three, is hard work and shows your dedication. Keep going, and don't give up! Unfortunately, I cannot review anyone's manuscripts. Editing is not my strong suit, and for legal reasons my publisher has advised against doing this too. It's a shame, but I've heard of writers trying to help an aspiring author out and then getting accused of plagiarism. If you'd like, I can recommend the names of some good freelance editors. Just let me know. I hope to see you at the next meeting, and again, I'm sorry for just now writing you back.

I reread the email several times, wondering if I've worded it strongly enough, while also wondering if anything I've written is going to set this woman off. In the end, I send the email as I've written it.

I lean back in my chair, perplexed and troubled, hoping against hope that this marks the last of any correspondence with Sarah.

It's closer to forty minutes when Rebecca knocks. I open the front door to find her on my porch, wearing stretch pants and an old sweater, carrying a bottle of wine.

"I look a mess," she says.

"You do not. Get in here."

She smiles and comes in. "Sorry I'm late. One of the boys didn't do all his homework, and then Ron and I got into it again. He thinks that's somehow my fault, even though I'm constantly checking up on what they're doing, and ... God, I just can't win with that man sometimes."

"I'm so sorry." I give her a big hug and rub her back. "Come on, let's sit down."

We settle in the living room. I bring out two wineglasses. She pours.

"I'm sorry about earlier," she says, eyeing me over the wineglass. "Really. That wasn't cool."

I wave it off. "It's no big deal."

"No, really," she says, still looking me in the eye. "I know you would *never* ... you would never with Ron."

I shake my head. "Absolutely not."

She laughs. "You don't have to sound quite so grossed out by it."

Oops. "No, I didn't mean it like that. I just meant, because you're my friend, and actually, I'd never hook up with a married guy under any circumstance. Not my thing."

"I know." She smiles at me. "And I'm sorry. When you suspect your husband is up to no good, it messes with your head. You begin to think all kinds of crazy things."

"I understand. Let's forget about it."

"Thanks." She takes a long drink of her wine. "Enough about Ron. Tell me about your guy. What's he like?"

"Oh, he's very sweet," I say. I feel a little bad, going on and on about how I met this really cute, caring, hot guy, when Rebecca's marriage is on the rocks yet again. But I can't help but be excited.

"That's wonderful," Rebecca says, her eyes drifting in the direction of her house. "It hasn't been like that with Ron in a long time."

"Well, part of me is waiting for the other shoe to drop," I

admit. "Brandon seems almost *too* nice, you know? And let's be honest, I don't have the best track record at picking men."

"Oh, right." Rebecca's eyes bulge a little. "Were you being serious in your text? You really went to the police station today?"

I nod. "I had to. Matthew is out of control. I don't know why I've been so blind to it up until this point. But ..."

I catch myself. I don't know whether I should tell her that Matthew was "seeing" the same woman that Rebecca suspected Ron was having an affair with, all those years ago. It nearly just slipped out.

"What?" she asks.

"It's—"

The neighbor's dog, the one that poops everywhere, starts yapping. Then Rebecca's dog, Lenny, joins in. The hairs on the back of my neck stand up.

"What's wrong?" Rebecca asks.

I haven't told her about the note at my back door.

"I, uh, want to see what that is."

I quickly leave the room and turn out the light in the kitchen so I can look into the backyard without being seen. Rebecca comes up beside me, glass of wine in her hand.

"You can't go by Lenny barking," she says. "If he *thinks* he hears a squirrel, he goes crazy."

I look out into the darkness. Lenny and the other dog are still barking wildly. Peering through the trees lining the rear of my property, I don't see anything.

"Amanda," Rebecca says, "are you alright?"

"I'm fine."

"Your hands are shaking."

She's right. "Just cold in here. I really need to turn the

heat up. Setting it to sixty-five degrees in winter isn't going to cut it."

"You're not worried that it's ... wait, *are* you worried that it's Matthew?"

The dogs are quieting down now. I still don't see anything moving around in the trees. Probably just some wild animal.

I hope.

I come away from the window above the kitchen sink and hang my head. Now I wish I asked Brandon to come over. I hate being creeped out in my own home.

"Amanda?" Rebecca asks.

"Sorry." I force a smile. "It's been a crazy few days."

"It has." She checks her phone for the time. "I'm sorry to cut this short, but I've got an early start at the office tomorrow."

"Alright. Thanks for coming over."

I walk her to the door. We give each other a hug. Rebecca holds on for a second longer.

"I'm sorry I ..." She can't quite say it out loud.

"It's okay."

Finally, she lets go of me. "I hate to even ask this, Amanda, but I have to know. Have you ever seen Ron bring somebody home?"

I shake my head no. "I would have told you right away."

"You promise?"

I nod. "You're my friend. Of course I would tell you."

She smiles sadly. "Thank you."

Then she's gone, and I'm alone in my house. I lock the front door immediately and then perform another perimeter sweep, checking windows and doors that I already checked and that I did not have any reason to open or unlock today. I grab my purse and make sure the newly purchased handgun is still in there, with the safety on.

From the darkness of the kitchen, I spy the backyard once more. I have one hand inside my purse, around the gun, when I unlock the back door and open it. It's another cold, damp night. I'm about to close the door when something on my deck catches my eye.

It's another envelope.

I really hope these messages are from Mom, but I still have a sinking feeling they're not.

I swipe the envelope and lock up. Now I've got the unsettling feeling that I'm being watched. I move to the front of the house and tear open the envelope.

Protect yourself. Stay away from the bookstore.

18

I sit out in my car for a few extra minutes in the parking lot of the bookstore. Peering through the big glass windows fronting the business, I see Brandon at work in the café. He's taking orders behind the counter and moving busily about, serving and bringing drinks to patrons seated in the small seating area.

I'm afraid to go inside.

All day long I thought about contacting Detective Taylor and handing the two cryptic messages over. These could be from Mom, but they could *also* be from Matthew—maybe my stalkerish ex is trying to scare me away from the place where Brandon works. Perhaps Matthew spied on Brandon and me the other day, and that has stoked the fires of his dangerous jealousy.

But if the notes *are* from Mom, I don't want the police knowing she's in the area. Especially considering the fact I lied to Brandon yesterday:

Mom knows who Megan Patterson was.

Ever since I went away to college, I've had ways to get in

contact with her. I'm disciplined when it comes to breaking our proverbial radio silence, usually only reaching out when I'm going through a difficult time. When I last sent her a message, it was right after the story broke about my identity, I'd lost some friends, and my job was in jeopardy.

I told her all about Megan Patterson, including my suspicions that the woman was trying to torpedo me at work. In my heart, I know Kimberly Dawn Allen is *not* a murderer, but the detectives almost certainly feel differently. If they thought these notes were from Mom and they discovered Mom knew about my contentious relationship with Megan …

I stop my train of thought. I've worried about this all day and am tired of going around in circles. Tamping down my fear, I decide to head inside.

I zip up my purse and get out of the car. Dirty, days-old snow is piled everywhere. I walk through the slush filling the parking lot. The bookstore is warm and smells like coffee. The meeting is supposed to start in a minute, but I don't want to walk right by the café without saying hi to Brandon.

A few people are queued at the counter. When Brandon catches my eye, I give him a smile and a tiny wave. He doesn't acknowledge me.

That's odd. Well, there is a line of customers waiting to place orders, not to mention a gaggle of people crowding the counter's pickup area.

Brandon addresses the woman at the front of the line with a strained voice. "Ma'am, I've already told you—"

"How dare you talk to me like that!" she says, loud enough for the whole bookstore to hear. "I cannot believe how you have treated me as a customer. You've been nothing but rude. I want to speak to your manager."

Brandon's face flushes bright red. "Look, lady—"

"Do *not* speak to me like that! Where is your manager? You deserve to be fired."

Brandon's eyes narrow. This is the first time I've ever seen him angry, and it's not a pretty sight. The veins in his neck are standing out.

"You have been so disrespectful," the woman goes on. She's got messy gray hair and looks to be in her sixties. "For my life, I cannot even *imagine* talking to a customer, never mind a woman, like you have!"

What has Brandon said? I'm getting a bad feeling about this. Have I finally seen a chink in his otherwise too-nice-to-be-real armor?

"Ma'am," Brandon says, and his voice sounds like he's about to burst, "I was *not* talking to you in any way. I just asked—"

"MOM!"

I jump at the sound of a man shouting behind me. He rushes to the counter and grips the older woman's elbow.

"There you are," he says. "We were looking for you. Where have you been?"

"This man here, you should have heard the way he was talking to me."

Brandon's angry expression softens as he looks from the older woman to this new man, who is about his age.

"What did you say to my mother?" he demands.

"I didn't say anything," Brandon protests. "I just asked her if she'd like something to drink."

"Of course I'd like something to goddamn drink!" the woman yells. "It's a danged café. Why else would I be here?"

The man's face softens as understanding fills his eyes.

"Why don't you get us a table, Mom? I'll order us something to drink."

"Okay, fine. But I want to talk to the manager before we leave."

Shaking her head, the older woman shuffles a little awkwardly to a table near me and sits.

"Young men these days," she mutters. "They have no manners anymore."

I crane my neck to get a better view of what's happening at the counter. The man and Brandon are deep in hushed conversation. The angry expression on Brandon's face evaporates as the man tells him something. Then Brandon smiles, and they shake hands, with what looks like real warmth, before the other man leaves with his mother.

I'm going to be late to the meeting, but I have to talk to Brandon now that I've witnessed this exchange. It takes forever for the line to move. Apparently, Brandon is the only one working at the moment, so he's taking orders and making drinks all at the same time.

"Hey there," I say when I reach the counter. "Everything okay?"

"Hey, you." He gives me a bright smile. "Two people called out, and my backup is on break," he explains, shaking his head. "Do you want your usual?"

He knows what my usual is already. This guy is the best.

"That'd be great. What happened with that lady?"

"Oh." He waves like it was nothing. "Poor woman. I feel terrible. Her son told me she's on new meds. She gets confused and easily agitated. He was very sorry about the whole thing. Apparently, she's prone to snapping at people waiting on her. When he told me about her condition, I felt *awful* about nearly losing my temper. I offered him a free drink, but he just wants to get her home."

Of course. Now I feel silly for even thinking that Brandon was rude to an older lady customer. He really *is* too nice for that.

"That's a shame."

Brandon checks his watch. "Hey, you're going to be late. Do you want me to bring the coffee back to the meeting space?"

"Do you think you can?" I look around. "With how busy it is?"

"My backup should return in a minute or two."

"If you're sure ... I don't want to make your job—"

"Are you kidding? I wouldn't miss an opportunity to interact with you some more."

"Hey, buddy," some guy calls out from the back of the line. "Can we hurry it up in here? I've been waiting, like, ten minutes already."

If it were me, I might give the guy a piece of my mind. But Brandon straightens up and, with a smile on his face, calmly explains to the customer how they're understaffed. I don't think that does much to change Mr. Rude's attitude, but Brandon is totally unfazed by it.

"Thank you so much," I say, reaching into my purse to pay. "That's so kind of you."

"Uh-uh." Brandon reaches out and touches my forearm, which sends a jolt of electricity running through my body. "This one's on the house."

"The house?" I ask.

"By house, I mean it's on *me*."

We both have a laugh at that. I thank him again and head into the back of the store, where our group normally meets.

The space is crowded, with more than the usual number of people attending. As I move through the space to take my seat at the long table facing the room, I get the feeling it's because of me. Several people quietly murmur to the person sitting next to them and then gesture in my direction.

"Oh, Amanda," Ken says, sitting in his usual spot. Front and center, the place of honor. "You made it after all."

"After all what?" I ask, feeling a little peeved by the attention and then Ken's snarky comment. People miss meetings all the time. People show up late all the time, too. This group comes with zero expectations, Ken is always saying. He's been late before, too, and he's missed meetings without giving us notice.

"I didn't mean anything by it." He smiles annoyingly. "Just wasn't sure you were coming."

"She shows up when she feels like it," a familiar voice says.

As I take my seat, I peer out into the group and spot Sarah Keller. Her face is down, her eyes on her phone. Louann, the older woman who's always knitting, is seated to Sarah's right. She is giving Sarah a surprised look. That confirms my suspicion: that snarky comment came from Sarah.

I decide I won't abide her rudeness again. I apologized in my email for taking so long to get back to her. If she's still angry about that, and if she's going to make these snide, disruptive comments throughout the meeting, then I'm going to ask her to leave. Most people come here to learn about the craft of fiction. And I'm taking time out of my day to help them where I can. We don't need this kind of distraction.

But just as I open my mouth to address her, Ken speaks:

"Now that we're all here. Let's get started. On tap tonight, we have—" He consults the notebook open on the table in front of him. "Oh, that's right, a manuscript, currently untitled, the space opera story. Let's dig in, and remember, please keep your feedback constructive."

I fold one leg over the other and then my arms and sit back in my chair. Sarah looks up from her phone to glare at me briefly, not quite long enough to cause a scene, before she peers back down and continues to scroll. Louann is back to her knitting.

Workshopping a story is always difficult, especially in an environment like this. Sure, most of the people here have read a lot of books. But only a handful have actually *written* one. That makes a *big* difference when it comes to offering constructive criticism. It takes all my willpower not to roll my eyes when a young woman in the front row is first to raise her hand to offer feedback and comments that there are "a few too many W sounds on the first two pages." The next person to comment starts with, "I don't read space operas, or sci-fi really, or that much fiction at all, but ..."

Oh boy.

I take out my phone and open the manuscript submitted for this week's workshop. It's five pages long, the first four of which are all exposition. While a few more people offer their feedback, I only manage to get through three pages. In addition to the long exposition dump, the manuscript has a lot of other hallmarks of the first-time writer: head-hopping, unnecessary description, etc. No judgment here—the first two books I wrote are dreadful and will never see the light of day.

Brandon appears at the back of the meeting space with my cup of coffee. He nods and smiles at a bunch of people as he passes through the room—of course, everybody likes Brandon. He draws a lot of attention, and as he approaches, I get fidgety with embarrassment. I should have realized that him delivering my drink would look a bit ridiculous. Brandon, giving me a sheepish grin, seems a little embarrassed too by the whole spectacle.

"Thank you."

Everybody is watching us. Even the man offering feedback has stopped, mid-thought, to observe. Brandon nods his way out of the room. I want to slide under the table and die.

"You get your drink delivered if you're a *published* author," Sarah says.

This comment draws a few laughs. I want to explain that the café was extremely busy, they were understaffed, and that if I'd waited for my drink, I would have been *actually* late to the meeting (actually late, Ken, rather than on time). But the moment passes because the man offering feedback starts up again. I feel Ken's eyes on me. He gives me a smug grin, as if he approves of my acting like a big-shot author, getting the help to deliver my drink.

When the other man is done talking, Ken fills the silence. "Alright, thank you for that. Moving on. I think the panel up here has deferred on feedback to the group. But, tonight, I want to hear from everybody." He turns to me. "Why don't you start, Amanda?"

I love being put on the spot.

Typical Ken. We did not discuss this beforehand. He just had an idea and unilaterally decided to implement it, knowing full well we don't always get a chance to read the manuscripts.

I turn to the man whose book is being workshopped. His

eyes are wide, and his face is turning crimson. I make sure to smile.

"I agree with most of what's been said," I answer tactfully. "The best advice I can give you is to cut the exposition and get to the story proper more quickly. And keep writing. *That's* what makes you better. More work."

He seems grateful for the mild criticism, like he was expecting me to savage his work.

"Guess you didn't have time to read his story either."

This time, Sarah's comment can't be taken as anything but snarky. The whole group turns to look in her direction. Next to her, Louann puts her yarn down in her lap and folds her hands primly, but expectantly.

I glare at Sarah.

"I have had enough of your poor manners," I say. "You can—"

But before I can finish, Sarah shoots out of her chair.

19

I cannot believe what is happening.

One moment, Sarah is sitting in her chair. The next, she is on her feet. She bursts into the aisle and, with arms pumping, practically sprints to the table. I'm overtaken by shock, and I do the worst thing possible: I freeze. In those self-defense courses I took all those years ago, the instructor drilled this fundamental principle into our heads over and over.

Do something. Anything is better than nothing. Do not freeze.

Sarah looks like she's going to attack me. With my less-than-optimal freeze response, she could have literally hit me, and I would have been too stunned to do anything about it. It takes her less than two seconds to move from her chair to standing right in front of me, palms on the table, leaning forward, an angry and aggrieved look on her face.

"You think you're better than all of us, don't you?" she practically shouts. "Because you're Ms. Bestseller or whatever. I pour my heart out to you, and you can't be bothered to give me anything but a form response?"

I lean back in my chair, putting as much distance as I can between us.

"Sarah," I say, trying to remain calm, "back up."

I don't think she is even capable of hearing me. "I'll bet you didn't even read his story! You're too good for workshopping also."

"Sarah," Ken interrupts, "you need to calm down."

He rises and comes around the front of the table, slowly approaching Sarah.

"You're too good for *everybody!*" Sarah screeches. "Did you even read my email? Do you even care about my traumatic childhood? Do you care about anybody but yourself?"

I carefully get out of my chair and hold my hands out. I hate that my purse is on the table between us—with my gun in it.

"Sarah," Ken says, edging his way toward her, "you *really* need to calm down."

Sarah faces the group and flings her arms about to keep Ken at bay. "This woman is a cold-hearted bitch! Don't buy her books! I'll bet she's a psycho killer, just like her mother!"

Brandon appears again at the other side of the meeting space. With a concerned look on his face, he peers from me to Sarah and back to me. After the slightest of hesitations, he begins to move across the room.

"Sarah!" I say, equally angry and terrified at the same time. This woman is acting like she's capable of *anything*. "You need to leave right now. This behavior is—"

Sarah spins back around and reaches into her pocket. "I'll show everybody!"

"Stop!" Brandon yells.

But she doesn't hear him.

Sarah's hand starts to come out of her pocket. All I can

think is: she's got a knife. Or a gun. This crazy woman is going to kill me. I have no choice.

I lunge forward and, in one motion, take my gun out of my purse and point it at her.

"Let go of me!" Sarah yells.

Brandon somehow made it all the way across the room and managed to grab her arm before she could pull her ... *phone* out of her pocket.

"Let go!" Sarah yells. "You're hurting me!"

Brandon stares incredulously at the gun in my hand. The whole room is panicked. Half the group has ducked out of the way, like I'm going to start shooting up the place.

"What the hell's wrong with you?" Sarah screeches, her face purple. "Are you seriously going to *shoot* me?"

My hand is shaking. My God. I came *this* close to ...

"Amanda," Ken says, "please put the gun away."

My hand is trembling. I'm embarrassed for everyone to see how badly shaken I am by this crazy woman. Making sure the safety is still on, I put the gun away.

Brandon lets go of Sarah.

"You see?" she says, holding up her phone. "I've got the email right here. I'm going to read it to you!"

"Sarah," Brandon says, "you're going to have to leave now."

"*I'm* not leaving!" she shouts. "*She's* the one waving the gun all over the place. She could have gotten somebody killed!"

While I might have garnered more sympathy than Sarah from the group, no one jumps to my defense. Most people look like they'd rather not get involved in this messy business, which is infuriating. I wasn't the one who disrupted the meeting, charged the table, screamed, then reached into my back pocket. It was perfectly reasonable for me to react.

"Maybe it's for the best if you both leave," Ken says.

I'm stunned. Ken and I aren't the best of friends, but all the same I'm clearly in the right here. And if anyone read Sarah's email, they'd know—

"I'm sorry, everyone," Ken says, holding out his palms. "We are going to take five. When we resume, Sarah and Amanda won't be here."

"That's ridiculous," Brandon snaps, getting in Ken's face. "Amanda was only defending herself!"

Ken backs away from Brandon, wanting no part of him. "I think it's best—"

Brandon pokes Ken in the chest. "You want Amanda gone so you can hog more of the spotlight, like you always do."

Ken is still backing away, with his palms out. He's not a small guy. Considering how full of himself Ken is, how much of a big game he talks, it's almost comical how quickly he's backing down from an argument with Brandon.

"I don't want to fight," Ken says.

"No, you just want Amanda gone—"

"Brandon." I cuff his arm and get between him and Ken. "Please forget about it. I'm leaving."

"That's not right." Brandon turns his attention from Ken to the group. "Amanda shouldn't have to go. You all saw what happened. This is ridiculous!"

No one answers. Everyone avoids my eye as I look about the group.

Louann is standing in the corner with her arms folded. She's the first to speak.

"I'm sorry, but I don't feel comfortable knowing she's got a gun," she says.

Sarah's grin is pure evil when she turns once more to look at me.

"I don't know why you pulled that gun," Louann adds. "Sarah wasn't going to attack you. You could have killed somebody."

"Maybe she already did kill someone," a man mutters.

"Who said that?" I snap, hating how my voice cracks. "Who just said that?"

Nobody takes credit for what, I'm pretty sure, counts as slander.

"Amanda," Ken says in an irritatingly calm voice, "I think it's best if you go."

With tears in my eyes, I hurry out of the meeting area, clutching my purse with both hands. Brandon is trailing me, but I'm hardly aware that he's even there.

"Are you okay?" Brandon asks from the passenger seat. We made it to my car but are now just sitting in the parking lot of the bookstore.

I wipe under my eyes. Even though I didn't do anything wrong, I feel humiliated. Everyone in that meeting is thinking that I'm just as crazy—or crazier—than Sarah. Even worse, there are people in that meeting who probably wonder if I murdered Megan Patterson now. None of them will have read the email Sarah sent me. None of them, other than Brandon, witnessed how she treated me on Sunday. Without that context, I have to admit, I probably look just as batty because I pulled a gun on her.

"I'm sorry that happened." Brandon rubs my shoulder sympathetically. "Ken's a coward. He should have taken your side."

I shake my head. "Yeah, well … that's Ken."

Brandon balls a fist. "I'd like to give him a piece of my mind."

"Don't do anything rash," I say.

"What?" Brandon asks, his chest puffed out. "I'm not afraid of Ken, of all people. I know how to fight. I did Muay Thai for years."

"What's Muay Thai?"

"Asian kickboxing, without the pads. Oh, and you use elbows, knees, and your head if you want."

I cannot picture Mr. Nice Guy getting into a ring with someone, never mind headbutting or elbowing them to death.

I reach for his balled fist. "What I mean is, if you get into a fistfight with Ken at the bookstore, you'll lose your job."

"I don't even care. He's an asshole. He should have done the right thing. And what about the rest of them? Nobody said a word. Meanwhile, Sarah is carrying on like a complete psychopath."

I lean the back of my head against the headrest. I had thought of these people as more than colleagues. Some of them I saw as friends. It turns out they didn't feel the same way, apparently.

"Hey," Brandon says, "you're probably not in the mood to go out now. But if I could get a rain ch—"

"I need a drink," I say. "Can we go now?"

It's a neighborhood bar up the street, one I used to go to a lot when I was younger. When discussing the date with Brandon, I picked this one because it's a bar Matthew and I never frequented. It's got a jukebox, a dart board, and a pool table.

We get a booth in the far corner, where we can have some privacy. Brandon orders us drinks at the bar, a lager for him and an old-fashioned for me. The bar is half full, and here's the great thing about it: I don't recognize a soul.

Brandon returns with the drinks.

"So," he says, offering me a wry grin, "how about *that* for a writers' meeting tonight, huh?"

Brandon's silly humor cuts right through my anger. We're only a half hour removed from my pulling a gun in a bookstore, and here I am laughing.

"You're the best," I say.

He waves away the compliment. "Here, drink this. You know what they say about alcohol, right?"

"It's both the solution to and the cause of all the world's problems."

We clink glasses. I haven't had an old-fashioned in a long time. It's good.

"I have to ask." Brandon's eyes drift toward my purse. "Is that thing loaded?"

I nod. "Guns don't work so well without bullets."

"Fair point." He takes a swig of his beer. "Do you know how to use it?"

I nod, not wanting to tell him who taught me. "You point where you want the bullets to go and shoot."

"Makes sense."

I wrap my hands around my drink. The coolness of the glass stings my palms.

"I bought it because of Matthew," I explain, getting serious. "I don't know how he's going to react to the restraining order."

"You don't have to explain." Brandon holds out a palm. "I understand."

"I have to ask you something."

"Go for it."

I take another sip of my drink, which turns into a swig. "Am I totally crazy? Or did you think Sarah was reaching for a weapon?"

He is nodding along with me. "Oh, absolutely. I could hear her screaming from all the way in the café. That's why I came running. She was in your face and swinging her arms around. She was the obvious aggressor. I'm not trying to be insensitive, but the woman clearly needs help."

It's good to hear somebody else unequivocally take my side. Even if that someone is my ... what are we? We've been on one date, and I spent the night at his place. Do I get to think of him as my boyfriend yet? Honestly, I've never been good at this dating thing, or understanding the rules that everybody else seems to grasp intuitively.

"What?" Brandon asks.

I smother a smile. "Nothing."

"Ken had better call and apologize."

"Yeah, that's not going to happen," I say.

Brandon shakes his head. "Unbelievable."

I take another sip. A few minutes later, the alcohol has taken the edge off, and I feel a lot better. Brandon reaches across the table and takes my hand.

"I'm sorry you had to deal with that," he says.

This guy really is the best. "Forget it. I'm a big girl. I'll get over it."

Brandon looks away. "That lunatic will probably show up at the next meeting like nothing happened, but you? You're *persona non grata*. It's not right."

Brandon seems as upset about this as I am.

"I hope Ken uninvites her," I say. "With me gone, she'll probably find somebody else to obsess over."

"He won't uninvite her," Brandon says, balling a fist. "That frigging guy only cares about himself."

"You're not wrong about that."

"Somebody should put that woman in her place," Brandon says, his fist properly clenched now. "She is out of control. I think we need to call the police."

"Brandon," I say, squeezing his hand, "I really don't want to go back to the police station again right now."

His face softens. "Oh, right. I get it."

"I'm going to let it lie and see what happens. If I'm not around, maybe she'll just leave me alone."

"I don't know," Brandon says. "She has this strange kind of obsession, where she thinks you owe her something. I don't know if she's—"

"Hey." I give him my best smile. "Let's talk about something else."

Brandon stares at me dumbly for a second, then finally picks up on my mood. "Sorry. You're right. What do you want to talk about?"

"I think it's your turn," I say. "Tell me about your moo tie."

He pokes fun at my pronunciation. "My moo tie?"

I giggle. Even though he was mocking me, he did it in as nice a way as possible. "You know what I mean."

"I know, just busting your chops. Do you want to hear about how I put a guy in the hospital?"

"You put someone in the hospital?"

"Oh yeah." He waves a hand like it's nothing. "Guy had it coming."

I *think* Brandon is joking about the whole thing. But I'm not sure.

While we enjoy our drinks, sharing a comfortable silence, the bar grows more crowded. Brandon excuses himself to use the bathroom. While he's gone, I check my phone. I've got a missed call and voicemail from Ken. I listen to his message:

"Hi, Amanda. It's Ken. After the meeting broke up tonight, I talked things over with the other members of the panel. I hate to do this, but we think it's best if you don't come around for a while. This whole thing with that poor woman being murdered, whom you knew apparently, and then this issue with Sarah—it's just better if you're not around. Maybe when things quieten down, we'll give you a call, but until then—"

I don't bother listening to the rest of his message. I call him back.

"Hi, Amanda," Ken answers nervously. "Did you, uh, get my voicem—"

"What about Sarah?" I ask. "Did you banish her too?"

He laughs, but it sounds pained. "Amanda, we didn't *banish* you. Per se. We just think—"

"What about Sarah?" I repeat.

He doesn't answer for a moment. And when he speaks next, he completely ignores my question.

"Why didn't you mention that you knew the woman who was murdered?" Ken asks.

"I didn't even know that she—wait a minute. How do you know I knew her?"

"Never mind that," Ken responds dismissively. "The point is, well, it's kind of odd you didn't say anything about it. Put yourself in my shoes, Amanda. What would you think if, well, if *that* happened and it turned out I not only knew the person, but I also didn't like the person very much?"

"Ken." I feel like my head might explode. "Are you suggesting that I had anything to do wi—"

"No, of course not. But put yourself in my shoes—"

"Yes, this must be very difficult for you, Ken. I should have thought about how you'd feel being in charge of the writers' group. Must have slipped my mind since, you know, I was a little preoccupied worrying about a killer copycatting something from one of my books and then having to deal with that whack job Sarah Keller turning out to be an obsessive nutter."

"I understand you're very emotional right now, Amanda."

"You know what, Ken? You can go to hell."

I end the call just as Brandon is returning with the drinks. He sees the expression on my face.

"Who was that?"

I bring him up to speed. Brandon curses. Then, of course, apologizes for cursing.

"Let me ask you a question," Brandon says. "You're worried that Matthew might have had something to do with Megan Patterson's death, right?"

As much as I don't want to admit it, I have to face facts. "It's possible."

Brandon purses his lips. "What if it's Sarah?"

"Before Sunday, she and I had never spoken before. How would she know Megan and I didn't get along?"

"She seems like a stalker," Brandon says. "What if she's been digging up as much as she can about you?"

"But how would she know about Megan?"

Brandon sips his beer and eyes me over the glass. "Would it really be that difficult to find out in this day and age?"

I mull it over. "I guess not. After my book started selling, I did a few interviews. I got asked about balancing writing with a full-time job. Those interviews got posted online. People commented—"

"Are you on LinkedIn?" he asks.

"Yes."

Brandon grimaces. "She looked you up and identified your colleagues. Then she catfished, or whatever they call it, posing as an ex-employee or a friend of one. Maybe she pretended to be a reporter trying to do a story on you and asked about your work history. It wouldn't be that difficult for her to find out about Megan with a little online snooping."

A chill runs through me. I take my hands off my cold glass. I have to admit that it's possible that Sarah killed Megan.

Brandon gets up. I'm a little confused because he just went to the bar to get a drink, but then he slides into the booth with me.

"Mind if I sit here?" He winks. "I wanted to get a little closer."

I smile over at him and then rest my head on his shoulder.

"I'm sorry," he says.

"It's not your fault."

"I know." I can feel him shaking his head. "I wish there were something I could do."

"You're doing it."

He chuckles. "And frigging Ken ..."

"Don't get me started again," I say. "This all goes back to my mother."

He kisses the top of my head.

"What do you mean?" he asks.

"If I weren't the daughter of Kimberly Dawn Allen, do you think I would have been banished from the writers' group tonight?"

Brandon doesn't answer. "Tell me about her."

"About Mom?"

He nods. "What was she really like?"

I smile sadly before I finish my old-fashioned. Then I reach for the second one. If we're going to talk about Mom, then I need more alcohol to help power me through the conversation.

"She was a good woman," I say. "But also complicated."

20

TWENTY-ONE YEARS AGO

Bells above the door chime as I enter the diner. Since I'm sneaking around and not supposed to be here, my guilty conscience is overactive. I check the diner for suspicious characters, a habit I've developed over the last few years. You can never be too careful when your mom is an alleged murderer on the run. All kinds of whackos and nut jobs and reporters want to talk to you. Family members of the victim, too, which is its own kind of hell. Nan had to get the police involved when David West's cousin tracked me down. It was awful.

Anyway, none of the customers here takes an interest in me. It's that slow time at an eatery, between lunch and dinner, so it's not crowded.

I spot the woman I'm here to meet sitting in a booth at the back, like I requested. She looks about Mom's age. When our eyes meet, she gives me the slightest of nods, not wanting to draw any attention. She looks familiar—I must recognize her from one of the old news reports.

I move through the diner, keeping my eyes down.

Not that I'd like to live with Aunt Cece again, but this secret meeting would have been much easier to pull off while I was under her roof. As long as I didn't interfere with my aunt's social life, Cece didn't much care what I did. Nan, on the other hand, takes an active interest and must always know where I'm going and when I'll be home. She's also made it clear that I'm not to go "looking for trouble," a brief that includes not talking to people about Mom.

Nan thinks I'm staying late after class to help with the school newspaper. I felt bad about lying to her, but in the end, I *had* to talk to someone outside of my family about Mom, a close friend who knew her well.

Nervously, I approach the booth. A bowl of broccoli cheddar soup sits in front of the woman, steam lifting off it. She didn't wait for me to order, though to be fair, I'm almost twenty minutes late. I wasn't sure if I was actually going to go through with this.

The woman offers me a warm smile, like we've known each other for a long time.

"Hi, Amanda," she says in a small voice.

Now that I'm close to her, I notice the gray streaks in her dull brown hair, which is pulled back into a loose bun. She has crow's feet around her dark eyes.

"Hi ..."

I've reached that age where I don't know what to call adults I've just met. I'm eighteen now and about to graduate, so that makes me a grown woman. On the other hand, this lady is old enough to be my mother. Only a year or two ago, I wouldn't have hesitated. I would have called her Ms. Bombeck straight away.

"Please call me Nora," she says, reading my mind.

I give her a tight grin. I'm amazed I was able to find her

through this new website, MySpace, but I'm still not sure this was a good idea.

"It's nice to meet you."

I slide into the booth opposite her. A waitress wearing a mustard yellow uniform comes by. I ask for a coffee. Nan doesn't let me drink coffee, even though she herself does. She thinks it's bad for you. I usually sneak a cup when I'm out with friends on the weekend.

Nora has a strange look on her face. "I'm sorry," she says, "but it's uncanny. You look exactly like your mother."

No one has ever said this to me before. I wonder if that's because my family wants to pretend like Mom doesn't exist. They'd rather act like I resemble nobody, I guess.

"Really?"

Nora nods. "I'm so glad you found me. I think about you a lot."

"You do?"

Nora pushes her untouched soup to the side and folds her hands in front of her. "Kim and I were very good friends. You and I have actually met before. You were very little."

Nora mentioned this in our email exchange. "I'm sorry, I must have been very young ... I don't remember."

She laughs. "The last time I saw you, you were five, maybe six years old? You were starting kindergarten."

The waitress returns with my coffee. We tell her we're fine for now, and she leaves us again.

"So," I say, "you knew Mom for a long time?"

"We grew up together," Nora says. "I moved into her neighborhood when I was eleven, right in the middle of my big awkward phase."

I chuckle. "Oh yeah. I know all about that."

Nora blushes. Even though she's got to be in her forties,

she's still embarrassed by the memory of being an awkward tween.

"I didn't know anyone, and the girls in school started picking on me because I had a funny accent and dressed differently."

"Accent?" I ask.

"It's gone now," she says. "I grew up in the South. It only comes out when I visit relatives or when I've had a few too many drinks." She laughs at this. "Anyway, Kim stuck up for me. She had been friends with some of those other girls, but she didn't like how they were treating me. It really meant a lot."

I love how she refers to Mom as Kim. After everything that happened, Mom's name changed. She wasn't Kim anymore: she was *Kimberly*. And she became one of those three-name people: Kimberly Dawn Allen. That happens when people think you're a murderer.

Nora continues, "We became best friends. After we graduated high school, we went to work together at the credit company. That's where she first met him."

Him.

"David West?"

She nods. "David was about ten years older than us."

I do the math in my head. "Was David my father?"

"I always wondered, but I don't know. Kim wouldn't tell anyone, not even me. David *was* married, but it didn't matter."

"What do you mean, it didn't matter?"

"Kim and Dave had this instant chemistry. It was like a force pulling them together. They laid eyes on each other, and something clicked. And believe me, your mom was *not* the type to go for a married guy."

"What was he like?" I ask.

"It feels strange to say this, because the man was cheating on his wife. But Dave was nice," Nora says. "He'd been to college, and you could tell he was on the fast track at the company."

For the last nine years, my family has tried to pretend like Mom doesn't exist, leaving me with so many burning questions. Now I'm seated across from a woman who was close to Mom and is willing to talk. This is my best chance to get those questions answered. Now's not the time to be shy.

"That's why everybody accused Mom of being a gold digger," I say.

"Some people did." Nora grimaces. "But your mother wasn't like that. She just fell in love with a married man."

"When did the affair start?" I ask, needing to know all the details.

"I'm not certain," Nora says. "Kim kept that from me."

"Why?"

"To protect me. Workplace affairs ruin careers. She didn't want me getting in trouble if they were found out."

"Is that why she lost her job?" I ask. "Because David was a man on the rise and more valuable to the company than a secretary?"

"That's part of it," Nora says. "But not all of it."

"That's what my aunt always told me."

"Cece." Nora growls the word. "Your aunt *would* say that. She's always had an inferiority complex when it came to your mother."

I look at her sharply; her words ring true—I've just never thought of it like that. "Then what happened?" I ask after a pause.

"Kim broke it off with David. As much as she loved him,

at the end of the day he was married, and she felt guilty about the affair, especially when she found out his wife wasn't well. Anyway, *she* decided to leave. She didn't trust herself being around him."

I'm floored.

"But David's letter ... he made it sound like Mom was making demands? Like she was threatening him to make him leave his wife."

"I know that letter exists, but I don't believe a word of it." Nora shakes her head. "That wasn't your mother."

All the news reports referred to Mom and David's relationship as an affair. But now something Nora said a moment ago has struck home.

"They were in love?"

"Oh yes," Nora says. "Absolutely. She was heartbroken when it was over. And that's when she told me all about it. She couldn't keep it in any longer."

"Mom took that new job when I was starting school, right?"

"Right." Nora smiles. "You know, I used to babysit you."

"You did?"

"When you were just a baby. I must have done it a dozen or so times. Being a single parent isn't easy, so I was happy when Kim asked me to help. She could get out of the apartment and unwind."

"I'll bet." I haven't touched my coffee. I put cream and sugar in and swirl it. Then I sip. It's not bad, as far as diner coffee goes. "What happened after Mom changed jobs? That must have been around the time you last saw me."

"Right." Nora gives a sad smile. "We weren't working together anymore, and we were leading very different lives. She had you, and I was young and single. I had just met this guy ..." She rolls her eyes at her younger self. "Who was a total waste of time. I wish—God, I wish we had stayed close. Maybe things would have turned out differently."

"How would things have been different?" I ask pointedly.

She thinks about it. "If I'd been around, maybe she wouldn't have been so lonely. A married man was all she had for attention."

I'm not convinced Nora's presence would have made a difference, but I can also tell she feels the need to cling to this notion.

"At some point, Mom and David got back together," I say. "Did you know about that?"

"I didn't find out till after."

"Do you know how it started?"

"David came to the apartment one night out of the blue," she says, a faraway look in her eyes. "They hadn't seen each other for a few years, but he proclaimed he was still in love with her."

"That's it?" I ask.

"You have to understand, things were difficult for Kim. She was a single mother, getting no support from her family and working a crummy job. In a moment of weakness, she took him back. She regretted it later. But that's all I know. She didn't have time to tell me the rest."

It takes me a moment to understand what she's saying.

"Hold on," I say, leaning forward. "Are you saying you didn't find out about the affair starting up for the second time until *after* David was killed and Mom was on the run?"

"She came to me for help," Nora says.

"You *helped* her get away?" I ask.

Nora's eyes go wide. I realize how loud my voice has gotten.

"Sorry," I say much more quietly. "You helped her?"

She nods. "After everything your mom had done for me, I was determined to help. Though we'd drifted apart, I still thought of her as my best friend. I was willing to get in trouble with the law to help her. Besides, Kim is no murderer. I believe that, with all my heart."

"Are you sure?" I ask.

Nora reaches across the table and puts her hand on my cheek. "I'd bet my life on it, sweetie."

When she takes her hand away, there are tears in my eyes. I don't think Mom is a killer either, but for the last nine years I've been surrounded by family members who either won't tell me what they think, or who will outright say she's guilty. It doesn't help that the rest of the world thinks she's guilty as sin too.

"What was she like?" I ask. "Before."

Nora's smile is warm. "She was funny, very spontaneous. She liked mint chocolate chip ice cream; that's the flavor she always ordered at the sundae shop. We talked about boys a lot. Her favorite movie was *The Lost Boys*, you know the one with the vampires. We were kind of opposites in some ways. I was always the shy one. Your mom was very outgoing. She didn't let anybody walk all over her. I remember, at our first jobs, we were nineteen years old, never worked before, and some of the older women there tried to boss us around even though they weren't our managers. Kim wasn't having it. She put them all in their place.

"She could also be very quiet. There were times when she'd just stop talking. She could get like that for hours, I remember. Then she'd come out of her quiet time, that's what she called it, and act like everything was fine. She was also beautiful, just like you."

No one has ever called me that before. I find myself blushing.

Nora realizes she's embarrassed me. She changes the subject. "She was a romantic. A hopeless one, to boot. That's why I know she loved David. She would not have gone for a married man unless there was something deeper there."

"But he *was* married," I say.

I've never forgiven Mom for this. Sleeping with a married man. How could she?

"His wife was mentally ill. She had been in and out of hospitals a few times, apparently. He felt more like a care-taker than a husband, at least that's what he told Kim. It wasn't much of a marriage, but he felt like he couldn't leave her. If that's true—"

"Big if," I say. "It wouldn't be the first time a married man lied to his mistress, told her some sob story just so he could keep getting into her pants."

Nora recoils slightly. She wasn't expecting me to have such a cynical view. "You're too young to think like that."

"I've had nine years to do nothing but," I say.

She smiles, her mood melancholy, then grows insistent. "Kim was no fool, trust me. She would have seen through him."

I shake my head. "What about the letter, though?"

Nora pulls a face. "I can't explain it."

"Do you think ..."

I once proposed my theory to Aunt Cece and Nan. When Cece was done laughing, Nan told me to never speak of it again.

"Do you think David's wife found out about the affair, wrote that letter to make Mom look crazy, then killed her own husband?"

"I don't know."

That's not a yes or a no. "But do you think it's possible?"

Nora looks out the window for a moment. "David's wife was staying with family when he was killed. Her parents gave her an airtight alibi."

Her words are like a gut punch.

For all these years, I've been harboring a weird hope that I could prove someone else killed David. Lori West had always seemed the most obvious suspect.

"She could have paid someone to do it, though," I say, not willing to give up on my favorite theory yet. "She came from money, didn't she?"

Nora smiles indulgently. "I guess it's possible. But how could we prove it if the cops couldn't?"

"Maybe they didn't want to," I say.

Nora closes her eyes for a moment. "I'm sorry, Amanda. I've been down that road many times, but I always end up in the same place."

I'm angered by her defeatist attitude, but I bite my tongue when I realize this woman is the only one outside of my family who is going to tell me the truth about Mom. I don't want to make an enemy of the one person in this world who takes my side when it comes to Mom.

We sit in silence for a moment. I drink more of my coffee. Nora doesn't touch her soup.

"What happened?" I ask. "When she came to you for help?"

"We didn't have much time," Nora says. "The police were already looking for her. I gave her what money I had. It wasn't much, a few thousand dollars. But it was something. She told me she'd made a terrible mistake, getting back together with Dave, but that she wasn't a killer. And ..."

"And what?"

"She swore she was planning to break it off again."

"Did you believe her?"

She nods. "Anyway, I gave her the money. We hugged and cried and said goodbye. That was it." Nora wipes the damp skin under her watery eyes. "Nobody ever found out I helped her, though the police suspected me, I'm sure. After it all came out, after everybody at the office knew, they fired me. They told me they were doing away with my job function, but nobody else in my role was fired. I knew why they'd done it: it was because I was friends with Kim. Nobody wanted me around anymore; I was too much of a distraction."

"That's so unfair."

"That's the way of the world." She shrugs. "It's a shame because it was a really good job. I had trouble finding work afterward. Everybody knew who I was, and nobody wants to hire the girl who was best friends with, you know."

"I know," I say. "That's why I changed my name."

She nods sadly. "I'm so sorry, Amanda. About everything. Your mom was just doing her best, raising you on her own. She was a good person. I miss her terribly."

"Me too." I finish my coffee. It's getting late. I need to get home soon if I don't want Nan getting suspicious. "Did you ever hear from Mom again?"

Nora does not answer for a moment. Then she looks around the diner, as if checking for eavesdroppers. Finally, she turns in her booth and reaches down into her purse.

"Once."

"You did?"

Nora nods. "I promised her I would give this to you when you were older. I think eighteen is old enough."

Nora pulls out a big manila envelope. It's very worn, the edges disintegrating. But the tape sealing it looks intact. She's never opened it.

She passes me the envelope.

"If you ever see her again," Nora says, "will you tell her I love her? I miss her so much."

21

"That is incredible," Brandon says. "Have you talked to Nora since?"

"We speak often. I always call her on Mom's birthday, and she always calls on mine." We usually see each other a few times a year, though I wish it were more often. "She's had a rough life ever since. She never rebounded. Nobody ever gave her another chance. Life can be terrible like that."

"God," Brandon says. "That's so sad."

"I think of her as family."

We fall silent. I finish my second old-fashioned of the night. Brandon sits up to get a better look out the window.

"More snow," he says.

Wonderful. I don't like the thought of braving slick roads right now. I sit up to look out the window. A few light flakes drift lazily by.

"Want to come back to my place?" Brandon asks.

I really do. It's not just that I don't want to be alone tonight. It's that I want to be with *him*. But I'm embarrassed to admit those two drinks, which I thought I nursed, have gone to my head. I'm not usually this irresponsible.

"I shouldn't drive."

Brandon smiles. "I was going to suggest that I drive."

"But aren't you—"

"I stopped at one drink," he says.

"You did?"

He nods. "How about this? I'll drive your car. That way, you can leave my place tonight—or tomorrow—I mean, whenever you want."

He's making this decision really easy. "What about your car?"

Brandon waves a hand. "I'll get an Uber back here tomorrow. It's no big deal."

"Are you sure?"

"Absolutely. Wanna get out of here?"

Brandon settles the tab. I take his arm, and he leads me outside. I pass him my keys and am about to round the car to get into the passenger seat, but Brandon moves in front of me.

"Allow me," he says.

He unlocks the car and then opens my door for me. What guy does that these days?

I slide into the seat. My teeth are chattering from the brief exposure to the cold. Brandon gets in behind the wheel and starts the car. I blast the heat, which, of course, fogs the windshield. We sit in the parking lot and wait a minute while the defroster goes to work.

"Feeling any better?" Brandon asks. "After the lousy night you had?"

"Oh yes." I look over at him. "I feel a lot better."

"Good."

He leans in. Not only is he very handsome, but Brandon is such a good kisser. He seems to know just how much pressure to apply. I feel his hand on the back of my head, his fingers running through my hair. I rub his chest, feeling his toned pecs respond under his shirt.

When we finally come up for air, the windshield is still foggy.

Brandon makes a face. "Oops."

I laugh. "I guess we'd better wait till we get back to your place. Otherwise we'll never get out of here."

"That's going to be hard," he says.

We hold hands and stare into each other's eyes. I'm not usually this sentimental, but it feels right with Brandon. Eventually the windshield defogs enough that Brandon can safely take us home. He's a good driver, and I feel safe with him behind the wheel. He takes turns carefully on the snowy streets and never pours on the speed. By the time we arrive at his place, the light snowfall has stopped.

I'm glad I let him drive. The roads weren't great. When I go home—probably tomorrow, who am I kidding—I'll leave a twenty on the table by the front door. Brandon is one of those old-fashioned guys who thinks he has to pay for everything, but I don't know how he can afford it given his job. The least I can do is pay for his Uber ride to pick up his car.

There's not a lot of talking once we get through Brandon's front door. As soon as we're inside, I throw myself at him. We make it to the bedroom only half-clothed.

I don't know if it's the drinks or if it's because we've already done this, but tonight we're less inhibited with each other. I love the way he kisses. I love the way he does *other* things too.

It feels really late when I drift off to sleep, tangled up in Brandon's arms. It's wonderful.

And I forget all about Megan, Matthew, Sarah, and those strange notes.

A SOUND WAKES ME. For a moment, I'm disoriented, but then I remember I'm at Brandon's. There's a dull ache in my head. I should have rehydrated after we got back, but there really wasn't much time for that. I'll just pop into the bathroom and drink from the faucet if I have to. As I'm about to get out of bed, though, I spot the bottled water on the table next to me.

I mean, could this guy be any more considerate?

I gulp half the bottle. My head immediately feels better. I turn around to give Brandon a thank-you kiss in his sleep. (I'm okay if it wakes him up and then other things happen ...) But I find his side of the bed empty. It's still warm where he was sleeping, though, so he must have just gotten up. Then I remember the sound—it must have been him making it.

I put the water bottle back down. I hear another noise; sounds like it's coming from downstairs. I get up and enter the hallway. The stairs are right around the corner.

"Brandon?" I call out.

No response.

I don't know why, but an intense feeling of dread overtakes me. Did somebody break in? Did Brandon hear them, get out of bed to investigate, and get his head bashed in?

No. I'm being silly. Brandon has a security system. I clearly remember him turning off that alarm ... but that was the other night. This evening, we were tearing each other's clothes off from the moment we entered the house. Brandon did not pause to activate the alarm after we got in.

Maybe he forgot to set it tonight?

Oh God.

I stop before I reach the stairs.

What if the person who killed Megan is an obsessed nut job who's been following me around? I'm honestly not that difficult to find and, once found, not difficult to follow. My life revolves around home, yoga class, the bookstore, and the coffee shop. It wouldn't take an expert tracker to find me.

"Brandon?" I call again.

No answer.

I linger in the hallway, not quite to the stairs.

I'm being silly. Even if Brandon didn't activate his alarm, I would have heard somebody breaking into the house. I'm a light sleeper. And Brandon would have probably woken me up if he went downstairs to investigate a mysterious sound that suggested the possibility of an intruder.

It must be Brandon downstairs.

I laugh quietly at my irrational paranoia. While I compose myself, my eyes fall on the closet door in the hall-way. The one that was locked before.

It's slightly open.

I don't remember it being open when we came up here. Though, I was a little drunk and not paying much attention to my surroundings while Brandon and I fumbled with each other's clothes.

Brandon did not want me looking inside this closet the other night. But that has only piqued my curiosity. What could he possibly be hiding in here?

I decide to peek inside.

I'm expecting to find random odds and ends, the type of things you cram into an unused room when you're expecting company. But there's no junk in this closet.

THIS CLOSET HAS shelves filled with paperback novels. And there are more novels stacked on the floor, pushed up against the walls of the closet.

There must be hundreds of books in here.

I turn on the light to get a better look at his collection. I'm expecting to find romance novels or something of the sort: books that Brandon might be embarrassed by.

But that's not what I find.

All these books are murder mysteries. Many of them involve serial killers. Some of them are on the gorier end of the spectrum, approaching horror levels of descriptive violence and death. I recognize the names and titles on the spines. Many of the authors represented here work in the same genre as me.

I get a bad feeling in the pit of my stomach.

Brandon told me he didn't read this kind of book. I distinctly remember him saying that. Why would he lie about it?

And then I notice what's right in front of me.

All my books, front and center.

Unlike the other paperbacks, positioned so their spines are out, the covers of my books face out. He has both hardback and paperback editions of everything I've ever written. Resting on top of my books are some newspaper and magazine clippings. I know without looking what they are, but all the same I pick one up and read.

It's a clipping from an interview I gave.

I hear another noise. It sounds like it's coming from downstairs.

I drop the clipping, terrified.

Oh my God.

I thought Sarah Keller was obsessed with me.

But Brandon clearly is too.

There's no other explanation for this. Why else would he tell me he doesn't read in my genre, and that he's never read my books before? Why would he hide *that* from me? Why would he cut out interviews I've done and keep them locked away in a closet when I come over?

And then another thought occurs to me.

What if Brandon ...

Do something. Anything is better than nothing. Do not freeze.

Quickly, I scoot out of the closet and scramble into my clothes. I don't know where he is or what he's doing, but I'm going home. Right now. I don't want to be in this house a second longer.

I get dressed in record time. I tiptoe downstairs. I've already decided that I'm going to act like nothing's wrong if I encounter Brandon and have to explain myself. I'll tell him I have an early Zoom meeting with my agent and editor, so I have to get home.

I left my purse by the front door when we came into the house. Left isn't the right word. I more *dropped* the purse as we tore each other's clothes off. Oh God, I don't even want to think about the fact that I *slept* with this guy who has created a weird shrine to me in his bedroom closet.

I make it downstairs and look for my purse by the front door.

It's not there.

"Shit."

I freeze. That was Brandon cursing about something. There's a light coming from the kitchen. He must be in there. I wander through the house, skirting the kitchen, still looking for my purse. I'm almost certain I left it by the front door. Why isn't it there?

I'm trying to make a quiet sweep of the house when Brandon calls out: "Mandy, is that you?"

If he catches me trying to sneak around, how is he going to react? Then again, what is he planning to do with me anyway? I have no idea.

I tiptoe toward the kitchen to see what he's up to. I peek around the corner and stifle a gasp. My purse is open on the island counter. My car keys are sitting next to it. Brandon's back is to me. It looks like he has something in his hands.

I never leave my purse unzipped. Never.

Why did he go through my things? Why are my keys out?

With that sixth sense we all have, Brandon recognizes that I'm here. He looks up from what he's doing and calls out.

"Mandy?"

I wait a moment to see if he'll go looking for me. When he steps away from my purse, I can grab it and my car keys.

But Brandon doesn't move.

"Honey, is that you?" he calls out.

Honey. Now all those cutesy things he's said and done feel gross and creepy.

Suddenly, he turns around. It's too quick for me to duck behind the wall without looking suspicious.

Brandon gasps when he sees me. "Jeez! You scared the crap out of me."

That's rich coming from him.

He's holding something small and rectangular and mechanical in one hand and a screwdriver in the other. I don't know what the tiny box is, but it looks like he's been tinkering with it.

"Hi, Brandon," I say, my voice sounding stiff. I try to lighten my tone. "I just woke up and remembered I have an early meeting with my ag-itor. I mean, my agent and editor."

He doesn't react for a moment. "Oh? You didn't mention that earlier."

"Because I forgot." I smile. "I was just, uh, trying to find my purse."

"It's right here," he says.

"Okay."

For a moment I linger where I am. I don't want to get close enough that he can touch me. But I also don't want him thinking that I've realized something's wrong.

Brandon's face goes white. "Oh, you're wondering why …" He looks down at the purse and my keys. "Oh, gosh, this must look weird."

You can say that again, Brandon.

He smiles awkwardly. "I woke up to use the bathroom and saw that it was snowing pretty hard. See?"

He motions behind me. I steal a quick glance over my shoulder and look out the windows to the rear of the house. He's right: heavy snowflakes are falling quickly. The roads must be a mess. I hate driving in the snow, but I don't want to spend another minute here.

"I got your keys out because I wanted to move your car into the garage," he says. "I don't know why I didn't think of it earlier." He gives me a sly grin. "I mean, I can hazard a guess why."

My stomach does a little flip. I don't want to think about having sex with this man.

"I came downstairs to move your car into the garage. Only, here's the thing." He holds up the small box. "I normally use the garage door opener inside my car. I tried using this one, the one that's inside the actual garage, and it wasn't working. I thought it might just be the battery or a bad connection, so I was checking to see if I could fix it and get your car inside, out of the snow."

It sounds legitimate.

But I can't stop thinking about the shrine I just discovered upstairs.

"That's very nice of you." I force the fakest smile of my life. "I really appreciate it, but I'm going to head home."

"Oh." He stares at me. "But the snow. The roads are treacherous right now."

"I'll be fine." When he doesn't move away from my purse or keys, I steel myself and move in. Keeping my eyes away from his, I grab my things and zip my purse. "Sorry, uh, to leave in the middle of the night like this."

"Mandy," he says. "What's the matter?"

He sees right through the act. I might be an author who spends her days thinking about fictional worlds and making up people and places and events, but in reality, I'm a very bad liar.

"Nothing," I say, not looking at him as I breeze by. "I'd just better get home."

He trails me to the front door. I try the knob, but of course it's locked. Brandon comes up beside me, getting very close and staring at me. He waits for me to meet his eyes, so I force myself to look up. The man is inches away from me.

"Are you sure you're okay?" he asks.

"Yes." My voice cracks. "Fine. I just want to leave, okay?"

He takes a half-step back from me, his face falling. Then, with the saddest look, he flips the deadbolt and the lock on the knob for me.

"Did I ..." His voice trails off.

I pretend like I don't hear him. A cold wind blasts me when I open the door. The snow is coming down in piles. I stagger out into the cold, shocked by what I see. There's a couple of inches of snow on the roads. And a lot more covering my car.

Brandon is right behind me. "I'll help you clear the car off."

He's only wearing sweatpants and a T-shirt and slippers.

"It's too cold," I say. "I'll take care of it."

I fumble with my keys but manage to remote start my car. I keep the doors locked because I don't want Brandon jumping into the passenger seat in a desperate attempt to prolong my strained departure.

I don't bother to search my trunk for the snow and ice scraper. I just swipe at the windshield quickly with my arm and then do the same thing with the rear windshield and other windows. Honestly, there's still a lot of snow blocking my visibility, but I don't care. If it's really a problem, I'll stop somewhere up the road and take care of the rest.

"Mandy, honey, what's the matter?"

Brandon is shivering in the cold when I get into the car. The seat warmer feels amazing. Just as I'm closing my door, Brandon's hand shoots out to grab it.

"Please, Mandy, what did I do?"

"Nothing," I say, giving him that fake smile again. "I just want to get home."

His hand lingers on the door for a moment, and I start to

wonder if I'll have to slam the door closed and hurt the man so I can leave. But Brandon lets go and puts his hands into the pockets of his sweatpants and stands in the freezing cold as I put my seat belt on and adjust the seat and mirrors. Brandon had to move the seat back when he drove us here.

I back out of Brandon's driveway and get myself into the street. He's still standing in the driveway, looking miserable. Before I can put the car in drive, however, Brandon bursts toward the vehicle.

I shriek and hit the gas pedal. My wheels spin out on the snow. I'm not going anywhere.

"Mandy! I know why you're upset. Please let me ex—"

Finally, my wheels grab, and I take off. My car skids through the snow. I very nearly sideswipe one of his neighbor's cars that is parked on the street. After that narrow miss, I get my vehicle under control and reach the corner. Brandon is running down the street in his slippers, which must be soaked through. It would be romantic if I weren't so terrified of him. As I turn the corner, I look back once more in my rearview mirror, just in time to see him slip in the snow and go down hard.

I don't stop.

22

The roads are treacherous. There must be three or four inches of snow on the ground, and the plows haven't been everywhere yet because it's the middle of the night.

The drive from Brandon's house should take me twenty minutes, but in these conditions the white-knuckled trip takes double that. I have to backtrack twice, and by the time I pull into my neighborhood, it's really late. Brandon has called once and texted a bunch. It was too distracting to keep hearing my phone go off while I was trying to navigate the hazardous roads, so I pulled over to silence my phone. Needless to say, I've ignored Brandon's every attempt at communication.

I'm relieved when I discover my neighborhood has been plowed. But that relief disappears when I notice an unfamiliar sedan parked on the street across from my house. Its lights are on, and it looks to have been recently cleared of snow. I'm hoping it belongs to a neighbor up the street.

Perhaps someone couldn't get into their driveway because of the snow.

I manage to get into my driveway and put the parking brake on. I thought Sunday was bad—but today has been much worse. I can't wait to crawl into bed and sleep.

But my eye catches my phone screen as I go to put it in my purse. Against my better judgment, I can't help but wonder what Brandon has to say for himself.

I open the string of texts from him.

> Mandy, I'm so, so sorry. Please come back.

> I'll sleep on the couch. You can take the bedroom. Please. I only want to make sure you're safe.

> I promise I can explain everything to—

Someone taps on my window, and I scream.

Heart in my throat, my hand shoots out for the door lock button. After regaining my composure, and once I know I'm safe, I peer out the fogged window at the big, jacketed form in the darkness. It's a man. He's bending at the waist to look into the car—

Oh my God.

It's Matthew.

"GET AWAY FROM THE CAR!" I shout.

"Amanda," he says, peering into the vehicle, "are you okay?"

"What the hell are you doing here?" I ask.

"I was worried about you." He smiles, but he looks terrible. Judging by his puffy, red-rimmed eyes, I'd bet he's been parked out here for a while, waiting for me to come home. "Mandy, I'm sorry. I'm so sorry about everything. I was at the bookstore tonight and—"

"You were?"

Not that I want to brave the wintry roads again, but I could drive away if I have to. I could also be on the phone with the police in less than two seconds if necessary.

But those thoughts aren't really comforting. I was already freaked out by my discovery at Brandon's house, and now my stalker ex-boyfriend has shown up at my house in the middle of the night during a hellish snowstorm.

"Yes," he says, like he's ashamed. "I really wanted to talk to you, but I wasn't sure you'd listen. I hung around the back and was going to leave, I swear—I swear I was going to leave —but then I heard all that yelling and saw what happened. I'm sorry that lunatic confronted you like that. Trust me, it won't happen again."

I reach into my purse and wrap my hand around the gun. He is really scaring me.

"Matthew, can you back away from the car?"

"I saw you leave with that man from the bookstore, and I was jealous. I can't help how I feel. But I knew you must have been feeling horribly upset, and I know how much you hate driving in the snow, so I came here. I had to know you're alright."

"I'm fine," I say, which is the lie of the century. "Would you please back away from the car?"

"Amanda, are you dating that man? If you are, then I will leave you alone. Forever. I swear. But if you're not, then please just hear me out."

"I'm dating him." Lie of the century number two. "For the last time, will you—"

"Okay, okay."

Matthew holds his palms out and backs away from the car. I wait till he reaches the sidewalk before turning off my car and getting my house key ready. Then I sling my purse over my shoulder and keep my other hand inside it, on the gun. But the last thing I want to do is draw that weapon again.

I keep my eyes on Matthew as I get out of the car. He's wearing a big puffy winter jacket and standing on the sidewalk with his hands at his sides. Twenty feet separate us. It's not nearly enough space. I recall seeing Matthew run at the gym—he's fast.

I stay half turned toward him as I make my way up the snow-covered steps.

"Amanda," Matthew calls out, "will you please just talk to me?"

I unlock my front door. "No, Matthew. I've filed a restraining order. If you don't leave, I will call the police."

"You *what*?" he asks.

"You heard me."

"How could you do that to me? Do you know what that's going to look like with the charges that are pending?"

"I thought you said those were dropped."

"They're in the *process* of being dropped."

I'm about to enter my house, to finally leave things be, but something Matthew said a moment ago has just registered.

"Did you confront Sarah Keller after I left, Matthew?"

"I know you still have feelings for me," he says, not answering. "Your friend told me everything."

"What the hell are you talking about?" I'm at a total loss now. "I'm calling the police."

"If you do, you'll regret it!"

Terrified, I slip inside the house and lock the door. Before I can get my phone out, I'm surprised to hear Matthew's car as he drives off. I check out the window to make sure he's gone.

Then I slump against the wall and burst into tears.

23

It's almost noon when I wake the next day and find the world covered in a foot of snow. After twenty groggy minutes of lying about, I check my phone. Brandon called again this morning. There's nothing from Matthew, though I wonder if I should call the police and add to the report I filed. It's probably what I *should* do, but I don't want a repeat of the other day, where the detectives use the opportunity to grill me again.

Unable to make a decision, I find myself scrolling through Brandon's texts again—

> Mandy, I'm so, so sorry. Please come back.

> I'll sleep on the couch. You can take the bedroom. Please come back. I just want to make sure you're safe.

> I promise I can explain everything if you'll let me. Please, Mandy, just hear me out.

I understand you don't want to talk, so I'll
stop calling. What I have to say is too long
to text, so I'm going to email. I hope you
read it. Good night, Mandy.

I did not answer his calls, nor did I respond to his texts. What makes him think I *want* to read an email instead? Annoyed, I get out of bed, don heavy winter clothes, and leave my phone on my nightstand. I nuke some oatmeal and eat it while it's still scorching hot in the hope it keeps me warm while I shovel my driveway and sidewalk.

It's another cold day. They're not calling for more snow today, but the wind is cutting. Shoveling out is not going to be fun.

I clear my porch and steps, then work my way down the walkway. While I'm throwing snow, Rebecca's two boys come out of the house with a pair of shovels and cross into my yard.

"Ms. Christie, can we shovel for you?" the older one asks.

I could die of joy. "Yes, that would be great. How much do you charge for driveways?"

The two boys share a conspiratorial look.

"We charge ... twenty?" the younger one asks.

"Apiece," the older one quickly adds.

I'm all too happy to be extorted. The snow is over a foot deep, and it would take me two hours to move the rest. I can splurge the forty bucks, so I don't have to break my back.

"That sounds good. Thank you, boys."

They both grin and get to work. I stick my shovel in the snow so it's standing up and am about to go inside.

"Hey, Amanda!"

Rebecca waves to me from her porch.

"Hey, you!"

She's waving at me to come over. "I've got hot chocolate ready, and I baked cookies this morning."

Now that I've freed up about two hours of my time, I should really get to work. If my editor knew how far behind I'd fallen on my edits, she'd be upset, and the publisher might begin to question whether we're going to make our release date.

But after the insanity of the last few days, a chat with Rebecca will help clear my head.

I trudge over, and we go inside.

"Hɪ, Aᴍᴀɴᴅᴀ," Ron says, in as flat a voice as he can manage.

He's wearing old jeans that don't quite fit him anymore and a sweater that's a bit too short. Even though I'm good friends with his wife, he can't even muster a neighborly smile for me. I guess he and I are past the point of pretending to be on good terms.

"Hi, Ron," I say as politely as I can. "Nice to see you."

He grunts and then brushes past me on his way to the den, where he turns the TV up loud enough for the whole house to hear. Rebecca rolls her eyes and motions me to follow her into the kitchen, where the aroma of hot chocolate and cookies hovers in the air.

"Smells great," I say with an appreciative sniff.

Rebecca pours two cups of hot chocolate and offers me a bag of marshmallows. I plunk two big ones into my cup. Then I take a cookie. We bring our food and drinks out to the dining room. Ron is watching the news in the other room. A reporter is talking about the weather and how we can expect more snow in the coming days. Even though Ron is sitting three rooms away, the TV is loud enough—too loud, actually—where we are.

"He refuses to get his hearing checked," Rebecca says.

I bite my tongue and sip the hot chocolate.

"Delicious."

"I'm glad you like it. The boys shouldn't take too long on your driveway," she says. "I had to get them out of the house. They were arguing about everything."

"Oh, it doesn't matter how long it takes. It's worth every penny."

Rebecca's mug stops halfway up to her face. "Wait—you're *paying* them?"

"Yes."

Rebecca throws her head back in frustration. "I told them to help you. Not *charge* you."

"That explains the look, then." I tell her about the conspiratorial glance the boys shared when I raised the issue of payment. Rebecca is outraged, but I shrug it off. I wouldn't expect her boys to do all that work for me for free.

"So tell me about last night," Rebecca says.

"Are you strapped in?"

I share everything, even the incredibly embarrassing part where I pulled a gun on a crazy woman in a bookstore.

"I don't believe it," Rebecca says when I'm finished. "Brandon sounded like such a nice guy."

Last night I went from terrified to irate. But now, speaking with Rebecca, a sadness comes over me. After I graduated college, I thought I had all the time in the world to meet a nice man. But now, these many years later, I've only met a few nice guys. Without fully realizing it, I'd gotten my hopes up with Brandon. He made me feel so comfortable. And now I'm filled with disappointment. Brandon

made me feel really safe and happy around him. It didn't
hurt that he seemed kind, was handsome, and also great
in bed.

"Yeah, well ... that's the way it goes sometimes."

"Tell me about it." Rebecca's eyes drift past me, in the
direction of the den, where Ron is still blasting the news.
"Ron was the nicest guy I'd ever met. He was so sweet. In
college, when boys were hooking up with a different girl
every night, he told me he wanted to go steady. Sometimes I
think he's making up for missing out on those wild days,
when all his buddies were sleeping around."

Ron might only be sitting in the other room, but with the
TV volume cranked to migraine levels, he can't hear us.

"How are things going with him?" I ask.

"I've never seen a man so grumpy about not being able to
go into work," she says, rolling her eyes again. "It's like he
can't wait to get out of the house and be away from me. Or
maybe be around somebody else."

I reach for her hand. "I'm sorry, honey."

Rebecca's bottom lip disappears as she looks away. "Yeah,
well ... that's the way it goes sometimes, right?"

The TV news turns from the weather to another story.

"A young woman was found dead in her home earlier
this morning on the three hundred block of Aramingo Street
..."

I try to tune the news out.

Rebecca groans. "Ron! Would you turn that down,
please?"

No answer.

"I hate the news," Rebecca says. "And it's *all* he watches."

"I can't stand the news either," I say. "It's all sensational-
ized and warps a person's reality."

"I know what you mean," Rebecca says, looking in her husband's direction again. "Ron! Could you—"

There's a heavy knock at the door. Not a neighbor's rap. This has the sound of authority behind it. I get a bad feeling in the pit of my stomach.

"Who is that?" Rebecca asks.

"Who is *that*?" Ron bellows from the den. "Beck, could you get that? I'm working."

"How could anyone work with the TV blaring that loudly?" Rebecca grumbles, but she gets up and goes to the door rather than argue with Ron.

I put my mug of hot chocolate down and turn in my chair to get a better look. From where I'm sitting, I can see half of Rebecca as she opens the door. A flash of white light fills the foyer. I can't see who's there or hear what's being said over the TV.

"Beck, who is it?" Ron calls out obnoxiously.

I want to tell him to look for himself. Rebecca is not his servant.

"Ron, would you please turn that down?" Rebecca calls back.

Her husband grumbles loudly enough for everybody in the house to hear before turning the volume down.

"I'm sorry, Officer, but I was having trouble hearing you."

"Your neighbor, Amanda Christie," comes a familiar voice. "Your sons told me she was over for a visit. Is she still here?"

24

Detectives Rooney and Taylor are standing in snow boots on Rebecca's porch. Neither of them smiles when I appear in the doorway. I look out to the street and spot their unmarked car parked in front of my house.

It's blocking my driveway.

"Good morning, Ms. Christie," Taylor says, pushing his glasses up his nose. "We were wondering if we could have a word with you?"

"In private," Rooney says.

"Yes," Taylor adds, "at your house would be best, we think."

Rooney looks his usual irritated self. The foul weather isn't helping his normally cheery disposition any. I tell them I need to grab my things before we speak. Rooney actually steps into Rebecca's house to watch me don my coat, like he expects me to try to run out the back door or something.

Rebecca is giving me a petrified look. "Is everything okay, Amanda?"

"I'm sure it's fine," I say with a confidence I don't feel.

Ron has come into the foyer to make himself known. "What's going on here?"

Detective Rooney looks the man up and down and doesn't care for what he sees. "Afternoon."

Ron frowns, expecting more deference from a stranger in his own home. But Rooney doesn't bother explaining himself and instead follows me out. While we cross the lawn, Rebecca's two boys watch us with unabashed interest.

The detectives elect to keep their wet boots on and leave watery tracks through my foyer as I lead them into the living room once more. We take our same places as before. I'm in the armchair; Rooney is on the couch; Taylor remains standing with his tiny notebook poised.

"Before we begin, Ms. Christie," Taylor says, "I have to ask if there's anyone else in the house?"

"No."

The two detectives share a meaningful look that leaves me in a cold sweat. I know something horrible must be coming. The only thing giving me a sliver of hope is the fact they haven't arrested me yet.

"Where were you between the hours of eleven p.m. and four a.m. last night?" Rooney asks.

I'm thrown for a loop. I was expecting some type of lead-in, a series of questions driving toward some point. But Rooney has skipped that part entirely.

"I was ..." Even though I'm a grown woman and this is the twenty-first century, I still blush. "I was with a man."

"What man?" Rooney demands.

"His name is Brandon Turner," I say.

Rooney says nothing. But his skeptical eyes bore into me with anger and incredulity.

"Brandon Turner," Rooney repeats. "He your boyfriend?"

"No, not exactly."

Rooney makes a disapproving sound. Taylor jumps in.

"Ms. Christie, could you walk us through your evening last night? Why don't you start at dinnertime?"

I don't really want to share what happened at the bookstore. The more I think about it, the crazier my actions seem. When Sarah charged the table, I should have gotten up and backed away and immediately asked her to leave instead of freezing like I did, then staying within her striking distance.

But if I *don't* tell them, and they find out later, it'll look even worse.

I tell the detectives everything that happened. I make sure to preface my heated exchange with Sarah at the bookstore by showing them the unusual email she wrote me, hoping that it will paint my behavior in a better light.

"You pulled a gun on her," Rooney interrupts at the crucial moment. "Right there in the bookstore?"

"Yes," I say. "You have to understand, she was *not right*. She ran up to the table where I was sitting, got right in my face, and was throwing her arms around wildly. The woman was practically screaming at me; then, like I said, she suddenly reaches into her pocket. I had no idea what it could be, but given how she was acting, I was scared. So yes, Detective, I protected myself. And that was it."

Rooney's eyes slide away from me and drift over to Taylor, who gives the older detective a nod like they've just confirmed something.

"Go on, Ms. Christie," Taylor says. "What happened next?"

I tell them the rest: leaving with Brandon, going out for drinks, spending a couple of hours at his place, waking up to find my books hidden away in his closet, and driving home in the treacherous, snowy conditions. Just as I'm getting to the part about Matthew waiting for me in his car, Rooney interrupts again.

"What time did you leave Brandon's place?"

I really don't know. It was late, after midnight, maybe one or two a.m. But I can't be sure.

"I didn't pay attention to the time," I explain. "Once I opened that closet door and found out what he was up to, I panicked. I had to get out of there."

Rooney nods slowly, narrows his eyes.

"How about when you got home? What time was it?"

I have to think hard about it. I vaguely recall eyeing the digital clock in my car during the hellish drive home in the snowstorm.

"I think two o'clock or maybe three?"

I find accounting for my whereabouts incredibly difficult. Like most people, I don't bother to constantly check the clock and memorize where I was and what I was doing at such and such a time.

And yet, both detectives are regarding me suspiciously, like my failure to provide specifics is damning evidence of my guilt.

"And when you got home, what happened?" Rooney asks.

I grow even more nervous when I tell them about my encounter with Matthew. Their manner grows increasingly skeptical while I relate the story, making me doubt myself. By the time I'm done, I'm in a cold sweat.

"Everything alright, Ms. Christie?" Taylor asks. "You look like you could faint."

"I'm sorry. I'm still a little shaken up by everything."

"That's understandable," Taylor says.

Rooney grunts. "Okay, you left this Brandon's house between one and two o'clock and didn't get home till around two or three. That's what you're telling us?"

"That's right."

"It took you up to two hours to get home?" Rooney says, like it's the most ridiculous idea in all of history. "When the guy lives twenty minutes away."

"The roads were awful." I look Rooney in the eye. This man will not cow me. "And it was still snowing heavily."

"Uh-huh."

The detectives share another of their mysterious looks. I can't stand the suspense anymore.

"Can you tell me what this is all about?" I ask.

"Sarah Keller was murdered last night," Rooney says. And then he watches my reaction very closely.

"Oh ... my God." I look from Rooney to Taylor. "That's terrible."

"Is it?" Rooney asks.

"What kind of ques—of course it is."

He shrugs. "I knew this guy once. Real piece of work. His wife used to call us constantly, a coupla times a month. She'd say he was whaling on her. By the time we showed up, things had always quieted down. Every time she'd recant her story. The third or fourth time this happened, when she was telling us it was nothing, this guy was standing behind her with this big shit-eating grin on his face. He knew there was nothing we could do about it. Anyway, a few months went by, and we didn't hear from the woman again. I figure she finally left the guy, maybe moved back in with her mother or sister. Turns out, the guy was hit by a bus one night. Drunk, stumbling home from the bar, stepped out into the street, and wham. Dead on the spot. He'd been in and out of prison twice for other crimes, and he was physically abusing his wife. I remember hearing about the guy dying. And thinking —it's not terrible he's gone."

I stare incredulously at Rooney. The man described sounds horrible, but Rooney's attitude over his death is still callous.

Rooney, however, is not embarrassed. My incredulous stare just bounces off him like it's nothing. Meanwhile, I'm still trying to process this new bit of information. The woman I pulled a gun on in a bookstore last night is dead.

"Rooney." I'm done playing nice. "If you're implying that's how I feel about Sarah being murdered, then you're way off base. There was something not right about her, and she was incredibly rude and threatening toward me. But that does not me—"

"You didn't kill her," Rooney blurts out. "Is that right?"

His bald question unbalances me. As a result, I take way too long to answer.

"No. Of course not. That's ridiculous."

"Are you sure?" Rooney asks, like it'd be possible to be uncertain of a thing like that. "Because if you have some-thing to tell us, Ms. Christie, now's the time. The longer things go on, the worse it will get. Believe me when I tell you that."

I lean forward in the chair. "I did not have anything to do with it. I couldn't."

Rooney's smile is irritating. "How *couldn't* you?"

"I just mean ..." What do I mean? I don't know. I scramble for an answer. "I'm not that type of person."

"Let me tell you something, Ms. Christie," Rooney says.

"I've seen all *types* of people commit murder. Unlike your books, in the real world, there are no *types.*"

He's trying to get under my skin.

I know it.

And yet, it's working.

"But I couldn't. I don't ... I don't even know where the woman lives, for starters. I only ever got an email from her—"

"How do you know she was murdered in her home?" Rooney asks.

Uh-oh.

"I don't—I just assumed."

"Well, you *assumed* correctly."

I roll my eyes and pretend like his suspicion is outrageous. But I know how bad my statement just sounded.

"You wanted to know where I was between eleven p.m. and four a.m., Detective," I quickly point out. "Most people are *home* during those times, especially in the middle of a huge snowstorm."

"Uh-huh," Rooney says. "Well, for your information, Ms. Christie, Sarah lives—I mean *lived*—four blocks away in the apartment complex around the corner."

Four blocks away.

"You can understand our problem," Taylor says, almost apologetically. He scratches the back of his neck sheepishly. I see through him now. It's all an act. "You get into this very heated argument with her last night—"

"During which you pull a gun," Rooney interjects.

"During which you pull a gun," Taylor echoes. "And then there's a two-hour gap in time you can't really account for."

"Then there's the other thing," Rooney says.

"Oh, right." Taylor makes a face. "Do we want to tell her about it?"

Rooney looks away from me for a moment, like he's thinking it over. He's a better actor than Taylor. I don't know if this was planned or not.

He doesn't answer Taylor's question. Instead, he turns his cynical eyes back to me.

"I'm going to ask you again, Ms. Christie," he says. "Is there anything you want to tell us?"

I shake my head. He gives Taylor a quick little look, and the younger detective steps in front of me.

"Let's go back to Matthew for a moment," he says, consulting his tiny notebook for a moment. "Matthew said he was at the bookstore last night and saw your exchange, right?"

"That's right."

Taylor nods. "And then he said ..." He reads from his notebook. "I took care of her."

I don't quite gasp. But I almost do. A moment ago, I was too consumed by Rooney's suspicion toward me. I didn't even have a moment to reconsider what Matthew said in light of this new information.

"Yes, it was something along those lines," I say.

"Did he say it or not?" Rooney barks.

"I don't remember his exact words," I answer.

Rooney grumbles. Taylor ignores him.

"And have you heard from Matthew since he drove away last night?" Taylor asks.

I shake my head.

"No text or email?" Taylor asks. "Could you double-check for me?"

I take out my phone. There's nothing new except for a missed call.

From Nora.

"Ms. Christie?" Taylor asks.

"Nothing." I put my phone away. "There's nothing from Matthew."

"Is everything okay?" Taylor says.

Rooney is sitting forward. His gaze is piercing.

"Yes. I mean, no, not really. You just told me this woman is dead and ..."

I'm going to cry. I don't want to look weak in front of these men, so I bite back the tears.

"It's all been a lot."

Taylor closes his notebook and puts it in his pocket. Rooney rises from the sofa.

"Ms. Christie," Rooney says, "we'll have more questions for you. You'd better not leave town."

Taylor smiles like we're old friends. "We'll show ourselves out."

25

After the detectives are gone, I breathe a huge sigh of relief. With shaky hands, I pour myself a glass of wine in the kitchen and sit down and try to sort everything out.

There's only one reason they didn't arrest me on the spot: Matthew. They knew, probably from one of the neighbors across the street, around what time I got home. Someone must have noticed Matthew's car parked on the street, its engine humming and its lights on. But whoever was watching didn't know it was Matthew waiting for me or what he said. All that was news for the detectives.

I go online. That news report Ron was blasting in his den must have been about Sarah Keller. I find a bunch of reports, but none of them mention her by name. There are no other details about the crime other than the fact she was found dead in her home. Whatever the detectives were holding back from me, it's nowhere to be found in the news.

It's the middle of the afternoon, a bit early to be drinking, but the glass of wine helps to settle my nerves. My phone buzzes with a text from Rebecca. She's asking if everything is okay. I tell her it's fine, the police are just looking into something that really doesn't have anything to do with me. It's a lie. I can't ignore the fact that two women with whom I had contentious relationships were murdered in the last few days. It very much has *something* to do with me.

I pour myself another (smaller) glass of wine and return Nora's call.

"Hi, Amanda," she says in an eerily calm voice. "I was calling to see how you were."

There is a subtext here. I don't know what it is, but I know it's lining her words.

"I've been better."

"I figured." There's a pause. "I saw that news article the other day, and I got to worrying about you."

I close my eyes. "I'm doing okay."

"Come on, Amanda. How are you really holding up?"

"Well ..." I can't lie to her. "I'm not sleeping. And I can't get any work done."

I can feel it: I'm going to come apart. Everything that's happened is going to spill out of my mouth in a torrent.

"Things aren't good, Nora."

"I'm sorry to hear that," she says. "Why don't you come over so we can talk?"

I don't want to go anywhere. I want to stay in my house and actually get some writing done and wait out the storm, both literal and proverbial. In a couple of weeks, hopefully all this will have blown over ... I know that's wishful thinking, but honestly, that's all I've got to keep myself together at this point. My books might be about detectives, but I am not one. I can't go out and gather evidence and find Megan's and Sarah's killers (or killer?) and hand them over to the police, so I come out looking like a hero. That's pure fantasy. The truth is, I'm a thirty-something author who's never been in a physical fight in her life, let alone tracked down a vicious murderer or two.

I'm about to politely decline when Nora adds: "You could bring your laptop. I'd love to read that new story you're working on."

I've been pacing through the kitchen, but at those words I stop. Did I just hear her correctly?

"Amanda, are you there?" she asks.

"Yes, I'm here," I say. "You want to read my story?"

"Yes," she says excitedly. "I'd *really* like to."

"Okay." I check the time. "It's going to take me a while to get there, what with the weather."

"That's okay," she says. "I'm not going anywhere."

I end the call. For a moment I stand there, my mind racing.

Nora always reads my books. As a matter of fact, I always send her one of the proof copies so she gets to read the story before it hits the shelves.

But she doesn't read my latest work-in-progress on my laptop.

That's just a code phrase we made up, years ago.

There's something she needs to tell me. And she can only do it in person.

26

The main roads are clear of snow. But the skies are gray, and now they're calling for another dusting late tonight.

I pass through town and then a little stretch of country where rolling snow-covered fields stretch. The long ride gives me time to think.

Two women are dead. Both Matthew and Brandon were keeping big secrets from me. Matthew has a temper and possibly a history of violence toward women. Brandon is an obsessed fan who, apparently, knows how to fight and spoke nonchalantly about putting another man in the hospital. The cryptic notes at my back door aren't helping matters either.

Then there's Mom ...

I can't believe I'm even wondering this, but what if she was involved in these deaths?

Before I'm even done entertaining the thought, I shake my head at its stupidity. Mom isn't a killer. And even *if* she had killed these two women out of some misguided bid to protect me, then she would not have copycatted a gruesome murder out of one of my own novels.

All the drama and stress of the last few days has taken a toll. I am not thinking clearly.

It takes nearly an hour and a half to reach Nora's town, the same place I grew up. This is where I lived with Mom in that little apartment above the old man who chain-smoked cigarettes all day. And next to that boy who was a few years older than me and who secretly kept a dog even though you weren't allowed to have pets at the apartment complex.

I don't like coming here.

I pass what used to be the soda shop and candy store. Mom and I would walk there every Saturday afternoon. Now it's a small insurance business. Around the corner is the laundromat where Mom used to lug our clothes when the washer or dryer or both at the apartment complex were down, which was often. I used to sit on top of the machines while we were there and read novels that were much too old for me.

Nora lives in an older apartment complex on the other side of town. For a long time, she talked about saving up for a place of her own. But she hasn't mentioned that in several years now. I think she's resigned to the fact that she's never going to have enough money to buy a house.

It would be easy for Nora to blame Mom for the way her life turned out. Many people have grown resentful for a lot less. After David was murdered and Mom went on the run, Nora lost her position at the credit company and struggled to find work. Though she would never admit it, being known as Kimberly Dawn Allen's best friend closed a lot of doors for her. Struggling to make ends meet, she fell into self-destructive patterns of behavior, dating one bad guy after another. More than one of them cleaned out her meager bank account. To add insult to injury, last year she was diagnosed with lung disease.

With all the massive snow piles everywhere, it takes several minutes to find parking. I make my way into Nora's building and take the elevator up to the third floor. I've got my laptop with me, just for appearances' sake. My throat is dry when I knock on her door.

It takes Nora a minute to open up. I hear her move through the apartment, and then the door is opening, and my mother's best friend is standing there. Her hair is completely gray now, and she's a little out of breath from the short trip to the door.

"Amanda." She gives me a big smile. "Oh, it's so good to see you."

When we embrace, we hold onto each other a little longer than usual.

"Come in, sweetie."

Her apartment smells like cigarettes. Nora still smokes despite her lung disease and her frequent need for oxygen, but she never does it in front of me.

"I've missed you," Nora says after she gets settled in her armchair. Her oxygen tank is on the floor to her left. I spot an ashtray on the end table beside her, which Nora quickly covers with a newspaper.

"I've missed you too," I say. This woman is more family to me than my actual family. I almost sink to the floor as I sit opposite her on her old couch, which she's been meaning to replace for years. I take in the apartment. Nothing else has changed either. I can't help the drift of my eyes toward her oxygen tank.

When I was a child, I thought I was the only one who suffered when Mom went on the run.

"I'm sorry," I say, suddenly overwhelmed by it all. "For everything."

Nora waves that away. "I'm fine, Amanda. Don't you go worrying about me."

"You know, with my next advance I could—"

"No," she says. "That's your money. I don't want a single dime of it."

I nod, but when that next advance comes, I'm going to put some cash inside an unmarked envelope and leave it in her mail. If she asks, I'll deny I left it, and she'll be forced to accept it.

With everything that's happened in the last few days, I haven't had time to give my career much thought. But now that I do, I'm actually worried that my next advance is in jeopardy. The police are circling me like sharks in two murder investigations, and details of the copycat murder have already been made public. My publisher might not want to have anything to do with me.

Nora senses my dark mood. "What's on your mind?"

I fake a smile. "Nothing important. What did you want to see me about?"

"First things first." Nora gives me a smile. "I want to know if you're okay. Online, all these readers are talking about Megan Patterson and how her death mimicked what happened in *Serial Reader*."

I forgot that Nora likes to interact with readers in online forums, where she takes every opportunity to shamelessly plug my novels.

"And then that story about Sarah Keller came up too. Everybody's worried about a copycat killer."

I close my eyes and nod. A reporter must have gotten Sarah's name. "The police have come to my house twice now."

"They're saying somebody glued one of your books onto Sarah's palms and then taped her eyes open, like she was forced to read it while ..."

I recoil in horror, feeling like I'm going to be sick. That wine I drank earlier is threatening to come right back up.

I shake my head. "That's out of another book I wrote," I explain. "The one about—"

"*Wicked Furies*," Nora says with a little smile. "I've read it a dozen times."

"Someone must be doing this on purpose," I say. "When it was only Megan, I held out hope that her death was just a terrible coincidence. But I can't pretend any longer. Whoever is responsible, they're murdering these people, and they want the police to think I'm involved."

"I'm afraid you're right," Nora answers.

"I don't know what to do," I say. "I'm worried ... I think it might be my ex-boyfriend, or maybe even this other guy I just met ..."

Nora holds up a hand. "Before you go on, I want to say this: be careful what you tell me. The police were here a couple of days ago. Rooney and Taylor were their names. The less I know, the better."

"They were *here*? My God, Nora, I'm so sorry."

"You don't have to apologize. I'm too old and don't have enough to lose to be frightened by the cops."

A heavy, ominous silence descends. I shift nervously. Nora tries taking a deep breath but ends up coughing badly instead.

"Are you okay?"

She nods while she coughs into her hands.

I stand beside her and gently pat her back. Nora's eyes are watering, and her face is flushed by the time she's done hacking.

"I'm worried about Mom, too," I say.

Nora looks up at me. "What do you mean?"

I return to where I was sitting and tell her about the two notes I've found on my porch. "I think she's been trying to warn me—I don't know who else would have left them."

Nora thinks it over. "I guess ... but those notes don't sound like her to me."

Nora has hit the nail on the head. That's what's been bothering me as well. In the past, when Mom has felt the need to risk arrest by communicating with me, she always sends a very clear message that does not leave any room for interpretation. These notes, on the other hand, are incredibly vague.

"I'm so worried about her," I repeat, setting aside the authorship of the notes for the moment. "Forget about the police. Mom's too old to hunt down a killer."

Nora chuckles. "Kim's an amazing woman, and I could see her following you around to make sure you're safe. But I doubt she'd try to track down some murdering lunatic. She's not a superhero."

I give her a half-smile as I say, "I never told you what happened in college."

27

EIGHTEEN YEARS AGO

His name is Tevan. He's not my usual type. Frat boy who's known to sleep around isn't my normal cup of tea. All my friends have warned me away from him.

But here's the thing. Despite the cocksure heartbreaker image he projects, he's also an English major. We've had a lot of classes together. And I know there's more to him than just the college athlete looking to get laid. Once in class the professor tried to put Tevan on the spot, asking him to give his thoughts on one of Percy Shelley's longer poems. I remember a few people snickering. They were the ones who had reasons not to like him and were more than ready to see him make a fool of himself.

But Tevan started genuinely gushing about this poem.

And he didn't speak in vagaries, the way that most students do when they've been put on the spot but haven't done the assigned reading. He recalled specific lines of the poem; he talked about its meter and drew some interesting parallels to this other poem we'd read in a different class. He must have gone on for nearly five minutes. I'll admit his performance totally shocked me. By the time he was done talking, nobody was laughing anymore. So yeah, Tevan is a jock, and he's a frat boy. But he's also *more* than those things.

I check my hair and makeup once more in the mirror before leaving the dorm. I'm meeting Tevan for drinks at the campus bar. I turned twenty-one a couple of months ago, so there's no need for me to even think about using this fake ID I once picked up. (Not that I ever used it. I swear.)

The campus bar is a dive, but they serve food, and the drinks are cheap. When I arrive, it's noisy and crowded. Not exactly my scene, but Tevan was the one who suggested it.

"A lot of girls are put off when they come to a fraternity party," he said. "And I understand. It's not the best place to actually meet someone and have a real conversation. How about the bar instead?"

He scored some points with me when he put it that way. Most college guys aren't interested in Ms. Right. They only want Ms. Right Now. The fact that Tevan isn't trying to wow me with a huge frat party and instead wants to have a conversation tells me a lot. My friends are wrong about him.

He appears a moment later. All eyes turn his way. He gets a big reaction from everybody there, which is exactly the opposite I received. Tevan smiles and nods at a few people, but he doesn't keep me waiting. As soon as he's inside, I can tell he's really looking to find me among the crowd. I give him a little wave from the end of the bar, and his eyes light up. He strides across the room. Tevan is a wide receiver on the football team and has the physique to prove it. He's solid but not grossly muscular, like those professional body-builders with their veins bulging out everywhere.

"Hey, Amanda." He moves in and gives me a quick hug. A

little thrill runs through my body when we briefly come into contact. "You look amazing."

I smile, feeling the blush break out on my cheeks. "Thanks."

He's looking me up and down. "*Really* amazing."

Tevan might be the hottest guy I've ever been on a date with. It's a little intimidating. I don't think I've ever looked *amazing*, but Tevan sure seems to think so.

"Thanks," I say again. "Do you want to get a drink?"

"Sure do. What are you having?" he asks. "They have beer. And beer."

I laugh. "I'll go with the beer, then."

"Good choice." Tevan bobs his head. The bartender comes over immediately. "Two light beers, please."

I've never had somebody order for me before. It's kind of nice.

"Alright," he says, turning toward me on his stool. "Be honest. What did you think of *Dracula*?"

We're both taking a course on nineteenth-century British novels. Bram Stoker's *Dracula* is the latest book we've just finished.

"Honestly? *Frankenstein* was be—"

"Better," he finishes my sentence. "*Right?*"

"Yes," I say, nodding. "Totally. *Dracula* was kind of a bore."

"I completely agree," he says. "It was too disjointed. With *Frankenstein*, you've got a clear ..."

He sticks his arm out. "A clear ..." He can't come up with the word.

"Throughline," I say.

"Yes! Exactly. That's exactly what I was thinking."

Our two light beers arrive. He holds his out in front

of me.

"A toast," Tevan says. "To Mary Shelley, a better writer than Bram Stoker."

"To Mary Shelley," I say, giggling.

We clink glasses. I spill a little of my beer onto his leg during the process.

"Sorry!"

"No worries," he says.

I grab a napkin off a dispenser on the bar and, without thinking about what I'm doing, begin wiping down his leg. It's hard not to notice the muscles under those jeans.

"Did you do that so you could touch my leg?" he asks.

I retract my hand and blush deeply. I'm really embarrassed.

"Kidding," he says, playfully touching my shoulder.

"Well, the answer is yes," I say.

He's taken aback, not expecting this reply from me.

"Kidding," I say.

A big grin sweeps across his face. Tevan wags a finger at me. "Now I don't know if you are."

We're laughing again. We start talking about the books we've read for class, then the books we read last semester, then our favorite authors growing up. It turns out Tevan and I have a lot in common.

"Do you want to get some food?" he asks.

"I'd better," I say as the bartender brings us our next round. I'm usually good for one or two beers at most, spread out over several hours. This is number three, I think, and we haven't been here that long. "What's good here?"

"Nothing." He smiles. "But at least the portions are small."

"That's from a movie, right?"

He feigns ignorance. "I have no idea. I swear I just made that up!"

We order appetizers and tuck into our next round of drinks. The fries are greasy, but they're *so* good. And Tevan and I are having a great time. I've had more to drink than usual, but I don't feel tipsy yet.

"Hey, when we're done eating, do you want to go back to your place?" he asks.

I was expecting him to ask me to come back to the fraternity house where he lives. But I much prefer to go back to my dorm. I'd feel much safer there.

"Sure," I say. It's a short walk back to my dorm, but my bladder is full. "I'd better use the bathroom first."

"Alright." He smiles at me. "I'll take care of the check."

I was fully prepared to argue about who was going to pick up the tab. But instead, I just thank Tevan and then head to the bathroom. The women's room only has two stalls, so there's a line. A few girls I recognize from class are waiting ahead of me.

"So you're Tevan's date tonight," one of them says, emphasizing the word *tonight* a little too much.

"Yes."

She looks at her friend, and they roll their eyes at each other. They're both in sororities and run in much more popular circles than me. Normally I wouldn't engage because I can't be bothered with superficial people. But tonight, I've got a few drinks in me, and I'm riding high from my date with Tevan.

"What's *that* supposed to mean?" I ask.

The two girls share another annoying look, and then they chuckle. As if they share a mind, they both say: "You'll find out soon enough."

They resume ignoring me. Feeling peeved, I wait my turn. Like all women's bathrooms, it takes forever. By the time I'm out, Tevan has taken care of the check and has his coat on. I grab mine, but before I put it on, he motions at my beer.

"You've got a lot left. Do you want to finish it before we go?"

I'm not drunk, but I've had enough. "I'm kind of full."

"Oh." He makes a face. "I'd hate to see it go to waste."

I frown. What does he care? I mean, okay, he picked up the tab. But does he really care if he spent two bucks on a drink I only half finished?

Tevan waits for me to answer. It's a little odd. Somebody told me that he grew up kind of poor and is only here because he earned a football scholarship. Maybe that's why he's being, how to put this, a little cheap?

"Would you like it?" I ask.

"Uh, no." He shakes his head. "I finished *mine.*"

Okayyyyy.

The rest of the evening has been great. I don't want to ruin it over something stupid. I pick up the beer and take another swig. There's no way I'm chugging this beer till it's gone. The glass is still a third full, but I can't stomach any more. I put it back on the bar. We were having such a nice time before I went to the bathroom. But now he seems ... *off.* I don't know what happened to put him in a different mood.

"Sure."

It's gotten much colder outside. This light jacket I brought isn't cutting it.

"I'm freezing," I say.

"Should have brought a warmer coat," he says.

I give him a hard look. I can't believe how rude he's

being. It's not like I asked him for his coat so he could freeze or anything.

"Did I do something to upset you?" I blurt out.

He gives me an incredulous look. "No, of course not. I've had a great time, Amanda."

What is with this guy? Hot for most of the night, cold for a little bit, then hot again. I don't get it. Maybe he was annoyed because I took too long in the bathroom? That'd be ridiculous. He's twenty-one years old. He should know by now how slow it can be in the ladies' restroom—

My foot misses the curb. I stumble into the street.

"Hey, take it easy." He moves in and grabs my arm. "Are you okay?"

"I'm fine."

I'm not. The world is slowly spinning. And I'm having trouble staying upright. It makes no sense. I've gone from pretty much sober to sloppy drunk in the span of a minute ... what is happening?

"You don't look fine," Tevan says. "Come on, let's get you home."

"Just want to sleep ..." I think I say.

Tevan doesn't respond. With his arm around me, we manage to walk about a block before I lose my footing again. I start giggling hysterically.

"Jesus Christ!" Tevan snaps angrily. "Are you freaking telling me you're not going to make it to your dorm? This is ridiculous."

Giggle. "Why are you ... yelling at me?" Giggle.

Tevan helps me up. He's *so* angry. I find it hysterical. I know I shouldn't, but I can't help it. He pulls me off the sidewalk.

"What are you doing?" I ask.

"Come on," he says.

He pulls me into a narrow alley between the admissions office and an academic building. I feel him press me up against the wall.

"Where are we?" I ask.

I feel like I should be afraid, but I can't quite feel afraid.

"Quiet," he says. "This is what you wanted."

His hands are all over me. I know what's about to happen, but I don't want to think about it. I try to bat him away, but there's no power in my arms. I can barely stay on my feet. The only reason I'm still vertical is because Tevan is pressed up against me.

"Don't fight," he says. "This is what you wanted all night."

"Stop," I manage to say. "Hey. Stop."

I want to scream, but I don't have the energy. He's trying to undo my jeans.

"Come on," he says, giving me a creepy smile. "You know you want this."

"Help." But I can't even raise my voice.

No one's going to hear me.

"Be honest," he says. "You didn't think I wanted to *date* you, did you? I only bring the hot girls back to the frat house. Luckily for you, I like nerdy chicks too."

"Stop."

He's got my jeans undone. Thank God they're really tight on me. He has a hard time pulling them down.

"Stop!"

This time it's not me yelling. Tevan stops what he's doing and moves away. Without his weight pressing against me, I lose my balance and fall onto my hands and knees. The air is cold on my bare thighs and bottom. I giggle. I don't know why, but I do.

"Who the hell are you?" Tevan asks.

I look up. I can't see so well. Everything is a little blurry, like somebody switched the world out of focus. There's a figure standing on the sidewalk. I think it's a woman. A dark hood covers her head. She steps into the shadow of the alley.

"Get away from her."

It's definitely a woman. She seems significantly smaller than Tevan. If he wanted, he could run right through her.

"We were just fooling around," Tevan says. "Leave us alone."

"You were trying to rape her," the woman snarls.

"I was n—"

The woman reaches into her pocket and pulls something out. I can see that it's glinting. A knife, I think. A switchblade?

"Don't lie to me."

Tevan throws his palms out. The woman is standing between him and the street. He can't get away, not without coming close to that glinting steel.

"Help her with her clothes," the woman demands.

"Uh—"

The woman lunges forward. She's incredibly fast. The knife is against Tevan's throat now.

"Help her! Or I'll kill you."

"Okay! Okay! Jeez! We were just fooling ar—"

"Lie to me again, and I will decorate this wall with your blood!"

"Okay. I'm sorry! I'm sorry! I'll help her! I swear."

I still don't know why, but I'm finding this whole thing hysterical. Giggling, I roll onto my back. My jeans are still down around my knees. The cold stone beneath me presses against my bottom.

Tevan hurries over. "Come on, Amanda. Stand up."

"She can't stand up because you spiked her drink, you fucking asshole."

Tevan ignores the woman. He does his best to get me on my feet.

"You put something in my drink?" I ask.

Tevan is shaking his head. "No, that's not true. I swear—"

"What did I say about lying?" the woman hisses.

Tevan goes quiet. He manages to prop me against the brick wall again, only this time he's trying to pull my jeans up instead of down. They're really tight, though, so he can't quite zip them.

The woman moves in. Tevan jumps about five feet away from her like he's a flea.

Ha-ha. He's like a flea. That's funny.

The woman brandishes the switchblade again. "I've killed before," she says. "If I ever see you near this girl again, I'll kill you too."

Tevan's eyes go wide. The inner thighs of his jeans turn dark. Oh my God, he's just peed all over himself. I know I should take this moment more seriously, but that's the funniest thing ever.

"I'm sorry," he says.

The woman's head is still covered. I can't make out her face in the darkness. But then she says: "I'm Kimberly Dawn Allen. And I will kill you if you ever try to rape this girl, or any girl, ever again. You understand?"

Kimberly Dawn Allen? That's my mother's name. What a coincidence.

"I swear! I'm sorry ... please let me go. Please—"

"If you tell anybody about this, if you tell anyone I was

here, I will find out about it. And I will come and kill you. Do you understand?"

"I understand. Please, I swear, I'm sorry, I won't say anything. I'll never say anything. I promise! Please let me go. I'm ... I'm just a kid. I made a mistake. I'm sorry."

"GET OUT OF HERE," the woman snarls, "you pathetic little shit."

Tevan shrieks and runs out of the alley. It's funny. But I'm not laughing anymore. Because Kimberly Dawn Allen is the name of my mother.

"Mom?" I say. I'm having trouble focusing my eyes on anything, and she's wearing a hood in the utter darkness of this alley. I can't make out her face.

"You have to be more careful," she says. "Or you'll get into trouble."

Next thing I know, I'm leaning against her. I haven't seen Mom in a long time, and it's surprising to discover that I'm taller than her. She's a small woman, but she put the fear of God into a hulking college athlete. She walks me out of the alley and then helps me along the street.

"Mom," I say. Somehow, the seriousness of the moment reaches me through whatever drug Tevan slipped into my beer while I was in the bathroom. "Is it really you?"

"It's me. I miss you, sweetheart."

"Mom, why do you have to leave? Can't you come to my dorm? Can't you just stay one night?"

"I'm sorry, honey, but that boy is going to tell somebody. Maybe not tonight or tomorrow, but he's going to talk. It's not safe for me to stay."

"Oh, Mom, but I miss you. Why do you have to go?"

"You know why, sweetie," she says. "I'm just glad I was here, for once, to actually help you."

And there's only one way she could have known to be here.

When Nora handed me that manila envelope a few years ago, there were several things inside. Mom had left me several thousand dollars in cash. There were also the names and numbers of some people Mom trusted. I could contact them if I was in trouble or if I needed to contact her quickly, but they were only to be used in case of emergency. The last item was a piece of paper with a random, strange-looking link I later discovered led to the dark web. It was a way for me to leave email with Mom that was, theoretically, untraceable. Just the other day I'd messaged her because I hadn't written in a while, and I'd mentioned my date with Tevan. I was excited but also nervous, as he wasn't my usual type, and my friends had warned me about him.

"You got my message," I whisper.

"Yes, honey. I'm always checking."

Before I know it, we stop on the corner near my dorm. Mom stays out of the light, turning away from the building.

"Mom," I say, "did you mean what you said?"

"Of course. I really miss you, Amanda. I love you more than anything."

"No, not that ... what you said to Tevan?"

Mom doesn't answer. She looks past me. Through the fog enveloping my brain, I'm dimly aware of a group of people crossing the street and coming toward us.

"Did you really kill David West?" I ask.

I would never have asked her this question. Not in a million years. But this drug Tevan spiked my drink with has lowered my defenses. I have to *know*.

Mom looks into my eyes. For that brief moment, I

glimpse what she looks like under the hood. She's aged a lot since I last saw her. Living a life on the run has taken its toll.

"Don't waste a minute of your time trying to clear my name," she says, which doesn't answer my question. "Live your life, Amanda. And know that, no matter what, I will always love you."

"Mom, don't go."

"I'm sorry." Her eyes are watery. "I love you so much."

She's about to leave, but I grip her hard and force her into a hug. Mom rubs my back.

"I saw you graduate high school," she says. "I was so proud."

"You were there?"

I feel her nodding.

"I hope to be there for college graduation too, sweetie."

"Mom, I love you more than anything."

"Goodbye, Amanda."

She tears herself out of my grasp, then hurries down the street, away from the gaggle of drunken students hanging around outside the dorm.

28

Nora swipes a tissue out of a box next to her and wipes her eyes. I've never told her that story before.

"Was that the last time you saw her?" Nora asks, then shakes her head. "No, wait, don't answer that question. It's better I don't know."

I reach for a tissue and dab my eyes as well. As a matter of fact, I saw Mom again a few years later, but that night on campus was the last time I ever got to speak to her ... and to give her a hug.

"I have to say this," I go on. "Because if I don't, I might go crazy. But what's bothered me all these years is that Mom didn't answer my question."

"She didn't kill David West," Nora says.

"Then why not say that?" I ask.

Nora gives me a steady look. "Because she didn't want you spending the rest of your life trying to clear her name."

I'm floored.

Now that Nora has expressed the idea, it seems like it

should have been obvious all along. If Mom constantly proclaimed her innocence and railed against the injustice of her situation to me, then naturally she'd fear I'd dedicate my life to her cause.

"All the same, it didn't work." I shake my head. "Do you know how much time I've spent over the years trying to find new evidence and identify alternative suspects?"

Nora smiles sadly. "I know."

"And it's all come to nothing." There's a lump in my throat. "I've never been able to help her."

I look out the window at the cold winter bleakness. I would give anything to clear Mom's name and have her back in my life, especially at a dark time like this. I wish I could contact her directly, but in the eighteen years since I opened that manila folder, the handful of people she trusted have either passed, moved away, or changed numbers. The link I used to send her those untraceable emails no longer works either.

There's a knock at Nora's door.

"Were you expecting someone?" I ask.

Nora doesn't answer. I follow her to the door. Nora opens it and peers up and down the hallway. There doesn't seem to be anyone there.

"Oh, it was just someone leaving a menu for that new place," she announces.

Nora reaches around to the outside of the door and picks up a little trifolded menu for a pizza restaurant. Before she closes the door, I notice another copy of the same menu left against the door catty-corner to us in the hallway.

Nora closes the door and gives me an indecipherable look. Puzzled, I watch as she carefully opens the menu. A tiny piece of paper that was hidden inside falls to the floor.

Nora bends to scoop it up. I can't read the handwriting on it from where I'm standing, but Nora's eyes go wide. When she's done, she holds it out to me.

Growing nervous at the strangeness of the situation, I take the paper from her.

Meet at the coffee shop. Come alone. Nora will follow in thirty minutes.

I recognize the handwriting.

It's from—

Nora grips my shoulders and peers into my eyes. "The shop is one block north, toward the library, and then one block west."

In my nervous excitement, I have trouble finding my voice. "Okay."

She gives my shoulders a squeeze. "Tell her I said hi."

In my haste to leave, I nearly forget my coat.

It's grown dark now, the streets busy with rush-hour traffic. I want to run to the coffee shop but know better than to draw attention to myself. At this point, it's better to assume I'm being followed, either by the police or by the person committing these murders.

I manage to keep my pace normal. It's a cold night, and the sidewalks are a mess with all the snow we've gotten recently. Five minutes later, I stop in front of the coffee shop. It's small and family-owned, not one of those chains without any personality. A two-sided chalkboard sign sits outside that reads FREE COFFEE YESTERDAY.

The storefront windows are fogged. There are booths in the front, but there are also tables and armchairs in the back where people can have some privacy.

It's warm inside, the air filled with the smell of coffee. I don't have to wait long to order my drink. It's ready a minute after I pay, and then I make my way into the back of the shop, where it's cozier and darker. I don't see Mom anywhere.

I sit in an armchair that's facing out toward the rest of the shop. The bell over the door rings a few times as people come and go, but Mom's still not here. Ten minutes pass before I realize I haven't even touched my coffee. I'm already amped on adrenaline, so caffeine is the last thing I need. But, to keep up appearances, I take a sip. When I set the cup back down on the low table in front of me, I feel a shift in the air.

"Don't turn around."

It's her.

Mom.

I fight the very natural urge to spin in my chair and look at her. It's been so long since I last saw her.

"Hi," I manage to squeak out.

"I apologize for all the theatrics," she says. "Having Nora contact you, then leaving a note inside a pizzeria menu. But, unfortunately, this is my life. I wanted to see if you were being followed. I was almost hoping you were."

"But what if the police found you here?"

"I'm not worried about the police," Mom says. "I've been hiding from them for years. No, I wanted to see if anyone *else* was following you."

"You mean the person who's ..."

I let that thought trail off.

"You look good," Mom says. "Really good. I'm so proud of you. You've grown into this beautiful, independent woman."

She must be sitting in the chair behind and to my right. Is there a back door to this place? Or was she waiting in the bathroom this whole time? No, she must have been out back, watching for tails. I trust Mom when she says I wasn't followed. Having avoided arrest for all these years, she's gotten very good at these sorts of things.

"I wish I could see you."

"I know, sweetie. But we have to be careful. We're both taking a big risk right now, just sitting here together."

"Were you the one leaving me notes?" I ask.

"What notes?"

My blood runs cold. I tell her about the two messages on my back porch.

"No, that wasn't me," Mom says. "I haven't been able to get close to your house in a long time. You've got a lot of nosy neighbors and loud dogs on that street."

If it wasn't her … then who was it who told me I was in trouble? Who told me to stay away from the bookstore?

"Someone is trying to destroy you," Mom says. "I don't know why, but I promise I'm going to stop them."

"Mom … what are you going to do?"

"Whatever I have to do to protect my child," she says.

I get a chill. The last time she talked like this, she had a knife to Tevan's throat.

"In a way this is all my fault," Mom says. "If you were anyone else's daughter, this wouldn't be happening."

"You don't know that," I say.

"I think Matthew is behind this," Mom says. "After you left the bookstore, that meeting broke up quickly. He was talking to Sarah Keller."

"You were there?"

"As soon as I read that news story about Megan Patterson, I came back. I've been … around. I hoped Megan's death was just a freak coincidence, but deep down I knew better."

That makes two of us. "What did Matthew say to Sarah?"

"I couldn't hear, but he got very agitated."

"That sounds like Matthew," I say. "He has a bit of a temper. It took me way too long to realize it."

"That happens in relationships," Mom says. "Love can blind us. You think you know someone, but sometimes you're wrong. Very wrong."

It's not hard to follow the train of her dark thoughts.

"Is that what happened with David?"

Mom grows quiet.

"I did love him," she says. "But even after all these years, I still can't believe David wrote that letter. I never once demanded anything of him, never mind threatened him. He had no reason to fear me."

"Who else knew about the affair?" I ask.

"Nora," she says, then sighs. "David and I liked to kid ourselves that we were discreet, but people at the office had to suspect as well."

"Do you think David's wife killed him?"

"She was hospitalized at the time."

"I know, but who else would have had a motive?" I ask.

She doesn't answer.

"Who called you that morning?" I ask. "I always thought it was her."

"It was David," Mom answers tentatively. "He was very upset."

"About what?"

"Amanda," Mom says, "I'm not here to talk about ancient history. I'm here to help you."

I don't care. When will Mom understand that she's as important to me as I am to her?

"It was the letter that sealed your fate," I insist. "All the other evidence was circumstantial."

"Amanda."

I don't stop. "Even the DNA doesn't mean anything. You were seeing him; it'd be easy for some of your DNA to get on him, his clothes, on items in his house. It doesn't mean—"

"*Amanda.*"

"You can't go on like this. We must clear your name."

"We have to make sure you're safe," she says. "I just want you to be happy."

"But I won't be happy," I say. It feels so good to finally get this off my chest. "Not until you and I can be together again."

"Oh, my precious girl. You've done fine without me. Look at the life you've built, all on your own. Without any help from Cece and hardly any from Nan." She mutters some less-than-flattering things about her family under her breath before continuing, "I don't want you to be Kimberly Dawn Allen's daughter, endlessly screaming at anybody who will listen that your mother is innocent. That's no kind of life."

I can feel the tears coming again. Our time together is always short, and I get the feeling we're winding down already. Ever since that day, when Mom promised she'd be back in a few hours and left nine-year-old me by myself in the apartment, I can count on one hand the number of times we've *interacted* in person.

She can't go on like this.

I can't go on like this.

When Mom speaks this time, her voice is closer, more above me. She must be standing right behind me now.

"You will be fine." Her hand grips my shoulder. I reach up to grasp it, but she pulls her hand away. "I'll make sure of it."

"What are you going to do?" I ask again, but afraid of the answer.

"What any mother would."

I feel her move closer to me. The urge to spring up and throw my arms around her is almost overpowering.

"Do you have to go already?" I ask.

"Wait here for Nora. She has something for you."

"She says hi," I answer, with a tearful smile on my face.

"Tell her I love her." Mom kisses the back of my head. "And I love you too, Mandy."

She moves away from me, and then, as before, the air in the room shifts. I can't help it: I look over my shoulder, but Mom's already gone.

I settle back in my chair and sit with my thoughts while my coffee grows stone cold.

NORA ENTERS the coffee shop about fifteen minutes later, carrying my laptop. She's out of breath as she crosses the room and sits down next to me. I give her a moment to steady herself.

"Would you like a coffee?" I ask, rising.

"No, thanks," she says, motioning for me to sit down. Then she lowers her voice. "How was she?"

"As good as can be," I say. "With being on the run and with her daughter a suspect in two murder inquiries."

"Sorry. Dumb question."

"No." I reach for her hand. "I wasn't being sarcastic."

She gives me a little grin. We hold hands as my mind circles back to my conversation with Mom.

"Whatever happened to Lori West?" I ask.

"I heard she changed her name and moved away. There was even a rumor going around that she got plastic surgery. She was tired of being recognized wherever she went. But I don't know if that's true."

"Did you ever meet her?" I ask.

"Oh yeah," Nora says. "Over at the Lee Mill Building, where we worked. She used to come around the office a lot. She was always baking something and swinging by the office unexpectedly. I think it was her way of checking in on David. I'm guessing she had her suspicions all along that he was fooling around with someone."

"What was she like?" I ask.

"She was ... I hate to say this because of what the poor woman went through, but she was *off*. She was always smiling, but you could tell it was an act. She let her guard down a few times. When she wasn't putting on a show for David's coworkers, her eyes were flat. Like there was nothing behind them."

"Do you know what conditions she suffered from?" I ask.

"We never knew for sure. One day it was schizophrenia; the next she was bipolar; then she had a personality disorder." Nora shakes her head. "You know what offices are like. People talk. Word got around that she *went away* a few times. I'm sure the gossip didn't help."

I want to sympathize with the woman. After all, Mom was sleeping with her husband. But, on the other hand, I can't think of anyone else with motive enough to kill David West.

Nora chuckles as she recalls an old memory. "All the guys around the office used to make fun of David for the scarves he wore. They looked so shoddy."

"Shoddy scarves?" The man came from money and made

a great living. He could afford expensive clothes. "Why did he wear them?"

"His wife made them," Nora says. "She loved to knit. But the teasing got so bad, David would come to the office wearing the scarf, then as soon as he stepped in the building, he'd rip that thing off and stuff it into his pocket."

Bizarre, I think, before I lower my voice. "Mom wanted me to say she loves you."

Nora reaches for my hand. "Oh, thank you."

We gaze into each other's eyes for a moment. I wish I could stay longer, but it is getting late. I'd better get moving before the temperature dips. The roads might freeze over again.

Nora lets go of my hand and reaches into her pocket. She pulls out a tiny envelope and hands it to me.

"What's that?" I ask.

"Your mother asked me to open a safety-deposit box," she says. "The name and location of the bank are in this envelope, along with the key."

"What's in the box?" I ask.

Nora looks around the room and lowers her voice even further.

"In case you have to ... leave town quickly ... there are things in that box that will help you."

I don't know what to say.

"I'm sure Kim's doing everything in her power to help you," Nora says. "But things don't always work out. That safety-deposit box is plan B."

Has it come to this?

If I run, I really am my mother's daughter.

29

A t least Matthew's not waiting for me when I return home.

I left in such a hurry earlier that I forgot to leave any lights on, so the house is dark. For a few minutes, I sit in my car. I realize I'm scared to enter my own home. The gun in my purse should be reassuring, but it's the opposite. Do I really think I'm capable of shooting someone?

Finding some courage, I unlock the front door and go into my house. I'm not in the best psychological frame of mind, but still, I can't shake the unnerving feeling that someone has been inside while I was out. Going from room to room, I switch all the lights on and examine every square inch of my home. Things *seem* slightly out of place, but I can't be sure. Wasn't the rug in the upstairs hallway closer to my bedroom door earlier? I thought that old picture of Mom on my dresser was angled more toward my bed ...

I realize I might be losing my mind.

The stress of the last few days is causing me to see things that aren't there and imagine the worst.

By the time I've done my forensic sweep of the house, I'm not reassured, I'm only more creeped out. There is no hard evidence that anyone has been here. And yet ...

I sit down in the kitchen. I should eat, but I have no appetite. In the end, I force myself to pour some cereal into a bowl, my go-to dinner when I don't feel like making anything.

While I'm eating, I open my laptop and go online. The media hasn't released any more information about Sarah's death, other than her name and the macabre details of her murder. But several of the articles mention Megan's killing as well, strongly implying a link between the two unusual crimes, and a few also make reference to my books. One article even states that the reporter attempted to reach me for comment, which is a lie.

The cat is officially out of the bag now.

When my cell phone buzzes in the absolute quiet of the house, I nearly jump out of my seat. It's Melinda, my agent.

"Hi, Mel," I say, then decide to rip the Band-Aid off. "I guess this isn't a social call."

"I wish it were, Amanda." She sighs. I know that sigh well. It's the one she uses to preface bad news. Over the years, I've heard it many times, like when this publisher or that press decided to pass on my book or reduce a print run or slash the marketing budget. "First things first, how are you holding up?"

Melinda and I have a good working relationship. I've come to think of her as a friend. Normally I'd share my feelings with her, but I just can't unpack everything again tonight. I need to let it lie.

"I've been better. So. What's the bad news?"

"Got a call from the acquisitions editor," she says in

deadly fashion. "Some of their other titles fell through. They had to take a loss on a couple of new releases and eat a lot of paper. Yadda, yadda, yadda. They've decided to *hold off* on your book for now."

Cowards. They wouldn't just come out and say, *We're going to wait and see if Amanda Christie is arrested and charged with murder.*

"What does that mean?" I ask.

"We can both read between the lines," Melinda says. "They're playing the wait-and-see game. Sorry, Amanda. It's not fair, but they can do it—they haven't violated any terms in the contract. Right now, you're looking at a year delay, hopefully nothing more, for the next book."

"If it happens," I say bluntly.

"It's going to happen," Melinda says. "As soon as you get clear of this, we'll get you back on track."

Less than two hours ago, Nora handed me the keys to a secret deposit box containing materials that will help me elude arrest. Right now, it feels like I'm closer to going on the run than getting back on track.

"Don't talk to the press, whatever you do," Melinda adds. "I've received a few calls but haven't taken them. If you'd like, I can prepare a statement."

"Shouldn't the publisher be doing that?" I ask. "They've got an entire press office."

"They should, but ... look, I didn't want to tell you this because I know you have a lot going on. But we've worked together a long time, and I feel I—"

"Mel, what is it?"

"The publisher might pull your books off the shelf."

"*What?* They can *do* that?"

"They're afraid of bad PR, and they're afraid of liability too."

"They think someone is going to *sue* them because some maniac copied something in a book of fiction they published?"

"They're not entirely crazy to think that," Melinda says a bit defensively. In the strange world of publishing, the intersection of writer-agent-publisher is a messy one. Melinda represents me, but she also has to work with my publisher on behalf of other authors. If she wants to keep landing deals for her clients, she has to play nice.

"How likely is that?" I ask.

"I don't know, to be honest. I'm going to reach out to them next week, when the dust has settled and cooler heads have prevailed. In the meantime, is there anything I can do for you?"

"Find the person responsible for these murders and hand them over to the police."

She laughs, but it sounds forced. I wonder if there's any doubt in her mind about my innocence.

"The best advice I can give you is to keep writing. You never know; they might change their mind tomorrow and want to push forward on the next book." She chuckles. "Next week, when all this blows over, they might want to rush it into production. How is it coming along, by the way?"

"I haven't gotten much work done this week, Mel."

She picks up on my tone. "Right. Of course not. Well, give yourself a few days. Recharge, then get back to it. You'll come out of this stronger. Who knows, maybe it will give you a few ideas for your next book."

Easy for her to say. She's got dozens of other authors as

clients, a couple of whom are topping the bestseller charts. I'm sure she wants things to work out for me, but if they don't? She has plenty of other lucrative irons in the fire. I *need* this to work out; she can more easily weather this particular storm.

"I'll call you in a couple of days," Melinda says. "To see how you're doing, alright?"

"Alright. Sounds good."

I end the call and hang my head. It feels like my life is unraveling. The urge to run is strong.

Yes.

Run.

If—God forbid—there's another murder, and I'm *not* in the area at the time of it, then that would go to show I'm not involved, right?

I shake my head. That seems like the most cowardly way to live my life. Run away, wait for somebody else to die, then come back to Rooney and Taylor and say: *See? It couldn't have been me.*

I am not thinking clearly.

I'm not the bravest person in the world. I'm not some hero out of a book. All I am is a regular person. But running away is not who I am.

It's all well and good to take such a high and mighty position, but still it leaves me in a bad spot. If I'm not going to run, then what *actions* can I take? This isn't some cozy mystery where the spunky single woman shows the police up, both identifying and then capturing a serial murderer. That's not real life.

So ... what can I do?

I come to the conclusion that there's only one thing. After an hour's research online, I find a good nonprofit that aligns with my goals.

It takes me a few minutes to set my phone up at just the right angle on my desk and get the lighting of the room perfect. After riffling my closet, I pick out a nice green shirt that makes my eyes stand out. I fuss with my makeup, then take a few minutes to write out what I want to say.

When I'm finally ready, I sit at my desk and hit the RECORD button on my phone.

"Hi. If this is your first time visiting my website, I'm Amanda Christie. Over the last few days, I have become aware of two horrible murders in my area. The killer, it seems, is copycatting events from my books. I will not go into details because I do not wish to give the murderer any more publicity than they're already receiving from the media. But I do want to address what's happened.

"Needless to say, I do not condone *anything* this person has done. I do not write books about death to inspire people to commit murder. I am opposed to violence in all forms, except in self-defense. I am horrified that someone has taken events out of my books, which are clearly fictional, and which I clearly do not endorse, and mimicked them in reality. I am deeply saddened that someone has twisted my life's work in this manner, and my heart goes out to the families and friends of these victims.

"Next year, I am going to donate one-third of my royalties to Homicide Survivors, a charity benefitting family members who have lost loved ones to murder. This certainly won't make up for what has happened this week, but hopefully it can help others in the future to cope with their terrible losses.

"In the meantime, the local police department has my full and ongoing support. I hope and pray that they will bring the perpetrator to justice very soon, before they can hurt anyone else. Thank you for watching."

I record my statement a few more times, then watch the clips to see which I like the best. I have editing software on my computer, which I sort of remember how to use, but this doesn't feel like a video that should be edited. After going back and forth, I pick one of the clips and then upload it to my website and social media accounts.

I plop down on my couch, in that weird contradictory state of exhausted and wired. I don't know what to do with myself. Within a few minutes, I'm back on the computer, checking the responses to my video. There are a bunch already, most of them on Facebook, but a few on my website itself. I'm slightly surprised to find they're all supportive. No trolls have popped in to imply, or outright allege, that I killed Megan or Sarah or both. It's a breath of fresh air reading these comments, and they restore my shaky faith in humanity a little after all the horrible dealings I've had this week. I'm about to close the laptop when my eye lands on a comment from someone with the username of Brandon_T:

Amanda is a great author and an even better person.

Eye roll. I click away from my website, but now I'm thinking about Brandon. Since I've got a little more distance on last night's strange turn of events, I'm curious to read the email he sent me. I don't plan on responding, or ever contacting him again, but I want to know what he wrote, kind of in the same way people slow down to gape at a traffic accident. Sometimes, you can't *not* look.

I scroll through my email and find the one from Brandon. He warned me it would be a long one, and he wasn't kidding.

Amanda – First off, I'm so, so sorry you had to find out I was a big fan of yours this way. I know what it looks like. Trust me, I really do. I understand why you were so scared and left in a hurry. If I were in your shoes, I would have done the same thing.

I don't know if you'll ever read this, but I really hope you do. Trust me, I don't expect anything in return. I don't expect you to respond or ever talk to me again. But I just couldn't let you go without telling you the truth. So, here's my confession—

I've been reading suspense thrillers and murder mysteries my whole life. It's my favorite genre. (I know, I lied about this too, but you'll see why if you keep reading. I promise.) I've always wanted to write my own but could never actually finish anything. School, work, relationships, life, blah, blah, blah, I've got all the same excuses as everybody else. I've tried so many times and given up on being a writer so many times, I've lost count at this point. I was thirty years old and told myself it was time to grow up, give up this childish dream. I was never going to be an author.

Then I discovered the first book you wrote.
I read it cover to cover in one sitting. I went back to the store the next day and bought all your books: at the time there were six more. I read each one in a day. I had to

know when the next was coming out, so I searched you online and found your website. You linked to a few interviews you'd done, and I was shocked to discover how, back then, you had a full-time job because you couldn't make ends meet with your writing. Your books were so good, I didn't understand how they weren't selling more.

In one of those interviews, the blogger was asking you all those typical questions an interviewer asks an author. Like, where you do you get your ideas from and how do you manage to actually sit down and write a book? Most authors will give BS answers here. They'll try to make their job sound much more difficult and romantic and mysterious than it really is.

You didn't.

I'll never forget this. You said you get your ideas from the same place somebody else gets the idea to go bowling. Then you went on to say that writing is just a job, like anything else. There are no shortcuts. You have to sit down and do it and, hopefully, over time you get better at it. I could tell this was not what the interviewer wanted to hear, because they kept trying to steer you toward more stock answers. But you didn't care. You were going to be honest. You were only going to be genuine. You removed much of the mystique of writing; you made it seem like it was similar to just going to work every day. And going to work every day was something I was already pretty good at.

It was your interviews that got me writing again.

That's why I became your biggest fan. Not only did I love your books, you also showed me that writers were just human beings, going about their work like everyone else. Your message really struck a chord.

I moved to this area for a job. I honestly had no idea you lived out here. But I was working on books and looking for an in-person writers' group to join. I could not believe my luck when I discovered this group and learned you were a member of it!

I'll be honest, the first time I attended a meeting and saw you, I was starstruck. I wanted to talk to you, but I was too intimidated. I spent an embarrassing amount of time having imaginary conversations with you.

I didn't want to tell you I was a huge fan, because, honestly, I'm a grown adult, and it's a little embarrassing to admit you admire someone when you're my age. That's why I kept it a secret. And when we started speaking, I was even more surprised when sparks seemed to fly.

This is the problem with lying, though: once you fib, you have to fib a lot more. That's what my mother always told me when she caught me in a lie. I'd already acted like I didn't know your books at all, so I couldn't then admit, after our first date, that I was secretly a huge fan. I guess that's what I should have done, but I wasn't thinking clearly. My feelings for you are overwhelming, and they made me behave uncharacteristically.

I thought about throwing out all my books and maintaining the charade. But I couldn't bear to do it. Your novels meant so much to me, throwing them away would have been like tossing out my favorite childhood toys. So I hid them in a closet and tried to think of the best time and way to tell you the truth.

Now, this is no excuse, but honestly there really wasn't a great time to bring this up. You have your own life, and right now you're dealing with your own troubles. Maybe this was me being a coward, but I justified holding off on being honest with you because I didn't think it was fair of me to put this on your plate too.

Needless to say, I handled this whole thing the worst way possible. I'm very sorry.

I really hope you read this. Meeting someone you admire is overwhelming, and I feared if I told you the truth, I'd have no chance with you romantically.

Again, I'm sorry. I know how hard you've got it right now. If you need anything, please let me know. Even if you don't want to meet in person, if you need me to do something, anything, I'll do it.

I CLOSE THE LAPTOP. I don't want to believe Brandon. Life would be easier if I dismissed him as an obsessed nutter. But here's the thing: I think I do believe him. Brandon is a decent guy. Sure, there are sociopaths out there who are expert at faking that kind of sincerity. But they're few and far between. If he was an actual sociopath, would he have shown that much patience with that older woman in the café? No way. Looking back now, I can't even believe I suspected Brandon was anything more than an embarrassed fanboy ... all the same, I'm not ready to talk to the guy. My life is messy enough right now.

If things ever go back to normal, then I'll think about contacting him.

But right now, it doesn't look like things will ever be normal again.

It's gotten late. I perform what I now think of as my security sweep, making sure all the windows and doors are locked. I save the back door for last, debating for a moment whether I want to check the back porch for another note.

It's been one hell of a day in one hell of a week.

I can't take one more thing. If there's a note out there, it can wait till tomorrow. I'm going to bed.

30

In the morning I rise early, with an uneasy feeling that more bad things are awaiting me. A warm shower doesn't improve my mood. While I eat oatmeal in the kitchen, still groggy from a poor night's sleep, my eyes keep drifting to the back door. I pretend I don't care if there's a new note there; I persist in finishing my breakfast and brewing some dark roast coffee.

It's supposed to be another cold day, with snow forecast. This time they're calling for eight to ten inches. As if on cue, a noisy truck whirrs by a moment later, spitting out salt as it passes. I don't know what to do with myself. I really should get back to work on my manuscript. My agent's right: publishers are fickle; they might change their mind today. You never know.

But the thought of sitting down to write seems ludicrous. Two women are dead, my mother is apparently hunting their killer, my ex-boyfriend is stalking me, and now even my home doesn't feel safe. If Matthew is intent on seeing me or getting into my house, a restraining order is not going to stop him. My gun might, but that assumes I'll be able to reach it in time and then have the gumption to hold him off at gunpoint—or even pull the trigger. And after my ordeal with Sarah in the bookstore, I don't really trust myself with a weapon.

And then there are the notes. I really have to check the back door to see if there's another one. But I need to work my way up to it.

At this point, I literally want to throw all my clothes into a bag and find somewhere else to stay. Home doesn't feel like home anymore.

But where else do I have to go?

I've stalled as long as I can. There's nothing else to do with my day except write, which I know probably isn't going to happen. I have to know if there's a new note waiting for me. Putting my coffee down, I stand on nervous, jittery legs and walk to the back door.

A tiny envelope is wedged between the back door and the screen door, presumably to keep it from getting soaked in all the snow covering my deck. Before bending to pick it up, I peer out into the backyard. Chances are this note was left for me yesterday, probably last night. The odds of anyone lurking out there this morning, in broad daylight, are slim. But I look anyway.

There's nobody there.

After closing the door, I take a deep breath, tear open the envelope, and unfold the single piece of paper inside. Again, all the letters and words have been cut out of newspapers or magazines.

Now you have to kill him.

My eyes go blurry as I manage to, somehow, stay on my feet. I'm dimly aware of the note leaving my hands and gently falling to the floor, where it lands and skitters under the kitchen table.

Oh God.

Kill who?

My mind races.

I start pacing. There's no question—I *must* turn this note and the others over to the police. I'm just trying to work out what's going to happen to me when I do.

My keeping the existence of these other notes a secret until now is not going to look good. I can make the case that the first two notes were ambiguous, perhaps only threatening toward me personally, not anyone else. But when you combine them with this latest, very unambiguous message, it paints a suspicious, rather sinister picture.

The detectives, especially Rooney, aren't going to believe a word I say.

Rooney will ask what the note means, but I won't have an answer. The only man who is arguably a danger to me is Matthew. But I don't want to kill him—I don't want to kill anybody—and, more importantly, I don't know who would *want* me to kill him either. I've only told a handful of people about the restraining order: Nora, Rebecca, Brandon. Nora would never tell me to kill anyone, and besides, she's in no condition to drive over here, sneak around in the cold, and leave strange notes without being seen.

That leaves Rebecca and Brandon.

Rebecca is one of my closest friends. I can't imagine her leaving me those notes. She knew of my history with Megan Patterson, but she didn't know anything about my contentious relationship with Sarah Keller. So why would she warn me away from the bookstore? And, much like Nora, I run into the same conundrum with Rebecca: why would she want me to *kill* anyone?

On the other hand, I must admit that Rebecca is uniquely situated. Nobody knows my comings and goings better than her. While I'm out, she could just slip out her back door, pretend to take the dog for a walk, and then leave a note on my porch. Nobody would see her. Nobody would even think twice about it if they did. We're constantly over at each other's houses.

Still ... I can't imagine why she would leave me those notes.

That leaves Brandon.

He doesn't know where I live. At least, I don't *think* he does. But what if he really is an obsessed fanboy? It wouldn't be *that* difficult to follow me home from the writers' group meetings on Sunday. It's *possible.*

But again, I run into the same conundrums I had with Rebecca. Why would Brandon first warn or threaten me that I was in trouble? Why would he tell me to stay *away* from the bookstore, his place of employment? And why would he suggest I kill another man, presumably Matthew? If he really was crazy-obsessed, and he thought Matthew was a threat, wouldn't he kill my ex-boyfriend himself?

None of this makes any sense.

My eyes catch the clock on the microwave. I've been dawdling in the kitchen for ten minutes now. I'm not going to solve this mystery by standing here and mulling everything over. I need to give these notes to the police. It will be a painful conversation, but necessary.

I put all the other notes in my purse and don a warm sweater, jeans, boots, and a heavy winter coat. I pour the rest of my coffee into a thermos and go to leave. But when I reach the front door, I get the oddest feeling.

Like I might never see the place again.

I take a moment to look around the house. This has been home for a long time, and the thought of never coming back here is deeply depressing. I stand in the foyer for a moment, closing my eyes, and I try to recapture that feeling of first walking in, when I was struck immediately by the utter need to live here. This was exactly the house I always wanted, neither big nor small, but cute and cozy in a nice neighborhood. I had to buy it.

It's all I have.

Outside, the air is damp. I can taste the snow that's coming. It takes a few minutes to defrost my windshield. I never remember to use the remote start.

The roads are still a mess, and now there's a layer of heavy salt everywhere. Two more trucks thunder by on my way to the police station. Now I'm second-guessing my decision to deliver the notes to the detectives. They have no reason to believe I didn't create them myself in a desperate bid to throw suspicion elsewhere.

But what if I don't turn them over, and something horrible happens that could have been prevented?

I pull into the left-turn lane at the next intersection and come to a stop at the red light. The police station is catty-corner to me. A cruiser pulls out of the parking lot while a few other squad cars with their engines on sit idle along the street.

My phone buzzes.

It's a call from a number I don't recognize. Normally I don't answer because this would indicate, ninety-nine times out of a hundred, that it's spam. But the last few days have all been one-in-a-hundred type of days.

"Hello?"

"Amanda!"

It's my mother. She's never called me before.

"Mom, what's wrong?"

"Honey, where are you?"

"I'm, uh, actually about to pull into the police station."

"DON'T GO THERE! Keep driving."

"Mom, what's—"

"There's no time to explain. Just listen to me."

"What's wrong? Mom, you're scaring me."

"Honey, I don't know what's happening, but you've got to listen to me really carefully now, okay?"

She waits for me to answer.

"Yes, okay."

"Don't go back home. Don't go anywhere else, as a matter of fact. Drive straight to that bank Nora told you about, empty that box, and *go*."

Go? "What do you mean?"

The left-turn signal on the traffic light activates. But I don't move an inch.

"I'm sorry, honey, but you have to *run*. Right now."

"Run?"

The driver waiting to turn left behind me hits his horn. The policemen in their idling cars all turn to look in my direction.

"Yes, run! Don't go into the police station."

I pull through the intersection, making my left-hand turn. Honestly, I have no idea where to go or what to do. I'm only moving so the man behind me stops laying on his horn.

As I pass the cruiser stopped at the intersection, I feel the eyes of the driver follow me the whole way.

"Amanda, do you hear me?"

"What's going on?" I ask.

"Matthew is dead."

I jerk the wheel and hit the brakes. I have to pull over. The driver behind me blasts the horn again, giving me a nasty look as he passes. I'm literally parked on the street outside the police station now, which is probably not the best place to be given what Mom has just told me, but I can't help it. This is all too much.

"How do you know?"

"I was watching his house," she says. "When he didn't come out this morning, I decided to go in."

"Mom—"

"I'm so sorry, honey, but you have no choice now. You have to—*ahhhhh!*"

My mother lets out a terrible scream. I hear the phone being dropped and then some kind of scuffle.

"Mom?"

She doesn't answer.

"MOM?"

The call ends.

I ring her back, but she doesn't pick up. I'm crying while I type out a text to her: *Are you okay?*

I really don't think she is; it sounded like she was being attacked.

A knock on my car's passenger window startles me. I swipe under my teary eyes and look out to find a uniformed police officer standing on the sidewalk.

I power down the window.

"Good morning, ma'am. Is everything okay?" he asks.

"It's … fine." I put on a fake smile. "I'm … I just got some bad news, is all. I'll be fine."

It's not a lie.

The policeman takes a moment to look around my car, like he's searching for drugs or weapons.

"Where are you headed?" he asks.

Uh.

I take way too long to answer. "Oh, the store, I'm running an errand."

"What store?"

I start to power up the window. "The grocery store," I blurt out. "Thank you for checking on me, Officer."

The window is up before he can ask me another question. I think how I must look very suspicious as I throw the car into gear, then pull quickly out into traffic and drive away.

31

I head out of town in a cautious hurry, keeping within shouting distance of the speed limit so I don't get pulled over.

I can't wrap my head around the fact I received a note telling me to kill a man, and now Matthew is dead. I don't know what to think.

All I know is that Mom thinks I should run. And while the idea gives me some pause, I know Mom only has my best interests at heart, so I'm taking her advice.

When I get out of town, I pull over and park in front of a strip mall to catch my breath. Using my phone, I check online for news of Matthew's death, but there's nothing being reported.

Back on the road, I drive to the bank, which is close to Nora's apartment. It's just after ten o'clock in the morning when I step inside. Before I get out of the car, I go to take my sunglasses off but then remember I'm technically on the run. Better to leave them on.

The bank is located in an old brick building. One of the

tellers calls for the manager when I explain why I'm here. A few customers lounge in comfortable-looking chairs in the waiting area, while overhead a couple of TVs with the sound off, but captions on, air morning programming.

A man about my age wearing a nice charcoal suit and stylish glasses appears a minute later, leading me into his office. The room is small and stuffy, not quite big enough for his desk and the two chairs facing it. The manager asks me for some identification. I get that dread feeling in my stomach as I hand him my driver's license. His fingers dance on his keyboard while his eyes search a computer monitor I can't see from where I'm sitting. I wait, occasionally looking over my shoulder to check on the people in the lobby. Any moment I expect the police to come bursting in with weapons drawn, barking orders for me to come out with my hands up.

"Here you are, Ms. Christie," the manager says with a smile.

I take back my driver's license.

"Please come with me."

He leads me down a short hall into a small room. On three walls are rows of safety-deposit boxes. Most of them are small, but a few are noticeably larger.

"I'll just be outside," the manager says, pointing to the door. "If you need help with anything, please let me know."

"Thank you."

He smiles neutrally, then steps out into the hallway and closes the door behind him. My eyes immediately search the room for cameras. I don't notice any, but they have to be here, right? Unless they're not allowed to video you while you open a safety-deposit box? I don't know if there is a law for or against this and wish I knew, but an overwhelming sense of urgency compels me to act. I find my box, open it with the key Nora gave me, and pull out a thick manila folder.

I plop the folder onto the table in the middle of the room and open it up and peer inside without taking anything out. Sure enough, there's a bunch of cash. Two wigs, one red and the other blonde, are in the bottom of the folder. I root around without taking anything out, just in case there are cameras in here, and find several fake IDs and one curious item at the very bottom. It's a small gray box with three buttons. It resembles a key fob for a car.

Has Mom left me a vehicle to use, one the police won't be looking for?

If she has, though, I have no idea where the car might be. I root some more in the folder, hoping to find a note explaining what this thing is. After moving one of the wigs out of the way, I spot a folded piece of paper, but then another item catches my eye.

A pink comb.

I gasp at the sight of it. Could this really be ...?

I'm pressed for time, but I take a moment to examine the comb. It's not the one from Mom's childhood. This comb looks new, like it's never been used. The thought of Mom making a sentimental gesture like this chokes me up.

But I don't have time to be nostalgic. I've got to get out of this bank immediately. I can read the note Mom left for me later, when I'm somewhere safe.

While I seal up the envelope, I can't help but wonder how Mom got her hands on all this money, not to mention the fake IDs. How did she ever manage to come up with money while she was living on the run? I've puzzled over that question often, my mind going to some dark places when I do. Somehow, she got the key to the safety-deposit box to Nora. With a warrant out for her arrest, I doubt Mom walked into this bank. Then again, she must have used a bank at some point in the last thirty years, right? Either way, when news of the murders broke, Mom must have gotten the idea to set up a safety-deposit box for me.

I stuff the envelope into my already crowded purse, then leave the room. The manager asks if there's anything else he can do for me. I tell him no and keep walking.

As we enter the lobby, I notice some unusual activity in the waiting area. Several of the customers are now standing, one of them is pointing at the TV screen overhead, and a couple of employees have come out from behind the counter to watch with them.

The manager notices the commotion as well. "What's going on here?"

Everyone stops what they're doing and turns to look at me. And I *know*. Right away. Without even seeing the TV screen.

I've made the news.

The manager doesn't know what's happening, though. One of his employees mutely gestures at the TV while the others stare pointedly at me. I've already made up my mind. I am leaving. The manager veers to his left to see what they're all watching.

I feel everyone's eyes on me as I pick up my pace and stride toward the exit. The manager reaches the waiting area, and one of his employees quietly and hurriedly explains something to him. The door is only ten feet away from me when the manager says: "Excuse me, ma'am."

I don't stop. I don't even slow down. The door is right in front of me.

"Ma'am, would you wait a moment?"

I push the door open and break into a jog. There's no use in pretending anymore.

I zoom out of the parking lot. A chorus of angry car horns blares at me as I cut across traffic, make a dangerous left turn, and whip down another street. I don't know where I can go, but I have to move as quickly as I can.

32

I stay off the interstate. Using my phone, I find a relatively quick route that will take me out of the state. My white-knuckled grip on the steering wheel doesn't let up until I'm a good thirty minutes away from the bank. I find a secluded spot on a lonely stretch of highway to pull over, parking in a turn-off and practically nosing my vehicle into a line of trees.

Breathe.

I get out of the car to move around. My adrenaline is surging. My legs won't stop shaking. With jittery hands and a heavy feeling in my stomach, I use my phone to check the news.

Matthew Lopez found dead this morning ...

Authorities are searching for his ex-girlfriend. This woman, famous author Amanda Christie ...

Breaking News: What we are about to tell you is almost too incredible to believe. In a shocking and ironic turn of events, a note was discovered in Matthew Lopez's apartment. In this message, Matthew goes on to describe, in great detail, how he aided his ex-girlfriend in murdering Megan Patterson and Sarah Keller. He went on to claim that he began to fear for his own life when Ms. Christie threatened him ...

I stagger through the woods and emerge in a snowy field. A red house sits in the pallid distance on a little rise. I picture the family inside that home, living out their very ordinary lives. I wonder what that must be like, to have a spouse to come home to, to have children to raise. These are things I've always wanted, and in this moment of despair, these are things I want all the more now that I almost certainly cannot have them.

I lean my weight against a tree, then slide down its bark till I'm squatting in the snow. My breath comes out in ragged, foggy blasts.

For all these years, I've often thought about what Mom's life was like. Always on the run, shedding one fake identity for another, a never-ending grind of hiding and emerging, always looking over your shoulder. Just waiting to be caught.

Now I'm beginning to understand what it's really like.

I feel like I should cry, but all this is still too raw: I've been hit in the face, but I'm still in that half-ignorant state where I know it will hurt, but it doesn't hurt just yet.

Then my phone buzzes.

Hoping it's Mom, I pull the phone out of my pocket. The call is from the same number Mom used to warn me only a few hours ago.

"Mom?"

"Hello, Amanda."

33

I t's not my mother.

     I recognize the female voice on the line, but I can't place it.

"Who is this?"

"I've found your mother."

I shoot up, back on my feet. I repeat, "Who is this?"

"If you want to see her again, then you're going to do exactly what I say."

I *know* this voice.

"No, you're going to do exactly what I say," I answer. "You will let her go, or I'll contact the police."

The other woman laughs. "That's the emptiest threat I've ever heard. The police will arrest you for all these murders."

"I haven't killed anybody."

"Try telling that to them."

"I'm innocent. I'll take my chances."

"They're not going to believe you."

The way she says it sends a chill through my body. "Why not?"

"Because if they haven't already, they're going to find the murder weapons in your house very shortly."

The ground beneath me starts to spin.

The woman laughs again. "I've been to your house. It's pretty nice, though not as nice as mine used to be."

"You're the killer," I say. "You put the weapons there."

"It wasn't hard to get a key to your house," she says. "People are so predictable, you know. That neighbor of yours, Rebecca, I found where she kept your spare key. Right there in the junk drawer."

"You broke into Rebecca's house—why didn't you just break into mine? That doesn't make any sense."

"Oh, come on, Amanda. You write mysteries and thrillers. Do I have to explain everything to you?"

"You didn't break into my house because that would be too obvious."

"Ah, good. Now you're thinking like the hack writer you are. And by the way, you really *are* a hack. I've read all your *novels,* for lack of a better word. They're insultingly stupid and unintentionally funny. You don't know a thing about life. Your killers are laughable, and your heroes are zero-dimensional. I'd ask for my money back, but I never pay to read your shlock. I've left scathing one-star reviews of them all, and I make damned sure it's hard to find your books in stores."

So—she's the one who's been intentionally facing my books backwards on the shelves or misplacing them altogether.

"Who are you?" I ask.

"If you want to find out, you'll do exactly as I say. Or *I'll* tell the police where they can find your mother."

"NO! Don't do that! Just tell me what you want."

"Meet me at the Lee Mill Building tonight, at eight o'clock."

The Lee Mill Building? That's where Mom and Nora used to work.

I'm about to ask why she wants to meet there. But in that nanosecond it takes the words to travel from my brain to my mouth, I get an epiphany. Everything comes into sharp focus.

"Why are you doing this?" I ask.

It's a leading question. I think I know. And it remains unanswered.

"Eight o'clock. If you ever want to see your mother again, come alone."

34

Mom would tell me to run.

She wouldn't want me "wasting my life" trying to help her.

But I'd never forgive myself if I abandoned her. This woman risked incarceration *just to see me graduate high school.* And then college. This woman intervened when I was about to be date-raped in college. She's always figured out a way to be there, to help me, in big and small ways, all the while living on the run.

Her life cannot end like this, either in prison or ...

I have to say it.

... or murdered by this lunatic.

An oddly wonderful feeling comes over me: I don't care what happens to me. Mom is all that matters. If the police catch me, I'll take my chances in court, knowing that I'm innocent and didn't kill anyone. I'm not strong enough to live a life on the run like Mom has. I'd rather take my chances trying to clear my name.

After only a few hours of my own fugitive existence, I don't know how Mom lasted this long.

I take a few minutes to think everything over. You never know when your life is coming to a head until it's just about to.

When I'm certain, I drive to a mall about thirty minutes away. Donning one of the wigs and some big sunglasses, I head inside to pass the time and find something to eat. While I'm there, I take out the burner phone left for me in the safety-deposit box and download an app.

I need to lie low for a few hours, so I walk to the far end of the mall and buy a ticket at the movie theater for whatever film is about to start. It's some dumb romantic comedy, but it doesn't matter. I just need someplace dark to hide. When the lights dim in the theater, I take off my sunglasses and sit back. I'm vaguely aware of the movie as it plays out on the screen before me, but by the time it's over, I have no idea what happened. I sit through the end credits, then get up to leave when the cleaning crew arrives.

I use the burner phone to call for a taxi so I can pay cash. I'd rather Uber, but I don't want to leave an electronic trail. While I'm waiting, I take out one of the fake IDs from the safety-deposit box. According to this one, my name is Karen Cohen, which is easy enough to remember. Karen Cohen. Karen Cohen. Karen Cohen. I repeat it in my head over and over.

I wait outside a department store for the taxi, my sunglasses hiding my eyes. I've got my heavy winter coat on, a hood over my red wig, and a scarf covering most of my face. I don't think a passerby would pay me any mind, never mind recognize me. A cop might, but I'm over an hour from home, and I seriously doubt the police would think to look for me in this random mall of all places.

While I'm waiting, a light snow begins to fall.

Before the taxi arrives, there's someone I have to talk to. Taking out my phone, I dial Brandon's number.

"Hello?"

"Brandon," I say, "it's me."

"Oh, hey, Chuck," he says, sounding a bit theatrical. "Everything okay at the store?"

There must be someone standing nearby.

"Alright," he says. "Give me a moment."

I hear him walking; then a door closes. He doesn't speak for another moment, and when he does, it sounds like he's outside.

"*Amanda?*" He lets out a big breath. "Are you okay? The police are looking for you."

"I know." I can't help but smile. I'm the prime suspect in three murders, yet Brandon is *worried* about me. "I didn't do any of those things, Brandon. I—"

"I know you didn't," he says.

"How can you be so sure?"

"I told you before." He sighs, and there's a note of what sounds like regret in his voice. "You're a good person. Anybody can see that."

"Brandon, what's wrong?"

"Nothing," he says unconvincingly. "I'm just worried about you."

It's perfectly clear that he's holding something back.

"We might never get the chance to speak again," I say, my heart sinking. "So whatever it is, you might as well come out with it."

"You're a good person, Mandy." He's choking up. "You don't deserve this."

I suddenly feel that I could cry too. "Thank you."

He clears his throat. When he speaks again, his voice is no longer strained. Now he speaks with urgency.

"Mandy, listen to me." He lowers his voice. "You have to run. Let me help you."

"I'm not calling for help," I say. "I wanted to apologize."

"*Apologize?*" he asks, dumbfounded. "What for?"

"I should have stayed the other night," I say. "I should have let you explain."

"No." He's adamant. "No, you were right to leave. Finding all those books locked away in a closet, that must have been so creepy."

"I should have *listened*," I say. "When we found out Megan Patterson was murdered, you didn't rush to judge me. *You* listened. And when I told you about everything else, about Matthew, you could have ghosted me. I wouldn't have blamed you. All along, you've given me the benefit of the doubt, and I never once did the same for you. I thought you were too good to be true, so when I found my books in your closet, I felt vindicated. But the truth is, you really are a great guy."

"Don't put me on a pedestal. I'm not as good as you think I am."

His voice is so full of emotion; he sounds like he wants to die.

"I wish things were different," I say. "Maybe if none of this had happened, we could have ..."

"Forget all that. You need to run. It's your only chance."

I start to cry appreciative tears. "You're a great guy, Brandon, you know that?"

I hear him draw a sudden breath. Is he going to cry?

"I'm sorry." My voice is thick. "But I don't want to drag you down with me."

"Mandy ..."

"Brandon, if I get clear of this, could we go out again? I'd like that."

"Forget about me. Now listen to me, Mandy. I mean it. Run."

A taxi pulls up to the curb in front of the department store. I step out from behind a pillar into the light of the parking lot. I wish I could tell him why that's exactly the one thing I won't do.

"Goodbye, Brandon."

"Mandy—"

Before my resolve completely crumbles, I end the call.

AN OLD APARTMENT complex sits two blocks away from the Lee Mill Building, where Mom and Nora used to work at the credit company with David West. After I get out of the cab, I pretend like I'm going inside the apartment building. When the car rounds a bend, I turn around and gaze into the distance.

The Lee Mill Building has been closed for a long time now. I remember reading about it in the paper and discussing the closure with Nora. The old, now-derelict building sits in darkness up the road. When it originally opened back in my great-grandparents' day, it was a tire factory. Then it was converted into office space. The credit company where Mom worked was one of the first new businesses to move in.

I cross the road in darkness while the light snow turns heavy—it's already sticking on the streets. A few cars wobble past on the slick roads; one of them is unable to brake and fails to stop at the red light in front of the apartment building.

It's almost eight o'clock now. The air is getting colder, the snow is growing denser and denser, and I'm walking to what will probably be my death. I reach into my pocket and look down at my burner phone. After punching a few buttons, I confirm the app is running in the digital background. Unless you know where to look, you'd have no idea it's active.

The building's large entrance faces the street. I ascend stairs that have not been cleared of snow, noting the lack of footprints. A few of the windows along the building's front are missing; some are shattered.

The door groans open. Inside, the air is just as frigid as outside. I take out my burner phone and activate the flashlight. I haven't been here in thirty years. I don't remember this foyer or the hallway leading into more darkness. There's a musty smell about the building, and somewhere water is dripping. Having been abandoned years ago, now it looks like a place where homeless people might shelter in bad weather, or where criminals come to make drug deals.

I take out my gun.

Pointing the phone and gun ahead, I start down the hallway. An old, worn sign on the wall lists the businesses that used to be located in this direction. The credit company occupied suite 300.

Shining the light from the phone down the hallway, I make out various objects. A few chairs are overturned on the floor near a rotting wooden desk. Old bits of junk and shreds of paper litter the place. That musty smell is stronger here.

"Hello?" I call out.

No answer.

I move silently down the hallway. My pulse throbs in my neck. The door to the first suite on my left is missing. I peer inside, seeing more abandoned furniture and a huge mess of trash and tattered, broken stuff. I press on. The next door is open, revealing a completely empty office inside. Suite 300 is only twenty paces away when someone speaks to me.

The voice does not belong to the woman who spoke to me on the phone earlier.

"Put the gun down, Amanda."

35

Brandon's words are followed by the unmistakable click of a firearm.

I freeze.

I know it's the worst thing I can do in this situation. But none of my admittedly scant self-defense training prepared me for the moment when someone points a gun at my back and issues an order. Ideally, I'd run. Less ideally, I'd whip around and start shooting. But I freeze.

Brandon's voice is the last one I expected to hear.

"Drop the gun," he says. "Please."

His voice is *alien*. Slowly, I lower my weapon but do not drop it. Then I begin to turn around.

"Don't make me shoot you. Please drop the gun."

"Okay."

I drop the gun. It hits the musty carpet with a dull thud, bouncing once, then stopping suddenly like some lifeless thing. Without being told, I raise my hands.

"Now the phone," he says.

I do the same with the phone. It lands on its screen and

flips over, the flashlight momentarily blinding me. Behind me, I hear a different sort of click, and then I'm bathed in light from Brandon's direction.

He comes around, keeping his distance and aiming a gun at me. It's a handgun, similar to mine, but his also comes with a silencer. As he passes, he collects my burner phone and stuffs it into a pocket.

I can't help it. I get choked up.

"Wh—why?"

"Your mother ruined our lives."

"Our?"

"That's right, honey." This next voice comes from the doorway just up ahead, the one opening to suite 300. It belongs to the same woman who called me earlier. "*Our* lives. Brandon, sweetheart, make sure to pat her down."

I feel his gun press into my back. All he has to do is move one finger an inch and I'll be dead. I stiffen at the thought, while Brandon runs his free hand up and down my legs and then checks my pockets. He finds the small gray box.

"Stun gun!" Brandon calls out, seizing the device.

I'd thought Mom had left me a car somewhere, but after reading the short note in the manila folder, I discovered that the box was a self-defense tool. Its three buttons activate a flashlight, an ear-piercing whistle, and a stun gun.

"What else?"

Brandon takes my wallet and keys, then roots around in my winter jacket, eventually finding the last item on my person.

"I got her keys and wallet," Brandon says. "The only other thing is a comb."

Brandon comes around to stand in front of me, still

pointing his weapon at me. He's holding the pink comb Mom left for me in his other hand.

"Figures," the woman calls out. "As vain as her mother. Now bring her in here."

Brandon has already pocketed my wallet, keys, phone, and the gray box. It seems like he can't be bothered to hold onto the comb, so he returns it to my jacket pocket.

He motions. "Let's go."

Before I can get my head around the fact that Brandon has been playing me this entire time, he's forcing me into the office suite at gunpoint.

"How can you do this?" I ask, desperate to reach some human part of him. "I thought we—"

"We weren't anything," he says. "Now do what she says."

I can't help but notice that he answers a bit too quickly. That could be because he's telling the truth now. Or it could be because he *did* develop some feelings for me but now must pretend like it didn't happen in order to complete whatever sick revenge fantasy is about to play out.

My only hope is that Brandon does care for me. And that I can reach that part of him. Thinking back over our last conversation on the phone, he *did* urge me to run.

He shoves me toward the office. "Go."

This is all my fault.

No rational person would have given me the benefit of the doubt when both Megan and Sarah turned up dead, killed in such gruesome fashions that were so eerily reminiscent of events from my novels. But Brandon did. Those developments didn't even give him pause. They should have. His reaction—or lack thereof—should have been a huge red flag.

Granted, there *were* times when I questioned whether

Brandon could be that nice. Whether *anyone* could be that kind. But every time those doubts arose in my mind, I dismissed them.

I guess I have Matthew to thank for that.

It's only now, when I'm being herded toward my death, that I realize what was driving me all along. After the fallout with Matthew, after enduring yet another bad relationship and another long, lonely stretch of being single, I was so desperate to meet a nice man that I ignored all the glaring problems with Brandon.

And now I'm going to pay the ultimate price for my poor judgment.

Again, the woman calls out, "Bring her in here."

Brandon jams the gun harder into my back. I have no choice but to obey. This isn't a movie, and what little self-defense training I did years ago hasn't equipped me for this scenario either. Besides, Mom is in danger too. What else can I do? If I'm going to die anyway, at least I'll get to see Mom one more time.

"Let's go, Amanda," he says.

I detect what I think is a note of sadness, possibly regret, in his voice as he speaks. But I could very well be imagining that. When people are about to die, they're prone to wishful thinking.

I look over my shoulder at him, hoping to spot some glimpse of humanity behind those eyes. Brandon holds my stare, unabashed.

"I don't care anymore," I say. "Shoot me if you must. Whatever. But know this: I'm only stepping into this office because it feels like my only hope of ever seeing my mother once more. Not because you told me to."

Brandon arches an eyebrow, surprised by my sudden

boldness. I'm just as astonished. The words came out of my mouth, but it feels like someone else spoke them.

He purses his lips, and this time I'm almost certain of what I see.

A touch of doubt in his eyes.

I step into the office.

"Hello, Amanda."

36

The office where Mom used to work is a chaotic, rotting, trash-filled mess. There are industrial-sized trash cans inside the suite, giving the impression that, at some point, a work crew came in to clean the place up but abandoned their project, deeming the place too far gone. A couple of battery-powered lights cast a blue glow around the office.

Amid this disarray stands a woman.

I know her.

She has gray-white hair. I normally see her at the writers' group meetings, wearing a KN95 mask. She rarely participates. Instead, she's usually got her head down, her eyes focused on whatever she's knitting.

"Louann," I say.

Louann is also holding a gun. But she's not pointing it at me.

"Come in," she says.

I don't understand what's happening. What does this woman have against me? What does she have against Mo—

Oh my God.

Everything clicks into place. I can see the whole picture now, with breathtaking clarity, even though I'm having a hard time *believing* it.

Louann motions. "Up against that wall."

When I stall, Brandon shoves me from behind. There's nothing gentle about it. Maybe there was no humanity in his eyes; maybe I didn't hear regret in his voice. Now I'm back to doubting myself again.

I stumble forward, losing my balance. I'm going to run headfirst into a pillar, but Brandon is suddenly there, grabbing my arm and preventing me from falling.

If they're just going to kill me, why would he bother to do that?

Brandon herds me toward the wall where Louann wants me. She stands there, admiring me like I'm some piece of artwork she's never been able to afford.

Until now.

"God, you look just like your whore mother," Louann says. "*Just* like her."

"You're David West's wife," I say.

"I *was*," she answers. "Till I had to kill him."

I've always suspected it was Louann. But actually hearing the words from the woman herself is still jarring.

"You murdered your own husband?"

"I—"

"Mom," Brandon cuts in, "could we just get this over with?"

Mom?

Brandon sounds like he wants to be anywhere else but here. His mother might be chomping at the bit to murder me, but he certainly isn't relishing this moment.

"Slow down, boy," Louann answers. "Your father screwed up my perfect moment twenty-seven years ago. Ever since, I've been waiting for this, and I'll not have you spoil it."

Brandon nods, turns his attention back to me.

"You're her *son*?" I ask.

"And David's," he says.

Oh God ... what if that means Brandon and I are ...

He can tell what I'm thinking.

"You're not *my sister*," Brandon mutters quickly. "Dad never got your mother pregnant."

"But how do you know?"

"It wasn't hard to get your DNA," Louann says. "Took it right off a coffee cup from the bookstore and got a paternity test. Your tramp of a mother got around. Somebody else knocked her up. That lying bitch, she probably told David you were his to trap him into leaving me."

It's all too much.

I'm shaking my head. Is she lying to me? I don't know. But given the fact that I'm being held at gunpoint, and I'm pretty sure they plan on murdering me, she doesn't have much of a reason to lie.

"You've killed all these people," I say. "Because you hate my mother?"

"I am what I am." Louann grins wickedly. "I didn't pick my parents. I didn't pick my genes. I didn't get to choose how I was raised. I didn't choose to be this way."

"*That's* your excuse?" I ask. "You couldn't *control* yourself?"

She scoffs. "I live in a place beyond excuses, you silly, prosaic woman. There is no right and wrong. There is only what is."

"You killed David, then left that note implicating my mother?"

"Yes. And I made sure your mother's DNA was everywhere." Louann crosses the room in a flash, surprising me with her speed and agility. She gets right in my face. "*I'm* the one who ruined your mother's life. It was the least I could do, since she ruined mine."

I realize I'm talking to an irrational, psychotic woman. But I still want to make some sense of her actions.

"Why didn't you kill my mother in the first place?" I ask. "If she's the one who ruined your life? Then David could have been all yours."

Her eyes narrow. "Even though I was pregnant, David still asked for a divorce. I realized no matter what I did, he was never going to be mine again. If I couldn't have him, then I wasn't going to let your whore mother have him either." The words tumble out of her in a manic stream. "The plan was to kill them both. I forced David at gunpoint to call her that morning and beg her to come over, pretending he wanted to share the good news of our divorce. Then, before that whore bitch arrived, David tried to be a hero. I had to kill him. The man attacked me, even though I was carrying his fucking child!"

Being angry that a man would defend himself is utter insanity, but clearly Louann—practically frothing at the mouth now—is too far gone to realize that.

"I was worried the neighbors heard our struggle and figured I didn't have the time to hang around to kill your slut mother. I'd already hidden the key to the safety-deposit box in his desk that would lead the cops to that fake letter I wrote. I left the rest of the evidence, including strands of your mother's hair I'd found on David's clothes, near the body. Then I ran."

"I knew it was you," I say. "I knew it all along."

"Yeah." She smirks. "But you could never prove it. I pretended to go upstate to see my parents, to get treatment, but that was all a lie. Unlike David, my parents were loyal to me. When the police questioned them, they gave me an alibi, and by then I was already checked into a ward. Everything worked perfectly, except your mother got away."

"She has suffered for it," I say.

"Not enough!"

I know that this woman could kill me any time she chooses, but I refuse to be silenced.

"You ruined her whole life."

"You want to talk about ruined lives? What about mine? What about Brandon's? David was the only man who'd ever loved me. He promised me a charmed life full of cocktail parties and country club memberships and trips to Europe. He promised me I'd never have to work a day and that our children would only have the best. That whore stole all that from me."

"So," I say, "where is my mother?"

Louann looks to her son. "Bring her out."

Brandon walks to the other side of the office and enters what appears to be a storage closet. He doesn't seem all that eager to be doing what he's doing, but that's a far cry from him turning suddenly into my hero. Even if he refuses to obey, he won't necessarily *stop* his mother doing what she wants.

A moment later he wheels my mother out. She's attached to a swivel chair with duct tape and ropes. Her mouth is gagged and taped. When she sees me, she immediately struggles to break free of her bonds, straining in a frenzy against the duct tape and rope. But her efforts are in vain.

Mom bites down on the gag; then she screams as best she can. It comes out muffled and choked. Her voice is hoarse like she's been shouting for a long time. I sense they've had her tied up and gagged for a while.

"Mom." I start to walk over. I'm going to hug my mother if it's the last thing I do. "I'm sorry."

Louann steps between us and jams the gun under my chin. "Don't you move an inch. You don't get to touch her!"

My jaw trembles at the touch of cold metal.

"What are you going to do to us?" I ask.

"I think you know this doesn't end well," Louann says.

"You ready, Mom?" Brandon asks, sounding nervous. "We got them both where we want them."

My mother lets out another anguished, muffled shout.

"Shut that bitch up," Louann orders her son.

Brandon hesitates. It's only a brief moment, but he definitely pauses. Then he hits her on the side of the head with the butt of his gun. Mom immediately falls silent as her head lolls to the side.

"Don't touch her!" I shout.

Louann clamps her free hand over my mouth. "Shhhhh."

"Alright, Mom," Brandon says again. "Can we do this?"

"Slow down, Bran," Louann answers. "I want to savor this. That bitch is going to *witness* her daughter's murder."

Mom makes a defeated noise as her head whips back up at those words.

"All this time," Louann says. She backs away but keeps the gun trained on me while she turns to eye Mom. "Every few years we hired a new PI to track you down, but nobody could. You were too good at hiding. It cost us a fortune."

She laughs.

"I should say, it cost my in-laws a fortune. I threatened to tell the world what their boy was really like, at home, when nobody else was around: how he didn't love me, how he slept around, how he put his hands on me. All lies, of course. But they did what I asked: they gave me a ton of money and told me to keep quiet. They had never approved of me, a girl from the wrong side of town who was also a little crazy. They wanted nothing to do with their grandson either, poor Brandon. But we've lived off their payoff ever since. While this whore here"—she brandishes the gun in my mom's direction—"was the prime suspect, there were whispers from enough people who thought I might have killed David. To get away from it all, I changed my name and went under the knife."

She runs her free hand over her face.

"I had that doctor carve my beautiful face, and I changed my name and gave Brandon his own last name too, a different one. All that. All those things. All this time, looking for you. I've waited more than half my life for this moment. I'd almost given up hope of finding you, then that story broke about Amanda being your daughter, and I saw my opportunity. Brandon and I moved into town together and began our work."

As I listened to her awful words, it all began to make sense. I was outed as Kimberly Dawn Allen's daughter a year ago. Brandon and his mom used that time to watch and study me, identify my enemies and my weaknesses, work out how to exploit my patterns of behavior. I thought how they must have squeezed a lot of money out of David's parents— that explains Brandon living in such a big house while working at a bookstore café.

Louann faces me again. The gun is so steady in her hand. No nerves. This woman is a monster.

"For the last year we've gotten to know everything there is to know about you, Amanda. And what an absolute boring waste of a life you lead, writing your silly stories about fake people. The highlight of your week is going to yoga, of all things. You're so *ordinary*. You're so *pathetic*. You're not even worthy of my hatred or vengeance. The only reason you're special is because you are your mother's daughter."

"You left the notes on my porch," I say.

She nods. "The notes were another link in the chain of evidence we were creating. We wanted you to give them to the police. The detectives would naturally assume they were coming from your mother. We wanted them thinking you two were working together to kill anybody who was a threat to you."

"Just like in that story you wrote," Brandon says, his voice neutral. "The one where the killer sends notes to the hero so the innocent person looks guilty."

I ignore him and keep my eyes on Louann. "But I was two minutes from walking into a police station this morning. If Mom hadn't gone to Matthew's house, none of this would have worked."

"I was due some luck." Louann shrugs. "Fate is on my side. The cops would have arrested you, and your whore mother would have suffered that way. Who knows, maybe she would have come forward and confessed to the crimes so you could go free? Either way, I would have gotten what I wanted eventually. Everything would have worked itself out."

I don't believe in fate, but she's right. Mom would have done anything to keep me away from prison.

My mind is racing. Things are coming to a head. Louann is going to shoot me. It doesn't matter that I can prove I was with Brandon the night Sarah was murdered: the police will simply think my mother took care of her on my behalf.

Brandon is standing to the right of and slightly behind Mom. He might have his mother's psychopathic tendencies, but he doesn't have her steady hand. The gun aimed at Mom is shaking. Brandon is nervous.

And maybe, just maybe, he has *some* feelings for me.

"The whole world is going to think," Louann goes on, "that you quarreled and killed each other. Mother and daughter, two killers. The whole world is going to think that Kimberly Dawn Allen and her girl were murderous, psychotic *monsters.*"

I look into Mom's eyes.

I've never seen her cry before. And this would be the time for it. We're beaten. But Mom's not crying. There's a hard, fierce look in her eyes.

With just a look, Mom always knew what I was thinking. Somehow, some way, she knew what was happening inside this brain of mine. But that was a long time ago.

Can she still read my mind after all these years?

Mom nods once, almost imperceptibly. She's done it. She's read my mind. She knows exactly what to do.

Louann smiles cruelly at me. "This is going to hurt, Amanda. A lot."

"Your son isn't going to let you kill me," I say.

Louann's smile slowly vanishes. "What the hell did you say?"

My body is trembling, but I put some steel in my voice. "Brandon loves me."

"What?" He laughs, but it comes out sounding shrill.

"What are you talking about?"

Louann keeps her eyes on me. I just need her to look away, only for a moment. I remember that much from my self-defense classes: a person can close a distance of fifteen feet surprisingly quickly.

"Oh, you didn't know?" I ask. "He keeps a shrine to me in that house of his."

"You're lying." Louann shakes her head. "You're a lying bitch, just like your whore mother."

"Don't believe me?" I challenge. "Then ask him."

"She's *lying,* Mom," Brandon says.

I suppress a smile. Now I *know* I've got him in a bad spot. It doesn't mean I'm safe—in fact, Mom and I are still probably going to die.

But there's a *chance.*

"He has all my books in that upstairs closet in the hallway. Hardbacks and paperbacks of each one. I think I even saw some foreign editions as well."

"Brandon," Louann says, keeping her eyes on me, "is any of this true?"

"No, Mom!" he says, sounding like a whiny child who's been caught red-handed—and who knows it. "Don't listen to her."

"You told him to get close to me," I go on. "But that was a mistake, because he ended up falling in love."

"Brandon." Louann's voice is icy. "You'd better not ha—"

"He warned me," I say, shooting a quick look at Mom. She nods, understanding that I'm about to make my move. "Brandon doesn't want me to die, but he's afraid of you, so he warned me. He told me to run."

"You're lying," Louann hisses.

"The police will be here any moment."

"She's lying," Brandon says, his eyes popping. "Mom, I would never betray you."

"Do you want to kill them?" Louann asks.

"I ..." Brandon hesitates. "I know why you want to kill Kim, and I won't stop you."

Louann motions with her gun at me. "And what about this bitch over here?"

Brandon takes too long to answer. Finally, he squares his jaw and stares defiantly at his mother. "She didn't do anything to us."

Louann squeezes her eyes shut for just a moment. "I can't believe you, boy. After everything we've been through together, now you turn soft on me?"

"Please, Mom."

"Think about it, Louann," I say, happy to add more fuel to the fire. "He was willing to help you murder three people he didn't even know: Megan, Sarah, Matthew. But he can't bring himself to kill me. That can only mean one thing—he was happy to see my enemies dead but obviously doesn't want to hurt me."

"SHUT UP!" she screeches.

She's very close to shooting me in a blind rage now, but I have to get her to take her eyes off me for this to work. I turn so I'm more facing Brandon, hoping my posture draws Louann's eyes toward her son.

"The police are coming," I say.

Louann's face has turned red with fury. But she hasn't looked at Brandon yet.

"I SAID SHUT UP!"

Louann takes one step closer to me, and I'm dead certain she's going to pull the trigger. But there's no gunshot. The shock of discovering her son has feelings for Kimberly Dawn

Allen's daughter is enough to throw her, at least momentarily, off her game.

I wince, using her action as the excuse I need to bring my hands back up. While Louann trembles with rage, I slowly lower my rear hand so it's hovering over my coat pocket. Everything is set. It's now or never. I have to get her to look at Brandon.

I can't keep my voice from trembling now. My adrenaline surges.

"Mom, I'm sorry," Brandon says. "I didn't mean for it to happen. But the longer I watched her, the more I ..."

A lone tear escapes from Louann's eye.

Brandon tries to harden his voice. "But I swear she's lying about the cops."

"She'd better be, Brandon. Or there will be repercussions."

Brandon lowers his head a moment, as if he's ashamed of what he's done.

"Look at him," I say. "Look into your son's eyes. You'll see the truth."

Louann wavers. For a moment I'm certain she's going to kill us first, then ask Brandon questions later. That would be the wise course of action. The rational choice.

But this woman is not rational.

Keeping the gun pointed at me, she turns her head to look at her son.

I reach into my pocket and rush Louann. At the same time, Mom pushes with her tippy-toes, and the swivel chair crashes into Brandon. Surprised by the sudden force of Mom's attack, Brandon fires his gun, seemingly accidentally. Louann senses my movement and whirls back around, gun pointed straight at me.

37

But before Louann can fire, I'm driving a three-inch knife into her belly. Her eyes go wide as she drops the gun and stumbles away from me into the column behind her, her hands reaching for her midsection. She grips the short pink handle of the knife.

The pink comb was a disguised weapon. After reading Mom's short note, I knew exactly what it was and how to use it. There's a tiny button along one side, above the teeth of the comb, that releases the handle and separates both halves, exposing the needle-like blade. Brandon had no idea, of course, so he gave it right back to me.

I stoop to pick up Louann's gun. Though the woman must be in agony, a murderous look fills her eyes, and she pushes away from the column to attack me. I squeeze off several shots. At this range, I don't miss. Louann's body shudders with each bullet, and she flies backward, her head hitting the pillar on her way down to the floor.

Mom is still bound to the swivel chair, unable to use her hands, and Brandon easily manages to get away from her.

Wide-eyed, he takes one sorrowful look at his mother. There's a lot of blood around her, and she's not moving. I point the gun at him.

"Don't, Brandon."

Tears streak his face as he stands there, staring dumbly at his mother.

"You killed her," he says, as if surprised.

I don't know what else he expected me to do.

"But I searched you," he says next, his voice pained.

I reach into my pocket with my free hand and toss the upper half of the pink comb at him. "You should have kept this."

Brandon flinches when the comb hits his chest before falling to the floor.

Mom has managed to get one hand free and is now ripping off the duct-tape gag.

"Amanda, you've got to shoot him."

I've already killed Louann. Even though I was totally justified in doing so, it's not an experience I wish to repeat.

"Amanda!" Mom urges.

Brandon stoops and picks up the gun he dropped when Mom crashed into him in the chair.

"DON'T!" I scream.

His weapon is aimed at the floor. Without raising the gun, he looks down at it. I can see his mind working.

"Brandon, put the gun down."

He won't look at me. "Megan deserved what she got. So did Sarah. And Matthew. They treated you horribly."

None of them deserved to die, but arguing with Brandon while he's holding a gun seems like a bad idea.

"Amanda, you have to shoot him," Mom urges.

Brandon finally meets my eyes.

"I do love you, you know."

"Brandon ..." I shake my head, sensing something terrible is about to happen. "Don't do anything stupid."

"I told you to run," he says, as if that warning were enough to make up for everything else. He gives me a sad smile. "Goodbye, Mandy."

He brings his gun up.

And I shoot him before he can fire. I hit him several times in the torso. He loses his balance, his gun goes flying, and he lands on his side next to Mom.

I hurry over to him, to see if he's still alive. There's a lot of blood, and his eyes are having trouble focusing.

"You have to run," he says, giving me one last smile. "The police will never believe you're innocent."

I reach into his pocket for my burner phone and hold it out for him to see.

"I recorded everything."

He closes his eyes and nods, looking almost happy. Then he goes very still. My eyes begin to well up. I'm not mourning this man, but I am deeply saddened by all this death his mother has wrought. It's all so senseless.

So meaningless.

"Amanda, behind you!"

I whip around to find Louann on her feet. She leans heavily against the desk by the pillar, pointing what must be Brandon's gun in our direction. She's unsteady on her feet and having trouble keeping the weapon still.

Louann's aim wavers between Mom and me. I get the sense she only has the strength for one shot, and she's trying to decide which one of us to kill. Before I can raise my own weapon, however, Louann makes up her mind and points the gun at Mom. Without thinking, I throw myself in that direction. Louann snaps off one shot and then slumps onto the desk before toppling to the ground. I feel a pinch, then land on my side.

For a moment, I think the bullet merely grazed me.

Then, all at once, the most agonizing pain I've ever felt hits me.

38

"Amanda!" Mom screams.

Mom has gotten herself out of the swivel chair. Before coming to my aid, she checks Louann's neck for a pulse. Finding none, she runs back over to me.

My side is sticky, and my leg feels warm from all the blood running down my body. I try to get up, but Mom gently pushes me back down.

"Stay still," she says.

I don't argue. I'm feeling light-headed, the pain in my side only getting worse. My body is one big throb.

Mom gentles the gun out of my hand, flicking the safety on.

"I've got you, baby girl," she says.

"I ..."

I'm fading. Is this what it's like to die? My vision is narrowing to a tunnel.

"You're going to be alright, Amanda," Mom says, but I can tell she's not sure. "You'll be fine."

She unzips my winter coat, and I sense her flinch at the sight of my gunshot wound.

"Mom ...?"

I make the mistake of looking down. There's a lot of blood.

"Hold on," Mom says.

She gets up and roots around.

"Mom ..."

Mom returns with a cell phone. She dials and waits.

I can hear the operator answer. "Nine-one-one, what's your emergency?"

"My daughter has been shot in the stomach. There's a lot of blood. We're inside the old Lee Mill Building." Mom gives the operator the street address and town. "Please send an ambulance quickly and the police."

"Mom ... you must go. They'll arrest you."

She shakes her head emphatically. "I'm never leaving you again."

EPILOGUE

"It's the big one," Melinda, my agent, announces over the phone.

I'm sitting at the kitchen table, my mother to my right. She gives me a proud grin.

"Okay," I say, taking a deep breath and preparing myself. I put her on speakerphone so Mom can hear both sides of the conversation. "What is it?"

When Melinda tells me the offer, I nearly fall out of my chair. Mom throws her head back and pumps a fist triumphantly. I ask Melinda to repeat the number—for a moment I can't believe I heard her correctly. But then she confirms the publisher's offer for my next advance.

"Congrats, Amanda," Melinda says when I've finally managed to get myself together. "You've definitely earned this one."

"Thank you," I say.

Mom reaches a hand out and rubs my shoulder, very proud of me. We'll call Nora later to share the great news.

With this money, I am going to figure out a way to help her buy the house she's always wanted.

I reach up and squeeze Mom's hand. We share an over-joyed moment, but then I turn my attention back to my phone call.

"Melinda, that's great news," I say. "But there's something I have to ask you."

"Okay," she says tentatively, picking up on my change of tone. "What is it?"

"I want an honest answer," I say, giving Mom a knowing look. "Did you leak my identity to the press?"

She pauses for a moment. "Amanda, I—"

"I talked to Avery over at Tory Imprint," I interrupt.

Throughout my decade of being a published author, I've attended dozens of writers' conferences and made plenty of connections. I'm not as plugged in as Melinda, but I do know people. Ever since I got out of the hospital and got Mom settled in with me, I've been quietly trying to figure out who leaked my identity to the press. Melinda has always vehe-mently denied it, and for the longest time I naively believed her. The thing is, Melinda has been my agent since the beginning of my career. She stuck with me through thick and thin, and I didn't *want* to believe she'd betray me like that.

"Oh." Melinda takes a deep breath. "Okay, don't be mad at me, but here's the thing. You were really struggling at the time, remember? And I liked your book, but I wasn't sure it was going to be the hit both you and I needed it to be."

"Is that a ye—"

She cuts me off. "And you were talking about quitting, remember? You were going to quit? You were afraid you were going to lose your full-time job because you were putting so much into your writing. Your life was—you were not in a good place, Amanda. With the books, with work, with Matthew, you really needed a break. I mean, the way you made it sound, you were going to be fired, and you were in real trouble, remember?"

"Melinda."

She doesn't stop.

"So I did what I thought was best. Remember you told me to do that? Early on in our relationship, you said always do what you think is best."

I did say that. But Melinda interpreted that expression pretty broadly if she thought it included leaking my true identity to the press.

"We were just sitting on this wonderful opportunity. For years, I mean, we sat on this wonderful marketing opportunity. There you were, daughter of Kimberly Dawn Allen, exorcising what must have been your many demons by writing these suspense thrillers. It was too perfect. And remember, for years, I said nothing."

"Melinda, I shared my identity with you in confidence."

"And I respected your wishes and your privacy. But things were reaching a crisis point, Amanda. As we sit here and talk about this three-book megadeal—your children's children won't have to worry about money, Amanda—it's probably difficult for you to put yourself back in that place you were, when the books weren't selling and you feared you'd lose your job."

"It's pretty easy, actually," I answer. "I'm a writer. Putting myself in different times and places is what I do for a living."

"I know that, and you're really good at it," Mel answers. She's oh so slick. She is an agent, after all. "All I'm saying is you need to take a step back and really think about where you were eighteen months ago versus where you are right now, Amanda. Obviously, it was your writing that got you to this point, but I have to say, and I think you have to admit, that I played a significant part in shaping your career. Remember when Cort Press was going to drop you? Remember when you didn't know how to finish that fourth book? I've been with you every step of the way."

"Until now," I say.

"Amanda," Mel says, her voice losing a little of her polish, "I understand you're upset with me, and you have every right to be, honestly. You're also riding high with this offer. With all these extreme emotions swirling, now is definitely not the time to make any major career decisions. You really need—"

"I *really* don't need you to tell me what I need," I answer. "You do realize, Melinda, that because you leaked my identity, Louann West and her son tracked me down, right? Three people were murdered, and then they nearly killed my mother and me."

"Yes, that was terrible," she says. "But, Amanda, you can hardly blame me for the actions of those lunatics. And look how everything turned out. Kimberly Dawn Allen was exonerated—"

People still refer to my mother like that, even though the whole world knows she's not a murderer. It drives me nuts.

"Her name is Kim," I say.

"Kim, right. She was exonerated, and now you two are reunited. I mean—"

"You will get your commission," I say. "But once this deal is finalized, you and I are through, Melinda."

She's still talking when I end the call.

I put the phone down. Mom smiles at me. We talked

beforehand about how difficult that call was going to be. Melinda wasn't exaggerating: she was with me from the beginning and helped me through some very difficult times. But I can't forgive her for not respecting my privacy when three people were murdered and it nearly got me and Mom killed.

Speaking of Mom, she looks so much better now. After living on the run for all those years, being able to settle down and live a normal life has restored her. She looks great. She looks so fresh and vibrant for her age.

We're making up for lost time. Mom moved in once the legal formalities were over with the police. We spend our nights watching old TV shows, drinking tea, doing crossword puzzles together. On Saturdays, she makes chocolate chip pancakes, just like she used to. She even comes to yoga with me. There's a cute guy who's started turning up in yoga class too. Mom caught me checking him out and knew, immediately, like she always does, what I was thinking, then proceeded to shamelessly chat him up. Never thought my mother would be my wing-woman, but here we are. Life is strange.

And, sometimes, wonderful.

I still think about how lucky I am. If I hadn't woken in the middle of the night at Brandon's house during the snowstorm, and if he hadn't forgotten to lock that hallway closet, then I would never have discovered that creepy shrine. If I hadn't seen that, I would never have thought to use Brandon's feelings for me against him.

Mom and I would have died.

I've talked about this with Mom. She thinks Brandon left that door unlocked and open because deep down, on some irrational level, he *wanted* me to know how he truly felt. Mom's probably right. She usually is.

The writers' group invited me back. Ken called me himself and ate a lot of crow, apologizing profusely over and over for the group's—he didn't take any of the blame himself, of course—shoddy treatment of me. After what seemed like a heartfelt apology, he went on to ask if I'd "as one writer to another, be generous enough to consider offering a blurb" for his upcoming book. Now that I'm a mega-bestselling author with an utterly ridiculous advance on a three-book deal, a blurb from me would do his next novel wonders. I told Ken I'd be back to the group eventually, because, despite my unpleasant experience with Sarah Keller, I truly do want to help other aspiring writers. But as for the blurb, I turned Ken down. He said he understood, given the "immense pressures on our precious time we all face," but I could tell he was miffed.

"How about we go see Nora?" I ask. "We'll take her out and celebrate."

"That sounds wonderful." Mom nods, practically glowing.

I'm still in my pajamas. I go to my room to get changed. The scar from the gunshot wound and subsequent emergency surgery is still ugly and pronounced. Before getting dressed, I run my hand gingerly over the jagged dark purple line in my side. Six months on, and every now and then I still get this random sharp jab of pain if I bend at the waist at a funny angle or twist my body suddenly. It means I need to be careful in yoga. I nearly bled out from the gunshot. I woke up a day later to find Mom sitting beside me in handcuffs and a uniformed police officer standing in the hallway.

I shake my head to clear the memory, pull on a butter-yellow sundress, and head downstairs to meet Mom.

"Mom, there's something I want to ask," I say as we drive to Nora's apartment, the car windows down on this warm summer day.

"You know you can ask me anything," she says. "And you also know I might not answer."

We share a laugh. "Was David my father?"

The truth is, Mom hasn't talked about a lot of things. She does *not* discuss her life on the run other than to provide vague details. Sometimes I get the names of places; even more rarely I get the names of people. But that's all. There are long periods of time she won't account for, time spent in places unidentified, with people I will never meet. In order to survive, in order to stay somewhat near me, Mom was forced to do a lot of things she wasn't proud of during those fugitive years, things she would never have imagined doing had she lived a normal life.

In the passenger seat of the car, Mom goes very still.

"David wasn't your father."

I get a lump in my throat. After learning more about David from Mom, I have grown to like the man. I used to judge him (and Mom) for having an affair, but the older I get, the more I've come to know that human relationships are messy and complex. Simpler minds would say David could have easily divorced his wife and moved on, but he was being held emotionally hostage. Lori wasn't *just* psychopathic—she was also incredibly manipulative. Every time David broached the subject of a separation, she would have some kind of breakdown; he'd experience tremendous guilt; then he'd feel obligated to stay and help her. Paradoxically, if the man had been coldhearted, then he would have cut ties with Lori. It was *because* he had a good heart and still cared about her that he stayed, even though she was poison. And the longer he stayed, the more difficult it became for him to leave. I do believe he loved Mom and wanted to be with her.

"Are you sure?" I ask.

"I'm sure, sweetie," she answers.

There's a long pause. This is the moment where Mom usually lets the subject of my father drop.

But, instead, she turns to me in her seat.

"The first time I ended the affair with David, I was heartbroken," Mom says. "It was the right thing to do, but it was devastating. I went out and got drunk and met a man at a bar and ... one thing led to another."

"Who was he?" I ask.

She shakes her head. "His name was Dale. He passed a few years ago."

I pull over. I can't see through the tears in my eyes. As I slump forward onto the steering wheel, Mom rubs my back.

"Why didn't you ever tell me?"

"He wasn't a good man," she says. "He got himself arrested right after we had our fling and went away for a few years. He was in and out of prison ... I didn't want everybody knowing your daddy was a criminal. I was afraid they'd treat you differently. Talk about irony. I'm so sorry."

I sit up and wipe under my eyes. "No, don't apologize. You were right. Your family treated me like I was diseased after everything that happened. You knew exactly how they would react."

"Still." Her eyes are teary. "I'm so sorry."

We embrace. There's nothing in the world better than a hug from your mom. A few minutes later, we're back on the road. The sky is blue, the road ahead of us is open, and my mother is with me. She always will be now.

THANK YOU FOR READING

Did you enjoy reading *Her Mother's Daughter*? Please consider leaving a review on Amazon. Your review will help other readers to discover the novel.

ABOUT THE AUTHOR

Brian R. O'Rourke has been writing stories since he was eight years old. A lifelong, avid reader, Brian believes that fiction has the power to change the world. He enjoys spending time with his family, exercising, playing the violin, and golfing.

He also writes mysteries and thrillers under the pen name Evan Ronan.

ALSO BY BRIAN R. O'ROURKE

The New Husband

The Only Son

Her Mother's Daughter

Printed in Great Britain
by Amazon

38259872R00199